ANOINTING

TO WAKE AND SLEEP NO MORE SERIES
BOOK TWO

Patsy,

Thanks for the support!

Ngozi T. Robinson

BY NGOZI T. ROBINSON

I AM Publications

Anointing

I AM Publications
(617) 564-1060
contact@iampubs.com
www.iampubs.com

Cover Illustration by Karen Silberman

ISBN: 978-1-943382-22-4

DEDICATION

To Ma, 1947 – 2002

PART ONE
A MORE OPPORTUNE TIME

CHAPTER ONE
THE THRESHOLD

Sheila was feeling like an orphan today. She had woken up with the sun and, for the first time in a long time, gone into her shrine room to pray. The corner room's four windows let the morning light pour in and illuminate the three shrines that she had. They greeted her like old friends, though she felt bad for abandoning her shrines when times had gotten tough with the recent death of her mother, who had been her spiritual mentor and best friend. Although she had decided that life was worth living, that she wanted God in her life, and that her husband was on her side, she still felt the grief of being motherless as painfully as ever. The cabinets sat with burned-out glass candles and bowls and plates with stale or rotten offerings that evidenced her neglect. At her Buddhist shrine, The Goddess of Mercy's statue stood silently. Sheila felt the goddess lamenting the fact that her offerings had not been attended to.

"Well, if you don't have mercy on me, who will," Sheila pleaded.

Her People of the Grey Dawn Native American shrine lacked that distinctive smell of fresh ground tobacco and mesa to call up the spirits that usually emanated from it. Her smudge stick lay in a large seashell, tempting her to light it and begin banishing the inertia that had seemed to settle in the room.

Sheila's Christian shrine sat in the corner. She had searched all over to find the carving of the empty tomb with the stone rolled away that sat on that cabinet. That was how she liked to think of Jesus, never quite where you expected him.

Praying here was hard. She hadn't prayed or connected to the Divine within her in so long that her actions felt rusty and unfamiliar. Sheila kept at it as long as she could, disappointed she hadn't fallen back into the practice as easily as she had hoped to. There was nothing to do but try again later. At least she was praying again.

She moved to the family room on the first floor off of the kitchen, where the warm tones and plush fabrics she had decorated it with welcomed her and made her smile like always. She stretched out on her favorite coach with the sun streaming in on her long, fit, caramel-colored frame from the glass doors onto their back porch. Her shoulder-length, straightened brown hair was pulled back, and she had her stern-looking reading glasses on. She had a pile of cards and packages of condolences from Ma's funeral that she was going through for comfort, but there was still one package she had not opened. She fingered the gold border along the thin green photo album, trying to find the strength.

Inside were pictures of her father, a man she had met only once in her teens, a few years before he died. A man her mother had always referred to as a test-tube daddy, but whom she had never been able to reduce to the term "biological father." He was Dad to her.

Sheila thought about how much she resented him for not being there, how the scar of his absence had affected everything in her life, especially her relationships with men. How many times she had rushed into things, driven by some unarticulated and unrealized desire to be loved and validated by a man? As she wiped tears away, she thought about how, in her heart, she had always known that they would one day meet so that they could talk and she could forgive him, and, maybe finally, he would have time and room in his life for her. Now that he was dead—for years now—that would never happen.

Sheila was feeling motherless *and* fatherless, and that cold pain spread through her and settled in bitterly.

She had always thought she looked more like her father than her mother. But, looking at the first picture in the album and sizing up the smiling, light-skinned, bald man standing 6’9” tall, holding an upright bass, she found he didn’t much resemble the memory she had created of him. She peered into the photo at a face that she didn’t much recognize or remember.

But, slowly, she began to see herself in that face, and she wasn’t sure how she felt about that. Did she feel more complete? Was there a sense of closure or outrage? She supposed she just felt lonelier.

When Raines Montoya walked in, she remembered why she loved her gorgeous, and, lately, pretty incredible, husband. She had always assumed it was the artist in him that had drawn her in. Slowly, she was coming to realize it was really his soul. Of course, it didn’t hurt that he was tall, built, gorgeous, and from an “established” Mexican family with money, either. Still, she closed the album and slid it behind her, having always preferred to process her feelings privately. After a wordless and mostly playful wrestling match, Raines held it in his hands.

“So…this is Dad,” he said coolly. “You open it yet?”

She nodded slowly. Standing, she shook off all the confusion of the feelings she had been wandering through. Raines saw that the matter was closed to her. After all that they had been through, he had to admit he was too exhausted to add yet another issue to the mix. But Sheila finally seeing pictures of the father she hardly knew was something they had to explore. Eventually.

“What’s on the agenda for today?”

“I guess I’m going to Ma’s to talk to the spirit of my dead grandfather,” she said, as if it were a normal to-do list item.

“Did you make a list?” Raines knew how much Sheila lived by lists.

“As a matter of fact,” she said proudly and not even minding that he was teasing her, “I did.”

“Can I see...in the spirit of partnership?”

“We are not partners.”

Raines started to rise up from the couch, drawing on all that effective Mexican Montoya royalty.

"You are not my partner," Sheila repeated before he had a chance to bear down on her. "Not on this," she said in a final tone.

"I thought you said we *were* partners," Raines said wearily. It seemed their marriage was getting back to "normal" after the coziness of the last two nights.

Sheila turned her back to him and took three deep breaths to steady herself. Then she sat on the couch and took his hands in hers.

"Raines, I don't paint your paintings for you. Being your wife means that you have my complete support. Whatever you need to do your job, I make sure you have. But I can never do your job for you. That's what I need from you now."

Well, he supposed it made sense. That alone made him suspicious. He sighed as he pulled her into his arms.

"What do you need from me?" He purred into her ear.

"I need some time from you to figure out what all this is. I promise I'll come to you with everything. Eventually."

Raines cracked a smile, "My wife is going to be a real-life superhero. What a ride."

"I'm not a superhero! I just have a lot of work to do."

"With the ghost of your grandfather teaching you to be a traffic cop between dimensions."

Traffic cop? Sheila stuck her lips out in dissatisfaction. "Well, when you put it like that, I think I prefer superhero."

Raines wrapped his legs around her, and they lay quietly as the sun rose higher in the sky. He fell asleep quickly, but Sheila was wrestling with a thousand ideas. The questions she had written earlier swam through her head, along with anxiety about the future.

Who had opened the window in her hotel room she had almost thrown herself out of? What price had her mother paid to reappear from beyond the grave to stop Sheila from killing herself instead of transitioning to the next level? What was she going to do about Massad, that worker of dark arts that Ma had restrained at her side? How would Sheila get her relationship with God back on track? What would she do about Ma's Institute? Who was that strange man, Hotep, to her? The last question was the biggest: what would it mean to fill her mother's shoes as the interdimensional gatekeeper?

Underneath all the queries and fears, though, was a quiet and steadying contentment. Ma had reached out to Sheila from beyond the grave to save her life. And that time, maybe for the last time, Ma had told her she loved her.

By the time Sheila had stilled her mind enough to sleep, Raines was waking up and hungry. He extracted himself from their embrace and made his way to the kitchen and rifled through plastic containers in the freezer until he found one marked "chili" and popped it in the microwave. He leaned forward against the counter while it heated, stretching his legs.

Raines let out a long moan as he allowed himself to remember the last two months. Sheila had lost her mother, her dead grandfather had appeared to tell her she was destined to take over her mother's role as inter-dimensional gatekeeper—whatever *that* meant—, and she had almost killed herself before his eyes trying to run away from her fate. Now, she had decided to replace her mother as gatekeeper, a role he still didn't understand and it seemed she didn't either.

It was not too much for him to handle, though it came close. He was a Montoya. The only things bigger than his refined and established family's successes were the secrets they had had to cover up in order to hold things together.

This was nothing new to him.

And now she was asking him to just sit and wait, keeping the home fires burning while she closeted herself up for only God knew how long. He headed toward the door of his basement art studio, forgetting his food in the microwave, which had beeped long ago. There was an Eden for him that would not fail to clear his mind and allow him to cast away his cares. It was only a paintbrush and canvas away.

Sheila sat on the edge of the couch, fighting off a nauseous feeling. It was time to talk to Grandfather. She closed her eyes as another wave of anxiety washed over her. She had been told she was strong, that she could do this, that she *had* to do this.

She willed herself into action. First, off of the couch and into her coat. Then, into the car and on the road. Finally, in her mother's home and up the stairs, until she stood with her hand on the door of her mother's shrine room.

Nausea got the best of her and she raced to the bathroom, barely making it. After a good rinse and tooth brushing, she opened the door to the adjoined bedroom. Ma's room looked as neat as it ever had. Had it really been two months? Her room still looked as though it were waiting to welcome her back. She went to the closet, stepped in, and embraced some of the clothes. They smelled like Ma. That wonderful scent soothed her, and, with a final deep inhalation, she headed back to the shrine room and walked in.

"Lift up your heads, oh ye gates," she recited. Somehow, there was a smile on her face, and she felt spiritual power pouring back into her. This had the same comforting feeling as hugging her mother's clothes. As she looked around the room at the half-dozen cabinets with their statues and offering bowls, it all reminded her of Ma, and she fought to hold back her tears.

Sheila sat before her mother's ancestral shrine, where all this talk of her destiny had started. Pictures of her forebears lined the top of the short cabinet. A bulb of cotton sat there, as if her ancestors had just finished picking it. A small coffee pot sat ready to percolate at the press of a button. Pouring a fresh cup of coffee into his mug and lighting his cigar, she called on the spirit of her grandfather.

A deep and anguished wail filled the room, and Sheila wept as she heard it. She remembered her grandfather's laugh from her childhood. It had always brought her joy. But she had never heard him cry.

She could hear the unspoken words inside that cry. It was a lament of all she had gone through since she had last been here. It grieved her self-pitying rejection of God, the lack of emotional strength she had shown, her rash and suicidal actions. The sobs spoke of her mother, what she had sacrificed of her own transcendence to protect and exhort her Baby Girl. The crying was also for future pain she could not see, but that was surely promised to her.

CHAPTER TWO
NIGHTMARES

Sheila lay as silently as she could, taking slow breaths. Sweat dripped from her face. She was tired of this dream, tired of the fear it poured into her. As she heard the distant clanging of footsteps at the end of the hall, her bodily involuntarily seized. She knew she had only moments before he would be upon her. Forcing herself to breathe, she worked on relaxing her muscles. Her right hand regained a sure grip on the knife she had chosen, and she breathed a little easier. She was pressed in between the grate above her and the one beneath her so tightly she could never hope to turn around and face him, but she still felt better with a weapon in her hand.

His footsteps stopped directly above her, and Sheila felt the weight of him press her even more tightly between the grates. 'Slow, even breaths,' she willed to herself. The wind got knocked out of her as he dropped to one knee above her. She felt the heat of silent tears track across her face as her fear overwhelmed her. His greedy, thick breath filled her ears. Tiny vibrations accompanied the sharp repetitive sound of him running the tip of his knife across the grate above her. He had gone from just hurting her to enjoying it.

A whisper of a thought was forming in her mind. Shuddering, she was trying to remember. As the knife plunged between the grates to slice into her shoulder, she exhaled a weak, "No."

Sheila woke sweaty, wracked with silent sobs, and wrenched in tension.

"I hate it," she wept. "I just can't anymore."

"You did better that time, though you're still progressing too slowly. Try again." The disembodied but now familiar voice of her grandfather filled the candlelit shrine room.

Sheila pushed herself up from the pallet she had made.

"You're going to drive me into the ground," she muttered, wiping at her tears.

"Until you learn to control your dreams, to reclaim and amplify your power, you can do nothing. I will not have you useless," he said sternly.

"I'm exhausted," she said, falling back onto her pillow and trying to will the tension out of her legs. "If I could move, I would leave," Sheila yawned.

"Are you sticking with the knife?"

"He has a knife. I have a knife." She turned to her side and fell back into a dreamful sleep.

"I don't think that's wise," he said, but Sheila was already asleep, finding her way back into her own personal Hell.

When she woke up struggling and shaking, familiar arms encircled her. She stopped fighting and leaned into Raines' chest.

"Thank God," she moaned. "I'm so glad you're here."

"When a man's wife is crying in her sleep, he has to do something about it." Raines' voice had a hint of restrained anger to it.

"I love you," Sheila snuggled into him. "Don't leave me."

"No, baby." He kissed her forehead. "You are too crazy to be left alone," he chuckled.

"I'm so tired," she breathed before falling back to sleep.

Raines let out a frustrated sigh. The nightmares were getting worse and more regular. Sometimes two or three times a night she woke up crying or shaking. It was hell on him. What had Sheila gotten herself into?

CHAPTER THREE
CONQUERING

Sheila lay on the couch off of the kitchen reading. She had a pile of assorted books she had carted over from her mother's library. She was combing through anything she could find that related to dimensions, since her grandfather refused to tell her about her role as interdimensional gatekeeper until she passed her dream test.

These had come from a bookcase built into the wall behind another bookcase. She'd had no idea it was there until her grandfather told her. Her mother had many secrets, she was learning.

As Sheila read, she shook herself to stay awake. Sleeping had become the enemy in the last week. Her grandfather had told her she had to learn to control her dreams–that it was the first step to controlling herself and gaining power between dimensions. Then she had talked about the hunting nightmare that had been with her for longer than she could remember. Grandfather had instructed her on how to choose a spiritual weapon that she could use in dreams. It reminded her of something her mother had taught her. She had to prevail against the hunter in the dream to pass her first test.

Every other night, she slept in her mother's shrine room, and Grandfather put her through her paces, inducing her into a dream state where she relived being pinned in between grates and stabbed by the unknown hunter several times a night. She had advanced to calling her weapon into being but she was nowhere near defeating or even confronting her foe.

The complete endeavor was backfiring, she thought as she rose from the couch and bit into an apple from the kitchen island. Now, every time she closed her eyes, she was tortured by that dream. She looked like a dead woman walking but was terrified of sleeping. She was tired, frazzled, and a holy terror to be around.

She had quit her job and had another few weeks before her consulting work started, so the only person she saw was her husband, Raines. He was regretting ever having said he wanted her to be home more, she thought, as she leaned against a wall, trying to press some of the tension out of her back.

She knew she could pass this test of the dream. She wasn't sure if it would kill her before she mastered her fear, though. And she couldn't tell anyone about it until she had overcome it; she had decided that the moment Grandfather had told her what she had to do. Drawing arbitrary lines in the sand was one of Sheila's specialties. Not even she could break her own rules sometimes.

Sheila gave a start as she slid down the wall. She had started to doze off. Heading upstairs to put on some winter workout gear, she prepared to take an afternoon jog. She had to stay awake.

The blue mirror above the ancestral shrine in her mother's shrine room misted over.

"You are forgetting who you are. You should have mastered this dream long ago." Her grandfather's voice seemed to fold in on her from all directions. "Where is that insufferable swagger you used to have about the superiority of your spiritual powers? You could use it now."

"I came here just days after I tried to kill myself, and you started making me do dream work every time I close my eyes. I haven't had time to heal! How can you expect any better? I just hope you've figured out a way to keep me alive through all this."

"You need to draw your power without even thinking

about it in the most demanding of situations. If you can't yet do it in a dream, then we have a problem."

"Then we have a problem."

"Your problem right now is that you refuse to use the power, good sense, and guidance that God gave you. Break through that barrier now. I won't do it for you."

Grandfather's voice faded as the mist cleared from the surface of the mirror. She thought as she lay on her pallet, about how the mist in the mirror was a new thing. She closed her eyes and sunk into the dreams of another night of fruitless attempts.

Raines stretched out on a twin-sized airbed in the hallway of his mother-in-law's house. The last few nights Sheila had come here, he had insisted on accompanying her. He would have demanded to be in the shrine room with her, instead of the hallway, but his memory of the consequences from the last time he had overstepped his spiritual bounds restrained him. Besides, Sheila had been pretty terrifying the last few days. He was afraid of crossing her.

He stared up at the ceiling, thinking about how long it had been since he had hung out with his friends. His brother would say Sheila had clipped his wings. It was a little distressing, but he recognized that this was where he needed to be right now. As he explored an idea for a new series of paintings on the theme of the tabernacle, he wondered how long 'right now' would last, and if he would ever have the power and the right to walk into that shrine room where he was pretty sure, whatever else might be happening, his wife was suffering.

Sheila's hot tears made her angry. First she got angry with herself. Then she got angry with the situation. Then she got blazing mad at the source of the footsteps at the end of the hall. Before she knew what she was doing, a high-pitched scream erupted from her mouth, and she shook with all her might against the grates she found herself sandwiched between. "You have no power over me," she thought. The grate above her disappeared.

She stood up and looked around. Sheila had never seen the dream from this perspective. She felt authority pour into her as the noise from the distance turned into a shadowy figure at the edge of the light.

"I want to see your face," Sheila said. The figure stepped forward into the light and removed the black cape, revealing a dark, old, leathery face, deformed with hate as it sneered at her.

"You're *ugly*, but the cape's nice. It's a shame your blood will ruin it." And with that, she leapt forward. Sheila gripped the hilt of her knife, only to find that it had become a sword. She had only a second to register the change before they crashed into each other. Her first thought was that he was stronger than her. Sheila felt like she had bounced off of a wall when they collided. Her sword fell from her hand and the clatter as it hit the grate rang in her ears. Her attacker pushed her onto the ground and lay on top of her. He held her down with his forearm pressed against her throat. His knife raised, preparing to plunge into her.

Sheila looked into her attacker's disgusting face and stopped time. "No," she croaked. Willing his body to become lighter, she pushed him off of her and stood up. Visualizing a tomahawk of light until it appeared in her hand, she exhaled and said, "Let's try this again," as she allowed time to flow.

The man shook himself as he got his bearings. As he

stood up, Sheila hacked away at the backside of his knee with her weapon. "I never said," she squeezed out through gritted teeth as she continued to hew at the same spot, "it would be fair." She took a moment of pleasure at the sight of his calf severed from his leg. "You never were to me." She reared back to take a cut out of his neck.

Sheila came down on his neck with all her power, intending to kill him, but the tomahawk slid off his leathery skin. Sheila almost slipped and fell on the blood that coated the floor as she stepped back to regroup. The man rose, standing on one leg, and raised his knife.

"The problem," Sheila panted as she allowed her tomahawk to disappear, "is your weak mind." She looked at him for an entire minute. She watched him die. He shook, clutched at his neck as he gasped for air that he now couldn't take in, and he spit at her. And, because watching him suffer was no longer a thrill, she turned her back to him as she willed his neck to snap, hearing a gruesome crunch as she walked into the shadows. "At least you were consistent. I would have hated it if you had begged in the end."

Sheila woke up on her pallet, shaking with laughter and relief. "I won," she whispered.

"Yes, you did," Grandfather said. "Well done."

"You almost sound pleased. Don't start coddling me now."

"Get some rest, Baby Girl."

"That I will." For the first time in weeks, she fell asleep, unafraid and content.

As Sheila slept, the old, oval mirror in the gold wooden frame from which her grandfather spoke to her misted over as he retreated to his dimension. His breathing was ragged as he willed his severed leg to reconnect itself and fused his broken spine back together. He rubbed the side of his neck where her tomahawk had struck so forcefully, soothing away the trauma before it bruised and clotted. Now that she had defeated him, he allowed himself to feel remorse for the cruelty that had been required of him in this effort. He was proud of her. She had been bloodthirsty, but not overly so. He forgave himself for what he had had to do. He had pulled no punches, and was truly pleased that his granddaughter was learning to trust herself and use her power.

CHAPTER FOUR
GRADUATION

Sheila stared at their kitchen table. Raines had actually broken it in two. As he prowled back and forth in the kitchen, he looked like he would love to punch a hole in something.

"Killing you, night after night, in your sleep, on your grandfather's orders?!" He ran his hands through his hair and looked accusingly at her, "I see now why you didn't dare breathe a word of this to me before, I would have killed you myself…at least I would have wanted to."

"I love you too, dear," Sheila joked.

Raines, who seemed to have finally worn himself out, sat down in a chair beside her. Blinking, he seemed to notice that he had smashed the table in two. "Uh…"

"Yes, you certainly gave the table what for." Sheila laughed and leaned into him. His anger gave way—well, most of it—, and he held her.

"But you're ok now." He nuzzled her hair and took a deep breath. Sheila had tried her best to get him to focus on the positive. He had to do that now. The nearest table still standing was stone.

"Yeah, it's unblocked me or something. I'm so relieved. Now I can finally take care of some things."

"Oh, yeah? Time to be a superhero already?"

"Well, not yet. But there is the matter of the man who cursed my husband."

He froze and felt a churning in his stomach as memories and fear ran through him.

"Are you sure? Can you beat him?"

"Please, don't insult my powers," and she wiggled her fingers at him the way a television witch might when casting a spell. Dropping her hands into her lap, she sighed. "I think so, but I'm not sure. Yet."

"Well, be sure," he rubbed his hands on his thighs a bit nervously, "Not that I like the idea of my wife finishing what I…" He couldn't bring himself to say 'failed at,' but it echoed through his head.

Sheila turned his head towards her and looked into his eyes. "I haven't forgotten that my husband stood in the gap for me when I couldn't, when I wouldn't. I never will. You did your part. Now let me do mine."

He let out a breath. "Well done." He appreciated she wanted to make him feel like a man, that he was the head, especially at moments like this. He held on tightly to that thin wisp of truth, that he had stood for her when he needed to, and used it to fight the sickening feeling that he was sending his wife to fight a battle he knew he couldn't win.

"Now," Sheila straightened herself in her chair, "this is what I propose." She wrapped his arms around her waist. "You take me upstairs and, uh, remind me you're my husband." The hunger flared in his eyes, and she laughed knowingly. It had been a long week and a half. "And then, I'll show you how to protect yourself so that what happened with Massad won't occur again."

Raines strained attentively. He would have never thought something could appeal to him more than making love to his wife, but he wanted, felt he had to have, that power she offered him.

"Can we reverse that order?"

Sheila stared at him, then ran her hands seductively down her sides, accentuating her curves. "What?!"

"I know, believe me, I know. But, I have to learn this. I have to protect myself, to keep you from," he struggled for a way to say it that would keep his manhood, at least a little of it, "risking your safety for me." He didn't have the skill of dressing things up as well as Sheila did.

"Oh, don't you believe it," she said ruthlessly as she stood. "He messed with my ma. And I'm going to *hurt* him." She turned to look at Raines, and her eyes were full of fire.

"It's for *me*."

"Well!" he said, impressed. "It's good to see your fire back, so I'll give you this one. But what do you mean, he messed with Cathy?"

"The taint he used on you, you don't pick that up overnight. It took skill. It took…a certain disposition. He *fooled* me, but he wouldn't have fooled Ma. All that time, he was her right-hand man at the institute. She had to have been keeping him around to contain him, maybe even to use him. Men like that don't take to being caged. He gave her hell, I just know it." She smoothed her hands over her skirt. "And I mean to pay him back for it." There was more than a hint of a threat in her voice. "So yes," she shook herself, "we *will* reverse the order, and I'll teach you now."

For the next hour and a half, she took him through his paces with a demanding breathing technique, visualization, mantra, and posture work until he could execute all the elements of the curse block at once.

"That's enough for now," she held up a hand when he protested. "Certain things you don't master in one shot. Learn now, perfect over time." Sheila sank into her chair. "If you spend about forty-five minutes a day, not more than an hour, working on it, it should become pretty natural in a couple of weeks. But sooner than that, probably in a few days, you'll be able to maintain the block for long periods of time. You'll just have to think about it when you do." Sheila took his face in her hands and kissed him. "You're strong. A quick learner. I'm impressed." She ran her hands down his chest. "Just remember, God's in charge and you will be just fine. More than fine." The mischief was in her eyes as she moved to straddle him in his chair.

"Take me to bed," she mumbled as she sucked on his ear.

Flush with the feelings of the new and intoxicating power she had just shown him, Raines nearly bounded up the stairs with her wrapped around him. Then he devoured her with all the frantic needs that had been building since the last time she had touched him. He was determined to show her something he had mastered.

CHAPTER FIVE
BARREN

"Silence!" Grandfather's voice boomed. "I will not discuss the matter any further." The bluish mirror he spoke through was a furious mass of tumbling clouds.

Sheila spoke through clenched teeth, "I am getting tired of men yelling at me." She stretched her neck from side to side. "I have no intention of seeking your approval for the things I do, Grandfather. I will give you the respect of informing you on relevant matters, but I will never ask for permission."

"When were you going to *inform* me you are trying to conceive a child?"

Sheila looked dumbfounded.

"I am not bound. I do not require your information, but you will do well to remember you require mine. There is only one master in this room."

"What does my…"

"Your path requires intense physical, spiritual, and mental discipline—and risk. It will be a challenge just keeping you alive. You will not be able to carry a child to term."

Sheila thought back to the miscarriages her mother had experienced when she was older. Part of her mind was telling her it should be a relief not to have to worry about getting pregnant, but…

"We don't have much more time and must complete your training in mere weeks. Your work will be difficult because of the time that has passed with no gatekeeper. This is your life now."

"It's clear that it is not about me, but about the work. That's fine. You died when I was too young to really know you, so it doesn't matter that you show no more love for me than one would for a complete stranger." It did matter to her.

It tore at her, but she wouldn't tell him. "But just how far do you think this little venture will get if I have no descendants to…submit themselves to this job after me?"

"There's Jasmine. Or Corinne."

He was a cold man.

"I can't have children for as long as I do this?" Sheila felt suddenly bereft.

"You were supposed to have more time."

Sheila struggled to her feet, half blind with grief, and stumbled toward the door out of the shrine room. Suddenly, she was mad at everything, right down to the room's light pink walls for trying to cheer her up.

"We are not…"

"*No*!" Sheila bellowed. Her energy furled with such force that all the candles in the room fluttered wildly, then extinguished. Cups and bowls turned over, spilling their contents onto the room's half dozen shrines. The acrid, burnt smell of candle snuff filled the air. She left without bothering to close the door.

Raines had bolted up the stairs and was halfway up them when the fury on his wife's face stopped him cold. Then, in a turn that had become far too common, she crumpled onto the floor.

He wrapped her in his arms as she cried. "I'm sorry," she whimpered, "so sorry."

"Shhhh." He smoothed her hair and rocked her. "It's alright."

Raines struggled not to shake her like a rag doll and demand to know what happened. "What can I do? What can I do?"

Sheila looked at him and tried to stop sobbing. "I…We can't…I know I said I didn't want to before, but I never…Raines," she took a breath to steady herself and rushed the words out before they hitched in her throat, "doing this work means I can't have children." Sheila drew back from him and hid her face.

Raines' hands dropped to the ground, and he went numb. It let the air out of his hopes and dreams all at once. His family's words of how he'd never be happy with her rang in his ears. To be childless, it was the opposite of manhood. It was the antithesis of him! He rose from the ground and paced the floor of the hallway, wringing his hair through his hands, suddenly full of nervous frustration. Oh, his parents had predicted this! They had seen what he could not, that this woman really would be the end of him. He loved her, but this was not a Montoya's fate.

And. with that thought, he punched a hole into the wall, kicked the floorboards, and gave Sheila a murderous look. When he saw how afraid and anguished she was, though, he softened and became ashamed of himself.

"I'm sorry. I just can't deal with this. I don't know how. And I don't want to. I need to go home."

"Alright, I'll get my things."

"No, I mean *home.* Las Lomas."

"Mexico? Your family?" He had told her that his home was wherever she was, but now *home* had become his family's estate when the chips were down.

"They'll turn you against me…and when you come back, if you come back, you won't be mine anymore." She spoke quietly but matter-of-factly. Raines said nothing.

Sheila smoothed out her skirt and couldn't bear to look at him. She sighed. "Go, then. Just know *I* never betrayed *you* on purpose." She stood up, albeit a bit shakily and wearily. "Let's go to our residence." There was more than a little accusation in her voice.

CHAPTER SIX
FRIENDS

Sheila sipped her margarita and swayed a bit to the music playing through their hidden speakers in the kitchen. No husband? No hope for babies? No job? A ghost of an ancestor that barked orders through a mirror who was ruining her life? Seemed like a good time to get drunk. She carried the blender into the sitting room, where her girlfriends lay sprawled out on various chairs, couches, and pillows on the floor. They all held up glasses, eager for refills.

Maybe she had overdone it in the living room with the theme of comfort. The coaches were so big and cushiony it was almost like some of them had been engulfed where they sat. But at least they were engulfed and super comfortable.

"That's what I'm talking about!" Naima shouted. She lost her inside voice when she got drunk. "Our girl is back!" She gave over to a fit of giggles as she keeled over on the couch, somehow managing not to spill a drop from her glass.

"Yes, I come bearing an olive branch…well, they were out of those, so I figured liquor was quicker." Sheila plopped onto a couch beside Shareen, and they clicked glasses before slugging on their cold, frosty drinks. "Ah, that's good for what ails ya," she said a bit wistfully, staring off into space.

Shareen, whose entire nature screamed mother figure, pulled her into her generous arms, holding her even when she struggled, until Sheila finally gave up and wept. Shareen rocked her and said, "There, there," as she smoothed her hair.

When she finally had had enough of crying, she sat up and dried her eyes as she looked at her four best girlfriends in the world: Tannaz, Rhonda, Shareen, and Naima, surrounding her.

"I missed you guys." She let out a weak little laugh.

"Oh, we could tell," Tannaz said sarcastically, "what with all the calls and emails and visits."

"Oh, don't be picky," Naima said fussily. "You know we nearly had to abduct her *before* all of this."

"Yes," Sheila said a bit tenderly, "before all of this." She sank back into the couch and shook herself out of a threatening self-pity party. "Well, it's only *all* hit the fan since then, but that's life."

"I'll drink to that!" Naima giggled and raised her glass, looking surprised when no one else joined her.

"I think you have had enough," Rhonda said, chuckling as Naima drew her glass back protectively.

"What a motley crew," Sheila laughed.

It felt good to laugh. They fell back into the easy and nourishing camaraderie she had missed. After Ma passed, she couldn't even bear the thought of being around her friends. She felt too broken to contribute and too defensive to tolerate being cared for. But when Raines had packed his bags and left for the airport, for *home*, reaching out to them had seemed like the most urgent thing in the world. Now, in the warmth of their company, she couldn't think what had taken her so long.

"Just so long as you realize you're part of it," Tannaz said in an easy, amused voice. "You've got to be laughing *with* us or it just doesn't work."

"Here, here," Naima piped up, sloshing the unguarded contents of her drink onto the coffee table, looking perplexed at why her glass was suddenly empty.

"Well, I gotta laugh at that!" The room erupted in a laughter and merriment that lasted long into the night.

Long after Shareen, Rhonda, and Tannaz had left, and she had bedded down Naima for the night in the guest bedroom, Sheila sat with her knees drawn on her bed, staring at the wall. It felt so empty without him. And the call that should have come hours ago to let her know he had arrived safely had never come. The least of her problems was the possibility he was lying dead in a ditch somewhere. She knew he had chosen not to call her. She wondered if finally her spell on him was broken, if he would ever really come back to her.

She lay on her back and prayed, and cried, and dozed until they all merged into one. Finally, the harsh gray of dawn filled the room, and she anxiously freed herself from their bed to tend to her shrine room.

The night had been far too long. Sick with herself for missing Raines so much, and for having such a defeatist attitude, she needed to *do* something. Luckily, she supposed, there were ample tasks before her. A bit of a perverse smile spread across her face. She would start with Massad.

PART TWO
UNFINISHED BUSINESS

CHAPTER SEVEN
MASSAD

It was late in the evening when Sheila pulled up to the Institute for Cosmic Consciousness for the first time since her mother's funeral. Then, she had been so busy with details and logistics that she hardly noticed where she was or how she was feeling. Now, too, she had a task to do that filled the whole of her mind.

Nothing could stop the familiar, proud feeling that always overtook her when she was here. Her mother had built up this place from a dream in her heart. It was a place of spiritual collaboration that helped people and made them whole. Some would say this squat, eight-room complex was not much, but it might as well be Times Square to her in terms of grandeur. Ma had done something that mattered in her lifetime. She was gone too soon, but she had left something behind that could not be erased.

As Sheila entered the side of the building, navigated the short halls that still smelled like Ma's favorite incense, and walked into the rear of the lecture hall where Ma had given so many talks and trainings, she beat back the tugs from grief and memory to stay on task. From the look on Massad's face, he had sensed her coming.

She hadn't anticipated quite how angry she would be when she saw his face. How could she not have known that her mother's apprentice had been an evil one? Why had Ma bound him to her? There were so many troubling questions. This was the man who had put an actual curse on Sheila's husband that had taken both of her sisters to break. Power flared within her from rage.

In the hall where about thirty people sat, half of those heads turned in her direction. She was dripping with spiritual power, and none acquainted with reading energy fields could have missed her presence. She recognized many of the faces she saw. They were friends and colleagues of her mother's, a few friends and mentors of hers, too. A thousand memories threatened to swamp her, but she had to stay focused.

She was hunting. While her mother had favored defensive strategies, Sheila much preferred the attack.

"Greetings and the Peace of Christ to all! Massad, please see me in my mother's office at your convenience." And with that, she turned and left. She didn't have to use her psychic powers to tell Massad knew she was onto him and was gathering his filthy energies. Sheila felt the nervous excitement of knowing she was about to be tested.

"Jeremy," she unceremoniously grabbed the arm of one of her mother's closest friends as she spied him in the hall, speaking to some men she didn't recognize.

"Blessings, daughter!" Jeremy hugged her and praised God.

"I need you to hear me now on this." Sheila detangled herself and focused his attention. "Locate Massad as he leaves the lecture hall. Bathe him in unconditional love and walk with him to my mother's office. Stay outside of the office and come to my aid if I need it. Speak of this to no one." Sheila took a few deep breaths. "Are you with me?"

"Yes. We will speak later." And, with that, he withdrew from her, gave a look to the men he had been speaking with, and two of them followed him.

Sheila exhaled as she continued towards her mother's office. It was nice to have people she could count on, for whom no explanation was required.

She slowed after making the last turn to her mother's office. Clear as day, she could see several demons "loitering" in the hall in front of her mother's office. The stink of their energies offended and took her by surprise. Three imps were darting around like they always seem to do. Four daemons stood side-by-side blocking the way ahead. Those were all she saw, but she reminded herself there could be more. They couldn't have been stationed here for long. Massad must have just summoned them now. For her.

Sheila's stomach churned at the thought of how much power Massad must have to accomplish such a showing. She straightened and drew courage from the thought of who her mother was and the power of the God of Light she served. Clapping her hands three times, she held them with palms facing in front of her as she walked forward, reciting St. Cyprian's chant for the dispersal of demons. As demons always did, they tried to scare her out of her wits. Her jaws clenched shut at their effectiveness. Insidious thoughts about how she would never be her mother tried to worm their way into her heart. The otherwise bright hallway was suddenly dark, with terrifying shadows playing across her eyes.

Sheila stopped walking, put her hands at her sides, and closed her eyes. She drew her energies inward to her solar plexus. The cloistering demons, sensing her diminishing energies, wrapped so closely around her she felt like she was choking. But her energies weren't diminishing. They were focusing.

At that point of focus, she uttered one word, "No." With that spiritual declaration, a dazzling ring of white light pulsed out from her, clearing all darkness from its path in every direction. The demons couldn't even make a fuss.

Sheila leaned against the wall and put a hand to her stomach to steady herself. She wondered if Massad was as winded after that exchange as she was. From the curse he had put on Raines, she had known he was skilled and powerful. She had underestimated him.

"Ma, what were you doing with such a devil at your side?" Entering her mother's office and switching on the lights, Sheila saw that it had become Massad's office. Her mother's bookshelf was free of her texts, with slick-looking awards lining it instead. The worn, blue Turkish rug Ma had spent forever deciding on was gone, and the floor was black and gleaming instead.

She couldn't say she was surprised, but it still angered

her. She let that emotion rally her energies that had dipped a little after the dismissal in the hall. At least her mother's comfy couch was still here. She sat, closed her eyes, breathed, and prepared.

Sheila had come to the Institute after nine that evening. At 12:15 am, Massad opened the door to her mother's office and entered with a flourish. He had waited until the witching hour to have the advantage of his element, Sheila thought as she glanced at the clock and rose to meet him. He made to hug her but stopped short as she placed a hand in front of her and formed a hand sign of impassibility.

"Such mudras, child's play!" Massad uttered melodically. Sheila had forgotten the charismatic warmth of his voice. "Though I must congratulate you on your actions in the hallway. I confess I hadn't thought you capable of accomplishing that, not yet."

"What do you want, Massad?" Sheila sat and gave him the satisfaction of standing over her.

"You are nothing like your mother, you know. And you never will be. You'll never have her power, her wisdom. You have been nothing but a disappointment to her, and it's almost better that she's not here to see this pathetic attempt of yours. I want to rule this place. I *will* rule this place." Massad said without emotion or doubt.

Sheila's brows drew together in concentration as she continued to stare through his belly button. She spoke absent-mindedly. "Demons always want to rule. Failures and rejects are destined to serve."

Quicker than he could react, her hand shot out, grabbed his belly button, and twisted it to the right, hard and fast.

"Ow!" Massad yelped, looking pained and confused as he tried to move, but found he couldn't. He was rooted where he stood.

Without releasing her hold on his flesh, Sheila turned her gaze to his face. "As you served my mother, you will serve *me*. So help you God." She released her hand from him and fell back.

Massad, now able to move, stumbled back a few steps and leaned against the desk. He clutched his stomach, sending energies to cool the searing sensation that ran up and down his body, clustering around his chakra points.

With great effort, Sheila hoisted herself up off of the couch and straightened herself out. Everything about her seemed frazzled.

"I don't think I would have been able to do it, at least not so easily, if you hadn't underestimated me so. I'm not afraid anymore. And I will say this," she continued as she leaned down to collect her purse and keys. "I may be nothing like my mother, but I am becoming who she hoped I would be. But you continue thinking little of me. It's worked out well enough so far."

With that, she hugged Massad, continuing to add unconditional love to what she had planted within him earlier.

"I can't change your nature," she spoke into his ear as she continued to embrace her enemy, "but I can so completely repel it from you with the love of God that you cannot call upon it for your nefarious purposes."

She released him and stepped back to look at him. "But because your nature is black, the love I have placed inside you will *burn,* and you will suffer every waking and sleeping moment." Sheila almost clapped her hands in delight. "You can't remove what I placed there. You can't contain it. But, if you want peace," she placed a hand on his shoulder, "you have only to repent. Don't fight it, and God will receive you, change you."

Massad growled like an animal and spat in her face.

Reaching for a tissue, she wiped her face. "I'm happy to see that's the worst you can do. When I return, I'll thank you for having all the negative trails you have weaved throughout this building removed. And then we will speak."

"Goodbye, Massad," she said, walking out of her mother's office. As she closed the door behind her, she turned to face Jeremy standing in the hallway and fainted in his arms.

Sheila allowed herself to be treated a bit like a doll as Jeremy lifted her this way and that to place pillows beneath her head and under her knees. She was thankful he'd had the good sense to take her into a small prayer room off of the hallway so that she hadn't been seen. It wouldn't do for people to see her so weak. This small couch she lay on felt like it was giving her a hug, and the blue, purple, and gold mandala painted on the room's ceiling seemed to give her a comforting wink. She put her hand to the cool, damp cloth he had placed on her forehead and sighed.

"Thank you," she said weakly. "You are a lifesaver in more ways than you know." As he moved a chair to sit beside her, she placed a hand on his arm. "Thank you."

"Duty and love are gifts as much as they are obligations." Jeremy patted her hand and tried to ignore his fatigue and the aches of arthritis in his hands and shoulders that had flared up from catching and helping to carry her. "I missed you. We all did."

"I miss Ma, so I couldn't be here." They left each other to walk through their own thoughts.

She hadn't thought things would go as they had. She had expected and prepared herself to have a battle royale with Massad. Power against power in the no-holds-barred barn whipping she meant to give him. She valued life, but didn't hold it as sacrosanct as her mother had. She had been prepared to contain him by whatever means necessary—hurting him, taking his life, if need be.

Her experience in the hall had opened her to the

possibility that she might not be able to beat him in the manner she had expected. She had been meditating in her mother's office when, unbidden, the Soshinge chant was on her lips.

"Hi nyo nik-ko fu un mu
But though the light of the sun is veiled by clouds and mists,
Un mu shi ge myo mu an
Beneath the clouds and mists there is brightness, not dark.
Gyaku shin ken kyo dai kyo ki
When one realizes shinjin, seeing and revering and attaining great joy,
Soku o cho zetsu go aku shu
One immediately leaps crosswise, closing off the five evil courses."

She remembered a scripture that had always perplexed her. In Luke 2:35, Simeon foretold the life of Jesus to his mother Mary, saying, "And a sword will pierce your own soul."

Then she knew the answer. There was no darkness that light could not dispel, *and* that the piercing of light into darkness would hurt. She might not be able to conquer him, but she could change him.

Massad had come into her mother's office feeling as *she* had before, ready to fight. Her sitting so soon in his presence had seemed to please him. His standing and lording his power over her had suited her so much the better.

She smiled now, reflecting that the most powerful work was sometimes the easiest. She had planted one word deep inside his solar plexus—'Love.' While Massad had placed a taint in Raines for evil, she had planted one in Massad for good. She hadn't tried to best him; instead, she had realized that the effect of planting God's unconditional love within him would separate him from his evil powers.

Sheila had compressed the love energy and placed it

within him, threading it through his chakras in an almost imperceptible stream, which she had protected with a shield. When she had activated his solar plexus by twisting his belly button—the love energy uncovered and bloomed, searing to his soul—it caught him by surprise. It surprised no one more than herself that she too had been filled with love and became incapable of feeling the hate and anger for him she had been feeding off of. She wanted him to become a spirit of light. She probably could not have destroyed him or compelled him, but it had not been that difficult a matter to attach such a powerful light of love to him it left no place for darkness to rest.

Not that difficult a matter. She wanted to laugh to herself, but even the thought tired her out. The "easy" matter of it had left her more spiritually drained than she could ever remember being. She could barely move. It exhausted her even more to think that there was no one at home to greet her.

"I want to sleep," Sheila nestled deeper into the couch, grateful when Jeremy covered her with a throw, kissed her cheek, and left the room, turning off the lights as he closed the door. She closed her eyes and, when she should have been content with her victory and survival, she was filled with concern for her husband and what he must be feeling. Reaching out to retrieve the phone from her purse, she sent a quick text to Raines before falling asleep. The phone slipped out of her hand and made a soft thud as it hit the carpeted floor.

CHAPTER EIGHT
LOS LOMAS

Raines was enjoying being home. His brother, Carlos, had sent their driver to meet him at the airport, and, in no time, he was passing through the tree-lined boulevards of his family's residential community. He entered his family's compound and memories came flooding back of the fun and wicked things he had done under his parent's noses, sometimes under their orders. He sat out in one of the inner courtyards and enjoyed the lush, colorful landscaping that his mother always kept impeccable. How different the light was here, he thought, remembering his first forays into painting as a child.

He hardly bristled at the regular digs his family took at Sheila, and could only respond with non-committal grunts and monosyllabic answers to inquiries in that direction. This pleased his parents and had even emboldened the older and usually reserved Carlos to throw a party in his honor. Their parents had even opened the main gate to the compound, instead of the usual side entrances, so guests could arrive in style.

Theirs wasn't the biggest compound in the neighborhood, but theirs was *old* money that had an unbroken line to the present. Carlos was the politician. Raines was supposed to have been the artistic soul of the nation. But his stint in America had grown longer and longer. Then, when things had gotten serious with Sheila, how his parents had fought with him, saying that he was disgracing his ancestors by marrying outside of his race.

But, even then, they had assumed Raines would bring whomever he married back to the family to live in their ample compound and under their thumbs. His decision to stay permanently in America had almost led to him getting cut off by his parents. Now that he was here again, though, he knew that hungry glint that was in his family's eyes. They wanted him back, to take his place in their supposedly perfect dynasty.

Carlos laughed with Raines and they smoked cigars and drank tequila, as if all was well between them. Carlos flung an unending stream of beautiful women in his brother's direction. Raines resisted only slightly as women complimented him, ran their hands over him as if they had been longtime friends, sat on his lap, and laughed in his ears.

This had been his life before Sheila—art, women, parties, and games. He hadn't missed it much, but at the moment, it thrilled him to re-enter a lifestyle free of her influence and pain.

It didn't look like grief, but he was determined to ease the pain, to forget every obligation that brought him hurt. So when he stirred in his bed later that night and the familiar curves of naked women lay on either side of him, he chose not to remember how they had gotten there and what had taken place since then. It didn't please him that his manhood had lain lifeless as they had worked their most confident seductions on him. That, when he should have been doing what a man does with two beautiful women to release the angry, violent frustrations that lay inside him, he had instead lay listlessly, hardly watching as they tried to capture his attention.

He remembered how, the first time he brought Sheila here, she had said as diplomatically as she could that she thought something evil was here. Perhaps she had been correct. As he lay there as naked as the women beside him, he focused on the breathing techniques Sheila had taught him. They helped him feel less disgusted with himself. He was glad he hadn't had sex with them, but regretted he had not been able to burn off some of the pain and hurt that lay inside him by using their bodies, as he would have so easily and thoughtlessly years ago.

When he reflected on what had changed him so much

in the last few years, he could suspect it was only one thing—his wife. One woman stirred and placed her hand on his chest. God, he couldn't remember their names. Had he ever even known them? He plunged into a whirlwind of hurt and confusing emotions that left him unable to respond, for or against, as the woman woke and sleepily straddled him, using her skilled hands to coax him to life. He was a man after all, though he doubted it would have worked if he hadn't been thinking about Sheila.

Raines knew she was about to take him inside her. He knew he should have been able to muster up energy to stop this, but he just couldn't. He was about to cheat on his wife when he didn't mean to, didn't want to. The specter of that thought should have sprung him into action, but he still felt paralyzed.

As she took him inside her, he looked from her up to the ceiling and tried not to enjoy the feel of her too much. He could barely reach out to the nightstand to grab his phone when its notice tone beeped. "One unread text message." He tapped to read the note, and the picture of Sheila, one with her sticking her tongue out at him in a playful mood, popped up on the screen. Beneath it, her message read, "miss u."

"¡Maldita sea!" he muttered. Dropping the phone, he grabbed the hips of the women on top of him, meaning to draw her off of him, when he recognized a familiar pull. He let out a frustrated moan and dropped his hands. When she rolled off of him, he sat up on his elbows. Looking down, he grimaced to confirm what he had already known. He hadn't even worn a condom.

He wanted to slap the woman until her head spun. But he knew it wasn't her fault, at least, not most of it. All he could do was deal with things as they were now. Grabbing his phone, he sent a quick text in reply before showering, dressing, grabbing his bags, and leaving his family's estate without a backwards glance.

CHAPTER NINE
HOME

Sheila woke rested and calm as light shone in the prayer room at the Institute. She had slept a long time. As she rose, she heard the muted buzzing of her phone. It took her a few moments to sit up and gather herself. Finally, she figured out where she had dropped her phone and began smiling in advance when she saw she had a text from Raines. As she opened the message, she got concerned.

"U r my home. 4give me 4 more than u know."

Sheila let out a long sigh as she let her hands fall into her lap. She had an incredibly heavy feeling. Closing her eyes to the material world around her and the roiling emotions within her, she reached out to a clear place in her spirit. She hadn't made use of her clairvoyant powers in what felt like a very long time. They were rusty. Slowly but surely, she formed her intention—what she wanted to see. A scene laid itself out before her and she watched a woman having sex with her husband while another lay beside them. She saw him try to stop but fail, and the look on his face afterwards. She ended the vision as she saw him tapping his phone, presumably texting her.

Sheila sighed as she opened her eyes and lay back on the couch. She was a mature woman who knew what was what. She knew the disappointments, hurts, and confusions that had driven him to Las Lomas. His easy way with women had probably combined with that ball of emotions to put him in that bed.

Sheila was surprised. Raines was an honorable man. She had always been able to count on that without a second thought. She was as shocked as she was hurt that he had done such a thing. Holding back the tears, the wailing, and the hurt, she struggled to think over the issue.

She was sure he was sorry, sure he would do

whatever it took to heal the breach. She had known he would have to face the phantom of his old life when he had gone down there. Did it matter that it took the form of a woman and sex that he hadn't sought? Yes, it mattered! But what she had feared most was that he would have stayed in a place she couldn't go.

Three nights ago, she had lost him. Now he had made his choice. He was coming back to her, all of him—as broken and imperfect as he was. Her husband was completely hers, despite all the children that she couldn't give him. He would be with her, body and soul, now. He had made his choice after a painful and costly failure. And for her, there had been no choice for her to make from the first time they met. She was his. Sheila would concentrate on that.

She sent him a text before she rose to walk the labyrinth outside and cry her heart out. When she saw him again, she wanted to be free, as much as she could be, of the anger and hurt that lay deep inside her. She knew he was on his way home. She was his home.

A little after three that afternoon, Raines drummed his fingers on the armrest impatiently as the plane taxied toward the gate at BWI Airport. As soon as it stopped, he turned on his phone, nervous to see if Sheila had responded. He didn't know what he was hoping for. He read her text—"I know. Glad u chose me. Come home 2 me & we'll talk. I love u."

Raines let out a sigh that was equal parts relief and guilt. He often forgot that she was psychic. It didn't make a difference to him, since she always said it didn't work the way he thought, and they couldn't win the lottery. But when she wrote she knew, Raines knew she really did.

He had nothing to offer this woman except his contrition, so he would take her that, and not be intimidated by the weakness and indefensibility of his position. He hadn't a leg to stand on. Faced with Sheila's mercy, he could only feel even worse. But he would bear it. He had seen how soulless and rash his life would be without her.

He had always known it, but last night he had felt it. His was a cruel and reckless family. He had possessed talent, passion, and a sense of duty. He had felt upstanding and limitless. But the man he had become through Sheila made his former self pale in comparison. He could never go back to that old life and not see it for what it was, empty and harmful. Even if he couldn't have the children he had always wanted, she had already given him more than he had ever even known there was to have. If he stuck with her, he was sure everything would be all right. He had made that choice too late, yet she was still ready to forgive him.

As he waited in line for a cab and all the way home, he poured over Sheila's text again and again. She loved him. After a few minutes spent standing at his own front door, afraid to go in, that thought gave him the courage to enter.

Sheila was dreaming of walking through her grandmother's garden. She hadn't done that in years, and it was comforting. The beautiful flowers captivated her and the sweet scent of honeysuckle reminded her of her childhood summers in the country. She woke suddenly as Raines gently shook her shoulder. She gasped and drew back instinctively, then regretted it as she saw the recognition on his face that she had withdrawn from his touch.

"I…I'm," Sheila paused, putting her hand on her chest and trying to take some deep steadying breaths to calm her skipping heart.

"No." Raines sat next to her. "You don't have to say anything. I should be the one explaining myself."

Sheila finally got her breath back. "I know you have some things to say to me. I want to hear. And I have some things to say to you. I made some tea." She picked up a thermos that had been resting at her feet. "Let's go outside. We'll talk." She stood and held out her hand to him, but she just couldn't manage the smile she had wanted to give.

Raines took her hand as if it might break. He helped her into her coat, and they went out to sit on the back patio. She poured herself some tea and held the steaming cup close to her face, closing her eyes as she breathed in the peachy herbal fragrance. The sounds of birds filled the air as they went about whatever business birds have. Their chirps and calls made for a soothing soundscape.

Finally, she opened her eyes and, for the first time since he had returned, took a good look at her husband. It brought her equal parts comfort and sadness to see that he looked as bad as she felt.

"You said you knew what happened, but I still have to say it. I went home, I mean to Las Lomas. I didn't like life without you, but I was hurting and it felt good to escape to my family, who thinks everything I do is right and all you do is wrong." Raines accepted the tea Sheila offered and took a gulp.

"I wound up in bed with two women. Carlos had thrown a party…I let them touch me. I did nothing to stop them. I felt like I wasn't even there. I was so mad at you. One of the women got on top of me, and we had sex. I'm so sorry. Your text came in the middle of that and it was like a wake up call. I realized I loved you more than all the other things I want. I need you, and even when I'm mad or hurting, there's no solution without you. Whatever I'm going through, even if I feel you are the cause, I still want you and want to work it out with you, not by myself, not with someone else. But it was too late. I wasn't wearing a condom. I don't even know who she was. I'm sorry."

Sheila said nothing for a long time. She had struggled

to maintain eye contact as he spoke and, as soon as he had finished, she drew her knees up and buried her face in them, focusing on breathing through the waves of nausea that swept through her. Raines endured the silence as best he could. Finally, she brought her head up, soaked with tears.

"I believe you. We'll be alright, but I just don't know when. For now, I'm hurt, and it's going to take a long time for me to trust you again, but I want to try." She inhaled and let out a long exhalation. "That's what I have to say. Oh, and I'm so glad you came home." She managed a smile, because she was happy he had come back to her.

"I'm tired," Sheila sighed, "and I want to lie down. With you."

Both of them had had more words than they could bear, and were bundles of raw nerve. Raines came out of the shower in a t-shirt and some drawstring pajama pants to find Sheila perched nervously on the edge of the bed. Normally he only wore boxers, since Sheila insisted on keeping it like a hothouse on the upper floor, but that felt too intimate now. He didn't want to make assumptions. One look at her unease confirmed he had made the right decision.

Sheila patted a spot on the bed beside her, and he joined her. She leaned into him, and his arms encircled her. It gratified Raines to feel her let her guard down with him. He held her closer.

"Ow!" Sheila jumped back. "No need to crush me to death," she laughed as she rubbed her shoulder.

"Sorry." Raines looked mortified.

"Well, if you're going to lose your sense of humor, that's no good." Sheila scrambled to the head of the bed to grab a pillow and gave him a lighthearted whack on the head. She hit him harder than she had intended.

"Did you kiss her?"

The question caught him off-guard, but Raines searched his memory. He didn't think so, but he wanted to be sure. "She kissed me, but not on the mouth." That revelation stung them both.

"Raines, kiss me." Sheila had an almost desperate need to feel close to him.

He hadn't felt this nervous and unsure around her since he had proposed. He touched his lips gently to hers, then deepened the kiss when he felt how easily she opened up to him. Sheila leaned into his arms.

"I'm yours, completely," she sighed. "It's as much a gift as it is a responsibility. I told you when we wed I would never divorce you. I knew you needed that promise, and I was glad to give it. It means that when you fail me, I have no recourse. I don't leave. I don't even cut myself off. I just hurt."

Sheila looked him in the eye. "What happens to me the next time you're hurting?"

"I can't say I will be a perfect man and husband. I may cause you hurt again. But I know that from this moment on, I will never be so concerned about myself that I forget or disregard you. You come first—before everyone and everything. I'll do whatever it takes for you to find peace with me again—to trust me."

"I want you to get tested for any sexually transmitted diseases, and again in six weeks. And you need to find out who she was. In case…" she couldn't bring herself to voice her fear that some stranger might give him the children she could not.

"I will. I will." Raines hadn't even thought about ramifications beyond their relationship. He could have caught something, and he could have impregnated a perfect stranger. These new thoughts lay heavy on his mind. "I will."

Sheila got under the covers and lay down. Sitting against the headboard, Raines stroked her hair and rubbed her back, preoccupied with his predicament. Eventually they dozed, but the tension never left them.

PART THREE
TOMORROW AND TOMORROW AND TOMORROW

CHAPTER TEN
AFTER

Sheila woke up tangled up in Raines. She nuzzled his neck, trying to get a bit more rest. She still felt the exhaustion of dealing with Massad besides all the stuff going on between her and Raines. A woman in her position was entitled to sleep in, she thought. She tried to push back all of her complicated feelings and just enjoy being in her husband's arms.

The bedroom was always too hot, according to Raines, but it was just right for her. She knew he must be suffering in his t-shirt and pajama pants, but she appreciated he had worn them to make her feel more comfortable. Or maybe he did it because he didn't want her looking at his body, wondering where that woman had touched. His wearing clothes hadn't stopped her from doing that, so he might as well have been comfortable, she thought.

Mingled in with all the fear and nervousness, the hurt and love, she had to admit she wanted him. Last night when he had kissed her, she had wanted his hands on her, for them to be one flesh. She had needed that comfort, despite what he had done. But it still hurt. Even now, it burned her throat and sent her stomach into somersaults. But she was trying not to punish him out of spite.

Sighing, she prayed as they held each other that he hadn't caught some disease from that woman. She would have to wait 6 weeks to make love to her husband, so that they both could be sure. They had enough to work through without the threat of communicable diseases hanging over their heads. Maybe the wait would be a good thing. Her heart hurt. It had felt achy and tender since she had found out. The wait would take the pressure off her to get back to normal too soon and give her battered heart a chance to heal.

As Raines stirred, she felt a familiar sexual appetite

emanating from him. It would be a long 6 weeks, she thought. As he ran his hands down her back, Sheila began a diligent pinching endeavor that left only a few bits of his exposed skin untouched.

"Woman!" Raines drew away from her and his eyes flew open.

"Wake up," she laughed. "It's time to discuss what you're making me for breakfast."

His face looked confused and annoyed for a moment before recognition ran across it. He composed his features into an easy smile.

"Happy to. What do you want?" He wanted to hold her again, but was suddenly aware of the distance between them. He hated feeling awkward in any situation, much more so around his own wife. Still, he should be grateful that she had even let him in the house. He got out of bed, remembering that.

"You want it in bed or downstairs?"

"I'll take it up here. Roll the TV in and we can watch something."

Raines gave her a smile and headed downstairs, trying to figure out how he was going to get back to feeling comfortable around his wife again. It would take time, he supposed.

Over a breakfast that had taken him longer to make than it took them to eat, they watched a random cooking show in bed, making sarcastic remarks and little observations about the episode. When she had finally eaten more than enough, she pushed the tray away, took a few deep breaths, and told him all about Massad.

Raines listened with interest and a good deal of confusion whenever she threw terms casually about that he didn't understand.

"Sounds too good for him," he concluded.

"If I had played that game, I could have hurt him, but I might not have won." Sheila leaned back, suddenly tired again, and rubbed her overfull belly. "Plus, I need him cooperative. There are still a lot of unanswered questions I'm thinking he may have the answers to."

"So…what *are* you going to do about the Institute? How did it feel to go back there for the first time since the funeral?"

"Ah," she grumbled, "night before last was business, not a return. I couldn't let emotion in. I was focused." Sheila sighed. "It looks like I have to take over the Institute, doesn't it? I can't just let it die. It was her life's dream. Brief life, big dream," she reflected as she looked off into space.

Shaking herself, she scooted under the covers and pulled them over her head. "Every step pushes me further and further into someone else's life," she mumbled.

Raines pulled the covers away from her face. "One more time?"

"I don't want to be her; I never did. I loved her, respected her, but I never wanted the things she did. Different things, different goals. Now, what choice do I have?" She sighed and kicked her feet under the covers. "I'm pushed into a corner."

Raines set the breakfast tray off of the bed and held her. He wanted to say everything would be ok, but he didn't know that it would. So he just rubbed her back and kept her close. As usual of late, she cried in his arms and eventually fell asleep.

Raines stood outside the open door to Sheila's shrine room, hesitant about going in. Even with his strict Catholic background, albeit lapsed, her Buddhist shrine had always drawn him to it. The statue of the God of War had fascinated him from the start. When they had wed, she had given him permission to commune with him whenever he liked. This consisted of sitting in front of the shrine and pouring liquor into a shot glass, downing it, and leaving the last drink in front of the statue. As long as there was no cooked food at the shrine, he could do this.

It was hard to describe, but he had known from the first time she had included him in that ritual that there was something to it. It comforted him. He felt he was in camaraderie with a good and powerful friend. It made him uncomfortable to realize that, but he pushed all the difficult questions of the situation deep down.

Normally he would have just taken off his shoes, walked in and done it, but he had been skittish of all things witch-ish since Massad. So he stood at the edge of the doorway and wished for periscopic vision as he tried to see if any cooked food was on the shrine. Just the normal raw jasmine rice and mysterious red seeds in their neat bowls, along with some fruit stacked and a couple of lit candles.

It was all clear. He took a deep breath and walked in, sat before the shrine, and started pouring.

"And if you've got any marital advice, I'm listening." He nursed the shot of brandy he had been working on. It was still morning. Sitting there had calmed him down some. It reminded him there were a great number of things completely beyond him and his control. It brought the realization back that his wife was nothing if not an unusual woman whose mind didn't work like anyone else's he had ever known. So, that meant there was reason to hope.

It suddenly occurred to him that he should be painting. Wiping the rim of the tall shot glass, he set it down and carefully filled it to the top.

"That ought to tide you over," he chuckled as he walked down the stairs and allowed thoughts of his work to fill his mind.

CHAPTER ELEVEN
REUNION

Sheila paced back and forth in front of her mother's shrine room. The hallway on the second floor looked like she had worn a path in the carpet, but she must have been imagining it. As it had always been when she was alive, Ma's house was neat, with everything just so. Ma's house had truly been her castle, and everything, including this weird zigzag carpet on the second floor that Sheila had never liked, was just how she had wanted it. Every knickknack held a story. She knew some of those tales and perhaps she was looking back on some of those memories with fondness instead of blind grief. Being in her mother's house was hard and sad, but it also held gifts that Sheila was doing her best to cherish.

She had driven slowly and made a trip that usually took twenty minutes last half an hour. She had swept the house yet again for any signs of what was causing the stale smell everywhere. And, of course, things were eerily quiet. Sheila turned on some music for the plants. They had always thrived under her mother's care, but she was barely keeping them alive. She even tried talking to them. At last, she could find nothing else to do.

It wasn't that she was afraid of her grandfather, at least she kept telling herself that. She was trying her best not to hate him for…for everything, she thought. Yes, a petty person could see this entire business as his fault. She was working to keep from being petty.

The question was what would come next. She had passed her dream test. She had read. She had agreed, although it closed the door on her husband's dream. It had cost her. Now, there was precious little left to do but the act itself.

Interdimensional gatekeeper, Sheila scoffed. It sounded like something from a science fiction movie. Why hadn't her mother told her? Had she thought her daughter incapable of the job? Or had the love and intimacy that she had thought was so complete between them simply not been as strong as she believed? She shook that off, holding on to the equally precious and fearful memory of her mother's apparition from beyond the grave that day she had contemplated ending her life. No, whatever else, she decided, her mother loved her more than enough. So, why hadn't she told her?

She knew she was strong, stronger than her sisters. She could admit that to herself with little guilt or presumption. But she also knew that she had never matched her mother. Part of that was practice. It simply wasn't, or hadn't been until now, her choice in life, so she hadn't given it the discipline of practice and strengthening that it deserved. The bigger part was just raw ability. Pound-for-spiritual-pound, her wiry mother beat her twice over for power.

Now she was alone. For the first time since her mother's death, the *logistical* implications of her absence hit her. She didn't want to learn from her heartless grandfather. She wanted to learn from her best friend, her mother. She didn't want to do the job alone and jump in at full speed. She wanted to be apprenticed and brought along gently.

Sheila wanted more than a handful of weeks to get used to a reality that changed her life. She had always hated being backed into corners. It took all her restraint not to lash out blindly in rebellion at the prescribed picture of her life that lay before her.

Sheila scrubbed her palms over her face. She was afraid. What had she gotten herself into? What job was so difficult that it made having children impossible? Rarely had the use of her powers involved any kind of actual risk, and rarer still were the times she had faced such risks alone. Oh yes, she was spitting mad at the man in the mirror. And terrified.

When she couldn't delay it any longer, she entered

the shrine room, sat before the ancestral shrine, and called on her grandfather.

"You neglect your duties, child." Her grandfather's voice sounded stern. "We've work to do."

Sheila said nothing. She fidgeted.

"I need you here, focused and prepared. Your work starts tonight."

She snapped to attention. Then, a self-satisfied grin spread across her face, replacing the confused and anxious look.

"No," she said calmly and slowly.

"This is no time for your machinations."

Sheila stood, grabbed a throw from a bench, and stalked over to the mirror from which her grandfather spoke. It churned so blue and smoky that she could not see her own reflection.

"I could cover your mirror with this throw, dismantle this shrine, and never hear from you again if I wanted. And I want," she said threateningly.

"My mother always wanted me to have my own life. She *never* spoke of me following in her footsteps in this way. It's my life! Why should I change it; because you say so? Don't give me any story about life hanging in the balance. I'm unmoved by some over-dramatized plight of existence as we know it. What's in it for *me?*" she asked coldly.

"Selfish."

"Yes," she hissed. "I want something for me! I don't have it in me to live a lifetime's martyrdom, and you know it. What's in it for me?"

"It's your destiny."

"It's my curse! Do you expect me to run to it?"

"I expect you to do as you're told." There was violence simmering beneath the surface of his tone.

"The only person who could order me was my mother. And she's gone now." It stung to say it. "So the way I figure it, no one but God tells me what to do now. I know you know you're not him."

"The same fire as your mother," he said reflectively. "But a great deal stupider. You start tonight." he spoke with finality.

"None of this moves me," Sheila said decisively, but tiredly. Going toe-to-toe with her grandfather took grit. Everything of late only sapped her energy. "I don't need to be courted, but I will have *some* respect, and even some consideration, if not kindness. I am not a soulless droid. If you can't deal with that, then do it yourself. And I mean it." Sheila's tone was just as final as her grandfather's. She wondered, as she plopped back down on the floor before the shrine and endured a long silence, which one of them would give.

"I am sorry about Raines. I had no wish for that to happen."

Sheila blinked. It almost sounded like Grandfather had feelings.

"I'm glad you're dealing with it. He's good for you. And I can tell you, he contracted nothing that night, and the girl won't conceive, at least not from him."

Relief flooded into her. She doubled over on the floor in release.

"Thank you," she said, gratitude pouring out of her. She sat back up and asked, "Is there anything you can do for my heart? It hurts so bad."

"Would you really want me to?"

"I need not to feel this way. It's destroying me, all my good intentions. The betrayal and the pain—it's hard to see past them."

"You never asked me to treat you for the pain of your mother's death. Is this worse than your grief?"

"That was different. My mother's memory is tied up in that. I can't discard the grief. There's too much of her in it."

"If I shield you from this pain, you'll go back to

normal, but what you and he have will never be stronger. And it can be. It's your choice."

Sheila found she didn't like that choice.

"Fine." She supposed she would just have to endure it.

"But what I will do is give you a peaceful sleep. Your rest will be true rest. Bring out the padding and take a nap. You start tonight."

As she fell into a sleep that reminded her of dipping into a cool, calm pool, she wondered which one of them had come out ahead in that exchange. She sighed, and every hurt, tension, and concern simply slipped away. Sheila snored like a lumberjack through one of the most relieving naps she had ever had.

CHAPTER TWELVE
PREPARATIONS

Sheila yawned and stretched her way out of a blissful sleep. She woke to find darkness fast approaching as she glanced at the windows. The grim thought that tonight was here penetrated her sleepy brain.

Sheila sat up and gathered herself. Sitting in a lotus position and concentrating, she reached out with her will to light some of the darkened candles until they filled the room with a warm glow. As she placed her palms downward on her knees, she took stock of herself. She was terrified. But, somehow, she felt ready. As she kept pace with the approaching night by singing, praying, and chanting, she felt less frightened and more centered. Finally, she could no longer deny it was pitch black outside, that the time had arrived.

As she and her grandfather had discussed countless times, with him drilling her on it between her dream work until she could recite it in her most exhausted moments, she began the proper preparations for the room. It didn't bother her that her grandfather seemed absent for this moment. She had always known she would ultimately be alone in this. Maybe she had even scared him away with her tough talk, she mused.

Sheila opened a floor-to-ceiling cabinet that, in all the years she had been in this room, she had never seen open. She stood breathless for a long moment. What a treasure. Various wands, medallions, pots of powder, vials of oils, seals, and crystals lined the shelves neatly. She held her breath for the half minute that she had stared and wracked her mental Rolodex to identify as many of the items as she could. Slowly she exhaled, afraid to breathe too hard and disturb the energy that emanated from the cabinet.

She searched the shelves until she found the items she

wanted: a case of old chalk pieces burned from stones in the Isar River in Germany, a piece of Dragon's Blood resin, the charcoal and small ornate bowl to burn it in, a sheet of parchment paper that looked ageless, a vial of yellow sulphur powder, an old, used quill and a bottle of black ink from who knew where, a vial of pure and undiluted white camphor, a bottle of Chinese Florida Water, a large ancient Japanese foot warmer with kindling wood chips placed inside, and a few kitchen matches. When she finished placing the items in the middle of the room, she smiled. Ma loved antiquity.

First, she retrieved a very large compass from the corner, took the chalk, and made a perfect circle 6 feet in diameter. Next, she lit the small flat disc of charcoal inside the brass bowl and doused herself with Florida Water to cleanse herself of negativity and purify her while she waited for the charcoal disc to turn an ashy white-hot. When the disc was white, she placed a few large chunks of the hard dark red Dragon's Blood resin on it, and they smoked and released their scent and power immediately. The smoke cleansed and banished negative energies from the space.

Once she was sure that she and the space were clear, she carefully spread an unbroken trail of sulfur over the chalk circle she had drawn, going back countless times to ensure that the chalk and sulfur were even and unbroken. This was the basis of the circle she was casting, a sacred space where she could state her intent and carry out spiritual work in an empowered and protected environment. The chalk circle would hold and amplify whatever intent she formed within it, while the sulfur would ensure no spirit, evil or otherwise, passed the barrier. The hairs on the back of her neck stood on end as she felt the vacuum caused by the energies of the various shrines high-tailing it out of the room.

Sheila turned to face the small bottle of camphor, deceptively harmless-looking, and grimaced. She had never dealt with undiluted camphor before. She had used diluted amounts in aromatherapy to aid her in specific spiritual tasks—astral projection, to commune with the archangel Gabriel, cleansing crystals, and the like—but this circle casting required its undiluted use. It would enhance her spiritual powers, particularly her clairvoyance. Evil spirits fled from camphor like Satan fled from the name of Jesus.

Camphor could cause convulsions and other wretched reactions upon contact with skin. It would be a shame to die before she got this superhero gig on the road, Sheila thought wryly as she bent to pick up the bottle. She opened it as far away from her face as she could manage without risking dropping it. Using the dropper, she placed one drop in the exact middle of the circle and held her breath until the vial was closed again. She took a slow, hesitant inhalation, trying not to choke on the acrid smell that filled the room. She took a few more breaths to get used to it. Well, if embalmers could handle the smell of it, so would she, Sheila thought.

She was almost ready. The idea that it might actually be dawn before she would be ready crossed her mind before she stamped it down but it made her more mindful of her pace. She at least wanted to complete casting her circle before the witching hour began. She gathered up the items she had finished using, carried them to the edge of the circle and then, without stepping outside of the barrier, bent over and placed them on a nearby bench. Sitting down, not quite in the middle of the circle to avoid the camphor dot, she arranged the kindling wood in the foot warmer basin, closed the top, and placed it near the edge of the circle.

Lastly, she wrote her full name on the parchment with the quill and ink. She wavered a moment to think that her mom had used all these items to do as she was doing, and had held this pen and wrote her own name on a piece of parchment only months before. Gently putting that thought away, she folded the parchment toward her three times and placed it in her bra over her heart. Should anything go wrong, this would help her spirit find her body again.

Placing the ink and quill on the bench in the same

manner, she took stock of her circle. It felt completed. She walked its perimeter seven times, reciting various chants and shoring up its barrier by directing her energies. Now it was time to set her intent. What to say…superhero, unemployed, cheated-on housewife seeks inter-dimensional trespassers to banish? That was a bit too sarcastic, even for her tastes. Finally she settled on it in her mind and, with a loud clap of hands at her heart center, said in a clear, still voice, "The daughter will follow the mother here," and let the silence absorb, amplify, and steep in those words.

Turning to the mirror from where her grandfather usually spoke to her, she frowned. She had expected him to be here. They had talked about everything, except what to do next. So it was inconvenient for him not to be here now. She was sure it was intentional, and was not displeased to find that the ire helped stoke her spiritual energies to a full blaze.

She lay down flat to the right of the circle's center and prepared to put herself into a trance, as she would for astral travel. After saying the usual prayers for protecting her body, she reflected, remembering what she had read about the distinctions between general astral travel and inter-dimensional travel. She thought back to when she was a child and her mom had taught her how they could meet each other in the rainbow palace while they slept, and how they both remembered the same things that had happened in the morning, even though she had been sure it had only been a dream.

She felt ready to travel, but did not know what would happen when she got there. 'It will be bad,' Sheila thought, remembering what her grandfather had said about the damage of having the gate unguarded all this time. Slowly, her spiritual body floated up and out of her physical body, trailing a thin, silvery cord behind it.

Sheila felt herself drawn forward and upward through the astral plane until she found herself in a glowing clearing. To her right was a doorway that seemed made of stones of light. And, low and behold, leaning against those stones, as casual as you please, was her grandfather.

"You made it," he remarked without looking at her.

"Well, at least I know you weren't sleeping on the job," Sheila quipped, though she had to admit she was relieved to see him. She still didn't quite know how to be alone since Ma, especially now.

"Slumming, aren't you? What is it costing you to be here?" The astral plane was not a roaring hang out spot for deceased spirits of his power and purpose.

"A great deal, but intercession is being made so that my costs will not be…permanent."

Sheila shuddered. The spiritual and metaphysical workings at his level were something she could well do without knowing. She hadn't imagined he would actually answer her.

"So," she stalled, "this is the gate, then?" Sheila gestured toward the portal he leaned against.

He didn't reply, which she took to mean, 'Of course, you idiot.'

She started to ask if she was supposed to go through it, but she checked herself before it left her lips. She didn't feel like another silent insult.

"I'm sure you realize we have never talked about what goes on in there and what I'm actually supposed to *do*," Sheila remarked, a trickle of disquiet running through her.

"Just be yourself, especially with that stubborn, unbearable attitude, and you'll be fine."

"That is unhelpful advice."

"I'll be here," he responded, suddenly straightening and looking past her.

"Some coach you are," she sighed. And with that, Sheila walked past him and entered the gate.

CHAPTER THIRTEEN
THE GATE

Hell. Later, when she had time to think, she would say this was what she always imagined it would be like in Hell. From the outside, the doorway had looked innocent enough. As soon as Sheila had passed through that harmless-looking barrier, things had changed.

Noise. A riotous din of noise and a mind-numbing blur of movement and color assaulted her when she passed through the gate. Everywhere was chaos and discord. It attached itself to her like a leech, draining and disorienting her. It didn't look like an interplanetary battle scene, but it came close.

Something akin to the God of War was releasing a high-pitched wail of an attack that was aimed at her. He had locked his gaze on her as soon as she had entered. His attack ripped through her so hard she had to lock her jaws to keep her teeth from chattering. It seemed to reach in and reverberate to her spine. That pissed her off.

Clenching her fists along with her teeth, Sheila struggled to take a breath. She closed her mind to the chaos and gathered her energies. First, she would be done with all the nonsense. Fifth dimension energies littered the gateway like the unruly spirits they were. They lived for chaos and were having a field day.

Sheila had always thought of them as imps, although they weren't only that, strictly speaking. Many a fifth dimension spook was the reason grown men slept with the lights on. They were scary and could do damage. They couldn't hurt, but could disrupt things until a person lost their mind.

Since she had entered, they had begun playing a game of chicken with her, careening around her in their bright, eye-catching colors, then taking hairpin turns to speed towards her. They meant to pass right through her at that speed. If she hadn't had her barriers up, they would have, and she would have gone crazy on the spot. As it was, the resulting occurrence was just as bad; they collided against her shield about five inches from her body, erupting in a splash of neon and undulating colors like supernatural bugs on a windshield. It was disturbing.

'Oh, you *will* move for me,' Sheila thought with a bit more glee than she ruefully imagined her mother might have had. Opening her left hand, there was a small steady swarm of black mist there; her own little black hole.

"Come on babies," she invited, and couldn't help but chuckle as the ooze of the decimated spirits that had tried to run her through was sucked into the eddying black orb in her hand. She struggled for that chuckle not to turn into a more sinister cackle. She had to stay focused.

"You *will* leave. Now." She focused her intention and power behind the certainty of the result in the statement. Fifth dimension beings began, not to scream or howl, but to beg, plead, try to trick, and cajole. At least this was something she knew, she thought with some relief.

When all the imp spirits had been gathered into her orb, she held her hand to rest in line with her solar plexus. In her mind, she said, 'Stop,' and the small pulsing black eddy went stone still, turning suddenly solid and heavy. She let it slip from her hand and it hit the ground beneath her with a vague thud. As it rolled away from her, it quickly grew smaller and smaller, until it disappeared.

She wanted to allow herself a small sigh of relief, but the fierce and bearded being's steady assault on her made her jaw lock. It almost made her miss the jarring, but less harmful, attacks from the beings she had just dismissed.

Now that Sheila had cleared the gate of about three dozen chaos monsters, she could get a better picture of what she was up against. He was the definition of terror, over 8 feet of ancient terra cotta warrior on steroids. And what was worse, she grimaced, was that he knew she was afraid of him. He howled with a confident laugh as he ritualistically stomped his feet. The actions combined to shake the air, earth, her spine, and confidence to the core.

This wasn't some dream where she could have a do-over. He wanted to pulverize her. She would have turned tail and run to the gate, but she knew she'd be dead before she started. He wanted to break through the gate. She and the fast-fading bindings her mother had placed on the door before her death were all that was stopping this thing from wreaking in her dimension.

"You amuse me," he uttered. "I will chew your bones while you yet live." Laughter echoed.

"I had fainted, unless I had believed to see the goodness of the LORD in the land of the living. Truth works better than threat. You should try it." It shocked Sheila that her sarcastic confidence was here. She stalked toward him and rolled up her sleeves. Suddenly, she felt confident. "Why are you still here? If you could have gotten through already, you would have." Sheila tilted her head in an expression of mock pity, "Big, bad monster not know how to turn doorknob?"

The being snarled and flung itself towards her with more ferociousness than she could have imagined. Sheila slowed time, using the extra moments she had created to grab a handful of gray powder from a pouch that she had willed to materialize at her side. As time sped back up to whatever passed for normal in this dimension, the being screeched to a halt just short of her powdered fist.

"Oh yes! Where's the bravado now?" she queried. As she stepped forward, keeping her hand in front of her, the being retreated and diminished in stature. "I really appreciate a perceptive adversary. You have the good sense to be afraid."

With that, she opened her fist and blew the gray powder over the retreating threat. As the powder spread to cover him entirely and harden, it took the form of a slightly translucent warrior. Slowly, the being beat itself on the chest, fighting the demon trapped within its form. Sheila turned and was walking out through the gateway before she could see the warrior draw its sword and, plunging it deep into its armor, collapse into a pile of broken, lifeless, harmless stones.

Outside of the gate, Sheila dusted off her hands. Two more warriors sprung up where the dust from her hands settled and assumed guarding positions.

"Let me know when something's wrong." With that, she began her descent to reunite with her body.

Sheila woke in the circle with an exhausted laugh. "I can do it!" she chuckled. As she rose to a seated position, she went to raise her arms above her head in victory. It was then that she took in the state of her right arm. Red, swollen, and in excruciating pain from shoulder to fingers. The arm she had used to call forth the black hole and banish the lower energies and to call forth the warriors to destroy her foe and guard the gate was battered and almost useless.

It had seemed so easy in that dimension. But it had repercussions she hadn't expected on this plane. "Maybe he *could* have crunched my bones," she mused, to take her mind off the pain. As she stood, her arm inevitably changed position, causing her to swoon and see stars.

With her left arm, she used the kitchen match to light the kindling in the foot warmer near the edge of her circle. In it, she threw the papyrus with her name on it. Then she broke the circle with a sure brush of her foot. She cast some sulfur on the camphor, knowing that would neutralize it in a matter of moments. Sweeping up the chalk and sulfur from the circle, she poured that into the basin, where it glowed white-hot blue as it ignited. With a great deal of patience and pain, she scrubbed any remains of the circle from the floor.

Finally, covered in a sheen of sweat that was part hard work and part pain-induced, she returned the things she had used to the cabinet, except for the basin. It had ceased burning long ago, but was still warm and held contents she needed to dispose of off of the grounds.

Dawn crept in the windows. Sheila stifled oaths and cried out as she removed her sweater and positioned herself on a bench so that the direct light from the sun would shine on her injured arm. Half dozing, she recited a Native American healing prayer that came to mind.

"Mother, heal my heart
So that I can see
The gifts of yours
That can live through me."

She was asleep before she could see her arm regaining its normal color, size, and mobility.

PART FOUR
SUNRISE

CHAPTER FOURTEEN
DEBRIEF

Sheila woke up wondering if she was the Highlander. Her arm seemed almost normal again, and last night, she had been sure it was beyond hope. She had already been musing about how to explain it to the ER doctors. This was far too much like a TV miniseries for her tastes.

"Well, time to consult the director then," she said as she hoisted herself up. Walking over to her mother's ancestral shrine, she wished she could have just banged a big spoon inside a metal pot until her grandfather came calling, but she knew certain things had to be done in a certain order. Turning the percolator on next to the cabinet, yesterday's coffee reheated while she tended to the shrine. Clearing away old saucers and fruit offerings that were going off, she had everything looking refreshed and clean by the time the scent of hot coffee wafted through the room.

Looking up at the wall clock, Sheila noted the time. It really was too early to be calling ancestors up, but she had no doubt in her power to do so. She also didn't much care if her grandfather got his other-worldly beauty rest or not. Settling down before the shrine with a cup of hot coffee, she took the cigar from its place and relit it, blowing out a little smoke before she took a sip of the coffee. She let her thoughts roll over his presence until she could feel a change in the atmosphere. Sheila didn't even have to look at the mirror for his reflection. She knew he was there.

"You honor your descendant," Sheila said, bowing so low from her seated position that her nose touched the floor.

"It is my purpose."

"And so humble, too," she smirked.

"Sheila, you did well last night."

Sheila's heart swelled at the words. It surprised her that his approval should matter so much, but it did.

"Careless and arrogant," he continued, "but sufficient."

"When you say sweet things like that, I go all to pieces," she retorted in a flat voice. Sheila worked to dismiss her disappointment. Shifting her focus, she held out her right arm and asked, "Is it you I have to thank for this?"

"The injury you received last night was not a physical one. It was a spiritual one from overusing certain elements of your ability. But since your body and spirit are fused, and now that you travel between dimensions, it might as well be physical. You, and you alone, will be able to 'see' your spiritual wounds as physical ones. They will hurt like mortal injuries but will heal quicker because the spirit is replenished and renewed more fully more often in you."

"I *am* the Highlander." Sheila threw her head back and laughed, because if she thought too seriously about her situation, she might cry. "Grandfather, I am going off the grid for a few days. I'll be back. Please leave me be in the meantime."

"How many mistakes in a row would you like to make?" he said sternly.

"Oh," Sheila replied in a light and carefree tone, "at least one more."

CHAPTER FIFTEEN
RUNAWAY

Sheila gritted her teeth as she used her right arm, which was still quite sore, to drive home. With a long sigh, she rested her head on the steering wheel when she pulled in front of the house. She hadn't enough energy leftover even to breathe. But she lusted after a bath and her own bed with a fierce passion that had her peeling herself out of the car and heading towards her front door. Raines opened the door just as she was wondering where she would find the energy to turn the handle.

"My kingdom for a lift."

"That's a bargain." Raines gave her a hug and shifted to bear her weight as she all but collapsed in his arms. Hoisting her up, he took in the exhaustion on her face. "You don't look so hot,"

"Raines, you are to always tell your wife she looks hot." And with that, she fell asleep in his arms.

The afternoon sun was shining when she woke to find herself in bed. She looked around and had the familiar comforts of home to greet her. She had gotten pale blue paint in her hair when they had painted this room, but it was worth it to have walls that pleased her. Then Raines had worked his magic with the artwork. It was a bit too abstract for her, but he insisted the pieces brought the room together. She never won fights about art with him, so of course he had had his way. But their styles meshing together had become her joy, and she wouldn't have it any other way.

Luxuriating in a lazy stretch, she found Raines looking at her from a chair where he had been reading.

"How's my hot wife?" he chuckled.

"A thousand times better, thank you."

Raines put his book down and went to sit at the foot of the bed.

"I thought we were done with this fainting business."

"Now really," Sheila started defensively and a bit guiltily. "I honestly didn't faint this time. I fell asleep. There is a *big* difference."

"Same difference. You never…" Raines could see his wife winding herself up for a battle and gave up the lecture that had been simmering since he had carried her up the stairs and set her down. "I was worried, that's all."

Sheila cocked her head and looked at him. She wasn't used to him giving up. She supposed there were a lot of reasons they shouldn't be fighting now, though. Leaning towards him, she reached for his hand.

"Sorry." She and Raines both took a moment to enjoy holding hands, both wishing it could be more, but unsure. "I know you worry. It's your job, husband."

Raines smiled ruefully. A husband's job wasn't what he had been up to lately.

"What can I do?" he asked, full of sincerity and contrition.

Sheila stared at their joined hands for a long time, afraid to make eye contact. She thought, wanting to speak truthfully and fully.

"No more Las Lomas. Not on your own, anyway." She shook her head as she spoke, full of rage against his family's underhanded ways. Carlos. Yes, she had words for his brother when the time came. Clearing the red from her eyes, she looked at him. "My grandfather told me you didn't get any disease and that the woman is not pregnant. I love you, but it's hard to be around you right now. It can't be like it was, and that hurts. I need time. I need time away."

Raines' hand reflexively tensed around hers. "Away," he mouthed as his world spun away from him.

"I'm gonna visit my sister, Jasmin, in Tempe for a while. And, when I come back, I'll be better." Sheila looked at him, willing him to believe the truth of her statement. She feared he was too stunned to believe, though.

Raines drew his hand away and scrubbed through his hair, trying to snap himself out of his dejection. "Whatever you need. It's nothing I don't deserve. I just hate it. But it's not about me. If that's what you say you need, I'll support you all the way."

"Thank you, Raines. I *do* love you. I have to do my part to let the bitterness and pain go before it eats me alive."

"Are you leaving home for the same reason I did? Are the same demons driving you?"

Every now and again, he said something really wise.

"God, I hope not. I only know there's some black stuff in me. It's not *all* that's in me, but I can't pretend it's not there. It needs to get out, and I don't want it to infect our relationship. So, I can't be here."

"I'll miss you."

Sheila got off the bed and held out her arms for a hug. As he held her, she allowed herself to forget everything. All the dark, conflicted parts inside her melted away for that moment.

Sheila held his face in her hands as she looked up at him. "I know what's at stake. I have zero interest in losing you."

Raines rested his forehead on hers and closed his eyes, letting himself soak up being close to her. He was having some sense of how she must have felt when he left. He felt desperate to keep her with him, but helpless to stop her.

"Dear God, please bring her back to me."

Sheila held him close. "Amen."

CHAPTER SIXTEEN
THE HURT

Raines lay on the sofa off of the kitchen in the middle of the day, staring up at the ceiling. He had given up on trying to paint and was simply trying to control his rage. He had driven Sheila to BWI Airport two hours ago for her to visit her sister on the other side of the country in Tempe, Arizona. It had been a one-way ticket.

He was bubbling with anger. Before, he had been incredibly sorry, afraid, and horrified at what he had done to Sheila and their marriage. Now, finally now, he was angry. He hated himself with an incredible amount of energy. It was something he could do. It was the *only* thing he could do at the moment.

So, he lay on the sofa and scowled.

Sheila could not end her hug with Jasmin. She just kept hugging her…and hugging her.

"I saw you a couple of weeks ago." Jasmin squirmed her way out of their embrace and went to put her bags in the car's open trunk.

"And you didn't see me at your best." Sheila's head slumped in guilt.

Jasmin sighed and placed her hand on Sheila's shoulder. "I've forgiven you, but I see you have some more work to forgive yourself. But then, you've never been afraid of the work, so I know it's just a matter of time."

"So let's get to it," Sheila said with sudden gusto and popped into the passenger seat.

"I'm surprised Raines let you go, not that anyone can stop you when you make your mind up," Jasmin navigated traffic out of the airport and onto to the highway.

"Argh, ugh, and bleep."

"Come again?"

"I'm on a Raines retreat…He cheated on me." Sheila hung her head, embarrassed.

Jasmin pulled over to the highway's shoulder, turned on her blinkers, put the car in park, and stared at her.

"I could strangle him. I just hate him. I can't believe what he did. And I don't trust him. So, yes, he certainly let me go wherever I wanted. And now that I'm here, I see I brought all of my tension with me. *Some* escape."

"What can I do?" Jasmin was stunned. She saw Sheila as a sheer force of nature. She couldn't imagine anyone being unfaithful to her, least of all Raines.

"I thought about asking you to lay hands on me, to heal me. But Grandfather says that's cheating, and I kind of agree. So, I guess you being you is enough. The hard work's up to me to do." Sheila's voice had become more resolute, and it heartened Jasmin.

"Grandfather? Have you been channeling?" Jasmin thought jealously of how easily Sheila had taken to channeling spirits and ancestors. It had begun in puberty, with her almost effortlessly being able to call up the voices of those who had gone on before and just as easily dismiss them. Whenever Jasmin had tried, it had always been a struggle, like her will was fighting the other's, and they couldn't reconcile. She much preferred divining. It was easier and less dangerous to her spirit to call forth specific answers from the spirits through her pendulums.

"No. No need to call him, no need to give him a vessel. He called me, through the blue mirror at Ma's. We've got a lot of catching up to do."

Jasmin took a deep breath and swallowed all of her questions. "Well then," she said as she got the car back on the highway and into the flow of traffic. "You throw, and I'll catch."

At Jasmin's home, over ice tea, Sheila launched into her no-nonsense retelling of events. She kicked off her shoes, poured herself a generous glass of white wine from Jasmin's wine fridge, and ran her fingers through her hair. Jasmin had always accused her of lacking a sense of the dramatic. 'Content is king,' Sheila thought. 'She won't find this boring.'

"I went to clean Ma's shrine room. Our dead grandfather spoke through the mirror, saying Ma had been a gatekeeper between other dimensions and ours. That one from every line of our family held this post and it was my turn. I refused. When I went to New York for that work conference—that day I hurt you—I felt so bad I thought about killing myself. I might have. Ma appeared to me, really *appeared*, and told me she loved me and was proud of me. I decided to follow in her footsteps and do it." Sheila drained her wineglass and refill it. This stuff wasn't strong enough.

"You should be glad you never knew Grandfather. He's absolutely heartless. I had to do some difficult dream work, but finally I was ready, whatever that means. One trip to guard the gate and it took ten years off me. Jesus," Shiela's eyes relived horrors as she paused, lost in her thoughts. "But he's not content with just cutting my life short. He ruins my marriage, too. Tells me I can't carry a child *and* do this work. You or Corrine's progeny are on the hook, you know.

"I tell Raines, and he actually punches a hole in the wall. A hole! Leaves for Las Lomas, sleeps with some woman, unprotected. Comes back, sorry as anything. Suddenly, he realizes how much he needs me. Needs me more than he needs to have kids. He's all devoted now, *truly*. And I hate him. Almost as much as I love him." She drained her glass again and let her head fall back on the couch, willing herself to be drunk, hoping it meant she would feel less.

Jasmin rose and went to the liquor cabinet, coming back with two shot glasses and some coconut rum. Jasmin always liked mamsy, pansy fruity stuff, Sheila thought glumly. But it would do.

CHAPTER SEVENTEEN
HOTEP

Sheila had always liked Tempe, she thought, as they drove through the center of town the next morning. It was like all the beatnik hippies had converged there. She could see why Jasmin had chosen it. It was weird and mellow, just like her.

After their silent drinking bout last night, Jasmin had *rudely* awoken her for morning prayers. She didn't care if they were three hours behind; she would never be a morning person in any time zone. But finally, she was awake and had a list from her grandfather of materials she needed, so they had decided to take a trip out to a botanica Jasmin recommended.

The drive in Tempe's crisp heat was the wake up call Sheila needed, and she basked in the sun like a lizard. This was what she had needed, time to just *be*. She tapped on her phone and pulled up Grandfather's list. There was more than one thing waiting for her back home.

Jasmin pulled up to the curb in front of "Sailer's Botanica and Gifts," and Sheila prepared to size the place up. Botanicas were the new age, occult, or esoteric's home away from home. One stop shopping for rare incense, candles, cleansing and conjuring materials, and anything else she might need for her preparations. It was a place where you could ask for just about anything, and no one would bat an eye. Need a ceremonial knife, horse's saliva, bird feathers, a line on a goat for sacrifice? They had you covered. More or less.

Each one had a distinct personality. Some owners put conjures in the store to keep you buying. And some were too black for her, frequented by dark practitioners with nefarious purposes. So your relationship with a botanica was personal and hard fought. If she took a deep breath and felt the energies to get a sense of the place and felt at home, then she experienced the pleasure of making a new friend, discovering a new haunt. If she didn't feel at home…

Sheila stepped inside, breathed in deeply, and immediately felt on guard.

"See," Jasmin said quietly. The store had a library's silence you didn't want to disturb. But beneath what some might take for calm, something was very wrong. "I *told* you this place was ok. And wait until you meet the owner. To tell you the truth, I'm smitten with him."

"Well, this I have to see." Sheila looked at her sister as a mischievous grin stole across Jasmin's face.

Jasmin seemed…almost asexual. She was devoted to her art. Dancing was everything to her. Intimacies outside of that and family had been few and far between.

She had begun dancing with a troupe based in Tempe about 6 years ago. When the company had been looking for a part owner two years ago, Ma had given her the money to buy in. Now she managed, choreographed some, and most of all, danced. It was on stage that Jasmin became alive, truly free. Sheila had always known her sister was part whirling dervish, and she thought it was wonderful. Jasmin was free in a way she would never be. Even so, she had often worried that love seemed to elude her perfect little sister.

"Smitten, huh?" Sheila's eyes were full of playful delight. "This man must really be something, then."

"Yes," Jasmin said, suddenly a little girl again. "Hotep is wonderful. I can't wait to introduce you. Oh, there he is!"

Jasmin gestured toward a 6-foot tall man of medium build, with a chestnut brown complexion and a well-manicured mustache. Sheila's blood ran cold.

Upon seeing them, he stepped away from his customer and greeted Jasmin with an involved kiss. It surprised Sheila to see Jasmin greedily return that affection. He kept his eyes on Sheila throughout the kiss.

They untangled, and Jasmin started to introduce them.

"Mrs. Montoya," Hotep began before Jasmin could speak. "I did not expect to see you again so soon. Not on this plane, at least."

Jasmin looked back and forth between them with confusion. "Oh. I see you…"

Sheila raised a hand to cut her off. She allowed herself to take her time and truly see him. She couldn't describe what she saw because she had never seen it before. But the words escaped her mouth before her mind could even make sense of it.

"*Ha satan*," she uttered, barely above a whisper.

Hotep laughed, almost seductively. "Yes. I was wondering when you would recognize me." He pulled Jasmin closer to his side and watched Sheila's mind put the pieces together.

Christians had made Satan into a ruler of Hell, red with horns and a pitchfork. But the actual Hebrew, *ha satan*, simply meant the adversary/accuser. Surely he couldn't be *the* adversary. Was he *her* adversary?

When she had met him at Raines' gallery opening last month, he had nearly hypnotized her. And now that she allowed herself to remember him, she realized he was the man in the cave she had been having sex with in her strange recurring dream. The one that had started after her mother died.

Sheila took in his relaxed posture, and who was standing next to him. "Jasmin, could you step away from him?"

"Oh, no," Hotep purred, locking his grip on her waist. "But I want her to stay."

"Jasmin?" Sheila asked urgently, not daring to take her eyes off of Hotep. She didn't take in the confused expression on Jasmin's face. "We need to leave now," she said definitively.

"I…I" Jasmin looked between them with a pained

look.

"How can she trust what you are saying is good for her, Mrs. Montoya? After all, you used your power against your own sister recently, didn't you? Don't you want to see her happy? With someone she can trust?"

Yes, he was her adversary. The greatest weapon the adversary had was the truth, and he was wielding it skillfully now.

"Lately, you've been so out of control, so different, so damaged. Don't you think Jasmin has been through enough? Why did you even come here, for her, or for you? Where have you been to help her deal with *her* grief? I've been here, by her side. I've been walking to and fro, and I have seen it all."

He was good. She only had one recourse left. Turning to Jasmin, Sheila began, "I have no excuse. I'm wrong and I'm sorry. I beg for your forgiveness. I repent. I plead the blood, may unmerited grace cover my sins." She poured the whole of her spirit and intent into the words. She meant them to the depths of her soul.

Jasmin flew into her arms, and they shared a fierce hug. Sheila never took her eyes off Hotep. She mouthed words she was sure he understood. "The blood always wins."

Sheila held Jasmin at shoulder length and looked into her eyes. She was tempted to use compulsion, but she fought it. Once you misused power once, it was a slippery slope you had to fight, scrape, and crawl to keep from descending. "We need to leave here. We need to leave him."

"I…I love him," Jasmin pleaded. "He's the only one who speaks the truth. Like I do. I need him."

"There's a difference between what's true and what's right. He is my adversary. You will get hurt with him."

"I will get hurt without him. Your fight with him is your business. I'm not the one Mother chose, am I?"

"What?" Sheila asked in confusion.

"Mother was forever choosing you, and now even in

death, it continues! Hotep chose me. And I like being first." Jasmin's voice had a tone of finality to it.

"Do you know who you're with? Do you know what he is?"

"I'm with someone who loves me. He values me. These things are true." Jasmin went back to his side and put her arms around him.

Sheila could not respond to that. She would have had to tell her the truth, the *whole* truth, instead of twisted, half truths in which Jasmin had been ensnared. And the whole truth was he *did* love her, for how she could help him carry out his plans. He *did* value her—as the sister to the one he wanted to destroy. But that would crush Jasmin. It sounded pretty conceited, even to her.

"So call him by his true name, *ha satan*. I dare you," Sheila had almost given up hope. This was her last ditch effort to convince Jasmin.

"He just wants to bear witness," Jasmin insisted. "What lie has he told?" she challenged. "I think you could use an accuser; to keep you honest."

"You…align…with…*ha satan*?" She drew the words out slowly, barely able to conceive it.

"He's my other half," Jasmin said, as placidly as if they were making dinner plans. "I see the best of what is. He sees the dark. Together, we're real." She leaned into him and seemed to draw strength from the embrace. "I will always love you, but don't ask me to leave him. Not ever."

The air froze in Sheila's lungs. Inside she was apoplectic with rage; outside she was paralyzed in disbelief. Suddenly, she had a raging headache. She just didn't know what to do now, how to proceed. Sheila was rarely at a loss for words, much less uncertain of what to do. This turn of events had her positively stumped.

Well, when you were beat, you were beat, she thought. "I'll be out in the car whenever you're done." She turned to go, slinking out in ignominious defeat.

"I thought you needed to get some…"
"Don't," Sheila interrupted, and continued walking.
Hotep was all smiles.

After Sheila finished throwing a tantrum in the privacy of her sister's car, she could think more calmly about matters. Ruefully, she realized this must have been what her sisters felt like when they had visited and found her running from God as desperately as she could. She had found her way back. She prayed Jasmin would, too. Jasmin was the least into absolutes, of them, so this whole yin-yang thing of being with the accuser probably spoke to her.

Sheila knew what it was to be lonely, and how desperately a person could fight to avoid it. If she thought there was any way Jasmin could be happy in the long-term with him, she would have tried to reconcile herself to it. As it was, though, the most she could manage was a resentful truce.

Hotep, *ha satan*, she corrected herself, had unearthed some deep family tensions and Jasmin had thrown them in her face. She was forced to admit that she and Ma had had something special between them. She had never compared how she was treated to her sisters. But she supposed that was the privilege of the preferred child. She had assumed Ma had had relationships that were just as special with Corrinne and Jasmin, simply in different ways.

Ma had known Sheila would succeed her. She had spent a lot of energy lately being mad and perplexed that her mother hadn't prepared her for this future. But perhaps she had—all the extra time and attention, continuing to live near her even as it meant being far away from her other children. She could see that often their relationship had been to the exclusion of others, including her sisters. She felt both special and ashamed.

And just as in life, so had she been in mourning, with her grief excluding others. She was the only wounded party, or at least that was how she had been behaving. It tore at her to realize how little she had thought of others since her mother's passing.

Ha satan had put in neon lights, all to which she had been blind. That's what made him so effective—it was all true, it was all dark. But it was incomplete, and the conclusions he drew were the real trap. He wanted her to lie down and die in shame so he could dance on her grave and shout to the heavens that he had told them so. It was only natural to renounce Jasmin for her choosing him. It was only right that she kill herself because of her failures. The accuser had no comprehension of mercy, grace, repentance, favor, or love. She did, and it was up to her to grab at her salvation with both hands.

Maybe *ha satan* could provide her with some balance, showing her the faults and flaws in her blind spots. But she would use that knowledge for redemption, not damnation. And, unlike Jasmin, she would never ever mistake it for love. The accuser had no love in him. That she knew, without a doubt.

She had tangled with him and lost. But real saints, she knew, were those who endured until the end. She prayed without ceasing that she could endure.

CHAPTER EIGHTEEN
BOY'S NIGHT

Raines hadn't painted in days. He went down to his studio every morning, but he looked at his incomplete canvases as if someone else had created them. He had blown off his tutoring commitment at the local school, rationalizing that he was the last person who should be a role model for children right now. And he drank. A lot. He was out of just about everything, but had drawn the line at going to the liquor store for replenishment.

He also prayed. He didn't know all the voodoo stuff Sheila did, but he was developing some habits of his own that he thought could become something. It humbled him, but every night he got on his knees and said some prayers. He focused on the formulaic prayers he had learned as a kid. Using his own words was still too uncomfortable. Once he had tried the rosary, but that had been way too much commitment. And boring. In the mornings, he tried to read a bit of the Bible. It had gotten insufferable around Deuteronomy and he had skipped to the Psalms. The psalms spoke to him and his situation right now; things were awful, but David was convinced God would bring him out of it. Summed up his life in a nutshell, at least the awful part. He was still working desperately on the believing part.

He had always believed you bent life to your will. Your reality was what you made it. But he had made an absolute mess of things recently, so he supposed God was the only escape hatch left to him. He was banking on it. Sheila's tolerance had run out, so she had left before she clobbered him with a frying pan. She often joked that it was how the men in her family expired. He was sure he deserved it. But he was hoping for that second chance the Psalms promised. He needed a miracle.

"Any time you want to show up, God."

Raines looked at his phone for the fifth time in as many minutes. He and Sheila had been carrying on a texting love affair since she had gone to visit Jasmin. That was another reason he couldn't paint. The phone was always in his hand, waiting for her tone to sound.

He sent her snippets of Pablo Neruda, as he had done when they were courting. Also pleas for forgiveness and promises of change. She had surprised him by being very responsive. And she had given some apologies of her own; for being so shut down and separate in her grief, for not sharing more of how she had been feeling with him. For being so stuck in her own victimhood that she hadn't kept him from going to Las Lomas. How he wished she had.

And interspersed in all of those depths, there were texts where they just talked. What was he eating? What was she drinking? Was he painting? Was she doing anything superheroine-ish? That gave him hope most of all; normalcy. Or at least, the new normal, whatever that might be.

This morning she had texted that the distance and time were making her miss him. He had replied, completely serious, anxious even, that he could be there in eight hours. She had haha-ed and said not yet.

"Almost," she had replied.

She was almost ready to come home? Is that what she meant, or was it meant entirely different? He hated texting. And most of all, he hated texting his wife as their sole means of communication. It was humiliating, but he was in no position to set terms. He was more than willing to take what he could get under the circumstances.

Almost. He would take almost.

She had encouraged him to have a guy's night. "NO STRIPPERS," had been the only caveat, and it had been in all caps. After he was finally convinced that she meant it, that it wasn't a trap, he had invited the guys over for poker and beer, with some ESPN on in the background, of course.

He stood over the chili he was making and stirred. He

was overworking it; he knew. The key to chili was leaving it. That's what Luis had drilled into his head. As a kid, he had spent a lot of time in the kitchen with his family's cook, much to the disgust of his father. Luis had taught him patience. Chili had been the vehicle for that lesson.

"Put in everything you need, then wait. Just wait." He repeated Luis' words as if he might finally absorb that lesson. Yet, here he was, stirring his chili as if he could hurry it. He put the spoon down and replaced the top on the pot. It would be done when it was done. He forced himself to walk away.

When he wasn't obsessing over his wife, he found he was actually looking forward to spending some time with his friends. It had been far too long. They were all artists of some type. They were the only crowd that could keep up with each other's madness. To be an artist, particularly a painter, was to be absolutely insane. Most of the time, he was consumed with a vision that he was convinced would destroy him if he didn't get it out faithfully. But it was never perfect, and as obsessed as he had been with producing the vision, he flayed himself just as mercilessly for the flaws and missed opportunities that only he could see. The artist always suffered, no matter how much money you gave him.

His work was celebrated, and his financial comfort was secure, but he still spent most of his existence either feeling like a fraud or the muse's whipping boy. Sheila had come along and been the first woman he could remember who was more interested in him than in his artwork. And she seemed not to mind his insanity, how he would lock himself in his studio for days at a time, only to destroy what he had created. He was insane, and she loved him. He reasoned she was entitled to her own insanity, and it looked like she had found it. She had been his anchor. How would this new normal work, with both of them flying so close to the edge?

He hated change. It hurt his head to think about what their new life would look like. He knew that was a big part of why he had gone back to Las Lomas. When the chips were down, he had needed the reliable comfort of routine to soothe him. He knew plenty of changes were yet to come. He had promised he would change, that he *had* changed. But he wondered what he would do when the tumult of their life became too much. Where would he find the haven he craved?

He had a feeling it was in the budding spiritual life he had begun to nurture. It still made him uncomfortable, but he had been regularly spending time at Sheila's Buddhist shrine, communing with the God of War. It had become part of his routine to sit and talk to the fierce-looking statue as if they were friends.

Did that make him a Buddhist? How his Catholic family would howl. It was almost worth converting. But his time with the God of War anchored him. Perhaps he would find more anchors as he continued to explore. And then he could be an anchor. The idea of being an anchor for Sheila, not just an optional additive, appealed to him. But for now, he was going to drink beer, talk trash, and take his friends' money. It would be a blissful oblivion. He walked to the door to answer the bell as his first guest arrived.

Something had gone wrong. As near as Raines could figure, it had happened sometime around the second beer. That was when the losing had started. And it hadn't stopped until he had reached their hundred-dollar limit. So much for his plan to steal everyone's money.

"I would let you put your vehicle up for credit," said Hans, "but no one wants that piece of crap." Everyone laughed but Raines. Hans threw him twenty dollars in chips. "There is no such thing as altruism. But you have my pity," Hans continued. "Just pace yourself, because that is the last of it."

"Theoretical bullshit," George sputtered. "Hans, it's

enough that we read your books. Besides, I don't need your pity to take money from you." And with that, he laid out his hand. "Royal flush, philosopher king. Royal flush."

"At least I wasn't in that hand, so I could look at this as putting me up by twenty bucks. Thanks, Hans," Raines said,, and made a show of counting his four donated chips.

"Maybe you can buy your manhood back with those," Benjamin murmured.

Hans and George howled at that. Raines scowled. But Benjamin was shameless. And while he usually used his musical ability to write songs for some of the hottest artists out there, he was not above pulling a Weird Al Yankovic at the drop of a hat.

"Oh, I lost my balls to She-i-la,
And my boys won't let it rest.
Have you seen them?
Tell me, have you seen them?"

Benjamin crooned to the tune of the The Chi-Lites' "Have You Seen Her" while Raines' so-called friends doubled over with laughter.

"Ha. Ha. Well, you've told me."

"Relax," George, who was always the peacemaker of the group, said. Perhaps it was the sculptor in him that gave him the patience and foresight to be a good mediator. "We're just saying we ain't seen you since last year. Where you been, man?"

"Just dealing with stuff," Raines said, noncommittally.

"But seriously," Benjamin tried to sober up. "How is she? Even *I* loved her mom."

"Yeah, she was spooky, but awesome."

"Yeah," Raines said wistfully. "Sheila's hanging in there, I guess. Touch-and-go there for a while. Might still be…me losing all my chips to you scoundrels might push her over the edge. I'm only thinking of her, guys," he smirked as he lightened the mood.

"Don't let him win, then she might never come back from Tempe, man." Benjamin punched Hans in the shoulder.

"A visit to her sister out of town," Hans said in his perfect English. "I'm German, but I know what that means. What did you do?"

"It's private," Raines muttered as he dealt the next hand. The other three exchanged a look. They had been joking, but when Raines didn't joke back, they knew it was serious.

"Anything we can do?" Benjamin inquired. "I'll write her a love song, begging her to take your sorry butt back."

"She's not a 16-year-old K-Pop fan, so I don't think your song would appeal to her. But thanks." And with that, the group's irreverent balance had been restored. "Your money will do just fine. And I intend to take it."

Raines sighed as he looked at the mess they had made. He decided he'd call their cleaning service in early. He was no maid. He had managed to win back about half of his money, plus Hans' pity stake, so he ended up almost even. Not ideal, but acceptable, he thought.

It had been good to blow off steam with the guys, to be a cocky so-and-so for a little while. It seemed like a long time since he had felt he gave as good as he got, that he was in charge. It had been a good reminder that he was more than Sheila's whipping boy.

And he knew what he had to do now. Recent events had gotten him so discombobulated, it was almost as if he had forgotten who he was. He didn't wait for life to happen to him; he made the life that he wanted. Raines was a king, and it was about time he got his queen back. He packed a bag and booked a flight to Tempe, Arizona.

They had some things to work out, he knew. But they

weren't going to do it from different sides of the country. She needed to know he had changed. Maybe she knew that in her mind, but she had left because she didn't *feel* it in her heart. He intended to remedy that.

Talking to Jasmin could often be unsatisfying. She was too simple or too cryptic for Raines' comprehension. Sometimes she was distracted or frustratingly detailed. He couldn't remember ever experiencing her as cold, though. He thought it over as he drove to the airport.

He had called to let Jasmin know he was coming. He wanted to make sure they weren't on a three-day canyon hike in the middle of nowhere, which was more than possible with those two. He hadn't expected the distance in her voice. Well, he supposed Sheila had told her everything, and now she hated him. Nothing he didn't deserve, but it was still a blow. Another hole he was determined to dig himself out of.

The plane ride to Phoenix reminded him of the ride back from Las Lomas. The same nervousness, sense of impending doom, and elemental need to be with his wife coursed through him. He hadn't sweated her like this for a long time. Heading to Jasmin's home in Tempe in the rental car was when the real chaos took hold. He hadn't a clue what he was going to do. He had no moving speech planned, no grand symbolic gesture.

Unlike most things in his life, he was far from certain of the outcome. But he knew being apart wasn't helping. And that it just wasn't in him to not fight tooth and nail for what he wanted. Just hoping she would come back wasn't enough for him. He had to *do* something. He had about an hour-drive to figure out what that something was.

CHAPTER NINETEEN
CHOOSING

Sheila sat on the swing bench on her sister's Tempe home, soaking in the heat. She had always wished that "roasting" was a weather option and visiting her sister always made her want to abandon everything and move out here and have the cacti for company. The thin, dry air always welcomed her like an impatient lover. In that way, her visit was a success.

Jasmin and Sheila's conversations had been "pleasant" for days now. This was not what she had come for, Sheila bemoaned. She had wanted to clear her head, get away from Raines, from her grandfather, her assignments, even herself. But wherever you go, she thought, there you are. Hotep was also here, proving there was no time off from her new job. And where he was, the accusations and recriminations closely followed.

She was used to having to confront herself whenever she traveled to Sedona, AZ. The vortexes there were primed for karmic reckoning. It was one reason she had never been able to stand the place, however often her mother and she had traveled there.

But Tempe had always seemed a kind of never-never land to her; a place to escape from the vagaries of life and play with her pixie sister in the "what could be" world. Everything else had changed, been turned on its head. Why not this?

Her mother had been so full of joy. How did she do it? It was a question Sheila had often wondered, now more than ever. Dimensional gate-keeping threatened to consume her, Massad's evil bound to her restraints, and no partner by her side.

Sheila had never known her father. There had been men since then in her mother's life, but it seemed they were always passing through; amusements more than partners. At least that's how it had seemed to her. She wondered at the toll this life took on intimate relationships. She had already paid heavily, and she was just starting. Could it possibly get worse than this?

Sheila thought back to her grandfather. She could barely remember him when he was alive. He had died when she was very young; an unexpected death, not quite as dramatic as her mother's, but still too soon. She wondered if everyone who watched the gate would meet with such fateful ends. Maybe one day she would wind up stabbed just like in her dreams, way before her time.

But in the meantime, she had to live with the heartbreak of having been cheated on, of being unable to give her husband the children he longed for, of having dangerous men like the actual *accuser* trying to get a bead on her. She was hunted, alone, and out of control.

Her grandfather had been married, though. Years later, when Sheila had been a teenager, her grandmother made a comment that had barely registered with her at the time. 'I never really knew him.' It was a strange thing to say about one's life partner. But now that Sheila knew what he had done, what he had been, it made perfect sense. Her life wasn't exactly dinner conversation anymore. If she had never told Raines about any of this, he wouldn't have had sex with another woman.

What would she rather have had, a destiny secreted away from even her husband in exchange for a functional home life, or a place with a man who could know her, what she did and who she was, and all the consequences it brought to their doorstep? She honestly didn't know.

And that's why she was here, on her sister's porch instead of at home. She hadn't figured out how to live her new life, so she ran. It was what she was good at. She supposed that's what Raines had done, too. She could understand the mistake he had made, but that didn't make it hurt any less. If anything it brought the ache closer.

She wasn't the woman he had married. He wanted her anyway. But she knew that this wasn't the only time she would crush his dreams because of the demands of her assignment. And it wasn't the last time he would break her heart into bits with his "understandable" response. She didn't know if she could live like that.

Were these the kind of choices her mother had had to make? Ma had chosen to live a life apart. Her grandfather had chosen a life of veils. What would she choose? And would any choice be any less painful than the other?

Sheila was accustomed to being able to think or act her way out of any corner. The problem was that her life was nothing but tight, uncomfortable spaces right now. There was no place to which she could escape, much less be victorious.

Something aggravated her arrhythmia, and she lay down on the porch with her back on the wooden planks to try to take in deep, even breaths. She knew it wasn't *really* arrhythmia. They were panic attacks. Now, they seemed to threaten with every anxious thought. The thought of how powerless she was to control anything, even her body's reaction to stress, had her on the verge of tears.

That was how he found her, lying on the porch of her sister's house, fighting off tears and trying to breathe. It disappointed part of him he had once again found his wife in a state of wreckage. This was their life for right now. He knew he had to be part of the solution, to be as invested in her survival as she was, more so if they were going to stand a chance.

He sat in his car looking at her for a long time. He wanted to make sure, absolutely sure, that this was what he wanted. Sheila wasn't the only one who could rush into things without thinking through the consequences. He was susceptible to doing what he thought was right, as opposed to what was best. He wanted to make a decision that was both.

This was not the woman he had married. He wasn't the man she had wed, either. It was more than the vows, though they were serious enough on their own. Something in him had knit to her, and it actually hurt to be apart. He was a proud man. He knew he could survive without her. But he knew, perhaps for the first time only recently, that with her he could be so much more than he was. He also knew he could never be that man without her. Suddenly, what he was, wasn't good enough, and he craved more.

So yes, he would let her carry his manhood around in her purse if it meant he could get closer to the man he needed to be. His boys had been right. He wasn't free as he had been, but he could be stronger, more loving, purer than he had been in exchange. Raines wasn't going to let go of the gift Sheila offered him. He loved her. He needed her. And it was all desperate.

She was a bit of a disaster—might always be so. He had behaved unforgivably, yet she had forgiven. She just wasn't sure she could stomach him. Her mom had died, her dreams hunted her, she had to do God knows what God knows where, and her husband had abandoned her. He couldn't imagine he would have done any better in her shoes.

She didn't look like the heroes he had idolized as a child. But she was his heroine, his love, his responsibility. He chose her unequivocally. He was sure.

Three sharp knocks on his windowpane jolted him out of his reflections. Sheila was at the driver's side window, looking in at him. It seemed he had been in his own world.

He cut the engine and stepped out of the door, leaning against the car. They stared at each other for a long minute.

Without meaning to, they reached for each other and locked in a kiss that nearly drowned them. Surfacing for air at last, they held each other.

"You can't leave," Raines spoke into her hair.

"You'll do it again. You won't want to, but you'll do it again, and it will kill me." Sheila held her head against his chest and tried not to cry.

"Look at me. I'll give you a gun. Shoot me if you ever think there's a chance I'll hurt you like that. Hit me with a frying pan if you want, but you're not leaving me."

Sheila smiled. "A pot of hot grits might be more satisfying."

"You southerners and your grits. Fine, I'll be your Al Green. You can't leave."

Sheila was squirming in his grip now. "I don't know what I've gotten myself into. It's unfair to put this weight on you. I don't want to live in fear of you hurting me. It can't work."

Now it was Raines' turn to smile.

Sheila frowned. "Not the reaction I was expecting."

"Everything you've said is true. But you forgot one thing."

"Raines, I…"

He cut her off. "You forgot nothing is impossible with God."

Sheila just stared at him, mouth still open.

"Have you asked God if we're supposed to be together? If I remember anything your mother, Cathy, taught me, it's that nothing is an accident. *We* are not an accident, not a mistake. Put it to the test."

"Who *are* you?" It seemed she had been asking that question of him a lot lately.

"You're not the only one who's changing. I *could* live without you, but I won't. God wouldn't take you from me. I'll bet my stake on it."

Sheila wavered. The truth was: she *hadn't* asked God. She had been praying for relief from her heartache, for the ability to see clearly and not die in her boots from fear, but she hadn't asked the question. 'Should I stay with this man?'

People were making a habit of stating the obvious truths that she was blind to lately.

"I'm going to live in hope. You're not leaving me. I will do whatever you want. We're going to make a life together. I don't know what we were doing before, but from now on, I'm your helpmate."

If *ha satan* was her accuser, then Raines was her comforter right now. He reminded her that to be a believer was to invest in what *could* be and what *would* be over what seemed to be. He was asking her to speak life into their marriage.

"I have to be sure. Let me in the car."

"Ok," Raines said, confused. He went to open the passenger door.

"No, the back is fine." Sheila slid into the back seat and muttered, "Ten minutes," before she shut the door after her. In the back, she pulled her legs up to sit cross-legged and placed her hands on her knees. This would be the quickest astral travel she had ever attempted. Raines had said she should ask God. She knew he was right. But there was someone she needed to talk to first.

She coughed in the misty air that suddenly surrounded her. She hadn't been here in a long time. The rainbow castle. It looked like something out of Disneyland but more colorful. The things only a child's mind could dream up. But now, everything seemed old and broken down. It was the type of rainbow fantasyland castle that *used to* look nice. She and her mother would often meet here when she was a child. It was their little secret. And she was desperate that this place would still hold some tie to her mother's spirit.

She further centered herself and focused on one

thought, ‘Ma.’

A voice spoke to her out of the whirlwind. “It is good for us to be here together.”

Sheila almost swooned with relief at her mother’s voice. “Ma!” she cried out.

“Baby Girl.” Sheila could feel the smile in her mother’s voice, though there was no visible trace of her mother, not in the form she had known her.

“Tell me what to do,” Sheila begged.

“You know what to do. But you’ve never trusted yourself. That’s why you surround yourself with rules and reasons. I never understood it. You are my heir in so many ways, yet so unlike me. God is strange that way.” Her mother laughed, and it sounded so otherworldly it made Sheila shiver. “But truly, you have everything you need. It really is time. You don’t need me anymore.”

“I’ve always needed you. I’ll always need you.”

“The student should surpass the teacher. Else, the teacher hasn’t done her job. It’s time. I’ve been here. Been watching. You can do it. And you don’t need me as an intermediary.”

The air seemed to heave, and her mother’s voice grew deeper. “This world tires me, and I’ve taken my toll on it. When I leave, when I really leave, the rainbow castle will be no more. But your knowledge, all I have sown into you that God gave me, together with your own gifts, they are yours to keep. Use them.”

“I came to ask about Raines, and now you say you’re leaving me!”

“You need to make your own mistakes and take your own victories. You knew I would say that.” Her mother’s voice was amused.

“I…I just…the only time I ever felt sure of myself was when I was with you. And now I can’t be with you anymore. I thought there might be a lingering of you here. I just needed to feel sure about something again. When I was with you, my life never felt like a disaster. At least not after my teens, anyway."

"I held back the waters, in this place and in others. Now that's your job, and all the weight that comes with it…I would that things had been different. I wish I had prepared you more, but I was so afraid."

"You? Afraid?" Sheila could not think of two things more opposite.

"Afraid you wouldn't love me once you knew the fate into which I had borne you. Afraid I would fail in my assignment to teach you. Afraid you would be better than me, and that it would make me doubt my ability to do my job.

"I relinquished my ascendance as a Watcher to be here for you. Even in death, I was still so afraid. But now I am not afraid. I see things as they are. I behold you. And I am so proud." The mists heaved again. "And now it is time. There is still a place for me. I have to lay these ties down."

"You'll forget me."

"You always knew it would be so."

The words didn't sting any less because they were true.

"Trust yourself. Trust that God is enough. And know that our love is indestructible, even as I fade from this world. I have loved you with an everlasting love."

"Don't quote Jeremiah to me. He was the weeping prophet."

"You always resisted being a vessel. You will break if you don't yield. Is it not enough that we are destined to weep? The time you spend resenting that could be spent loving, living."

"Loving seems harder than it used to be."

"Great gifts are not easily won. There is a cost to be paid. You know that now."

"I think I do."

"You have to let me go. It will be easier if you let me go."

"How can I do that?" Sheila cried.

"Give me permission to go on this next journey in my path. Be happy for me."

"You never ask small favors."

"I never ask for what is not required."

Sheila's sigh took forever to escape. She closed her eyes and began a recitation from a movie she and her mother had both loved.

"*Even the 50 years of a man's life,*
is short compared to that of this world.
Life is but a dream, a vision, an illusion.
Life, once given, cannot last forever.

"Mother. I love you. I celebrate you. I release you." She choked the last words out past her tears.

The mist disappeared, and the rainbow castle crumbled beneath her feet.

Raines had seen Sheila in a trance-like state once or twice before. That did nothing to prevent it from scaring him witless. He had stood unmoving outside the car from the moment she had closed her eyes. What was she doing? She said ten minutes. It had been fifteen. Was he supposed to do something? She had warned him he was never to put his hands on her if she was meditating, never to move her or reposition her because she might not find her body again. He had thought she was kidding. Now he remembered them as sacred instructions that froze him in his tracks.

He could make a noise, he supposed, but would that be just as bad? He had just decided to honk the horn, hoping Jasmin was inside to ask for help, when Sheila's eyes flew open.

She came to herself, gasping for air.

"Water," she panted. Raines grabbed a bottle he had

purchased at the airport and removed the cap, handing it to her. "Spray me." He looked at her suspiciously. "I'm not all the way back. I need to feel something. Soak me."

He splashed her face with it hesitantly. "More," she uttered.

"I'm out. Let me get some from inside the house."

"No time." She could feel her spirit roiling. She had left half of her heart at the rainbow castle with the release of her mother's essence. And the rainbow castle was disintegrating. If she didn't reconcile herself, that part of her would be lost. "I need something. I need to feel something. Anchors."

Raines pulled her to him. "I love you," he said before he kissed her.

And just like that, she was completely present. Mind, body, and spirit as one. When they finally released each other, they both noticed a sliver of white mist escape her mouth.

"What was that?!"

Sheila lay back on the headrest to catch her breath. "That, I believe, was indestructible love. It is what my mother, and I had. And it is what we have."

"Have?"

Sheila roused herself from her exhaustion to turn her head and look at him. "Yes, *have*. We paid for it, we're going to redeem it. You brought me back, and I don't want to live without you."

Before she had finished her words, she found herself engulfed in Raines' embrace. "Ow!" she gasped. "Are you trying to break me? Where's that gun you promised me?" She joked, but eased away from him. "Seriously though, hands off the merchandise."

"You've got me at a loss for words," Raines said. He had released his bear claw hold on her but still kept her close. And he had to admit, now that her shirt was soaking wet, he had quite the view. She wasn't wearing a bra. He loved it when she got all Bohemian on him. "Are you ok?"

"No." Sheila sputtered. "I need you to take me home and take care of me. I'll try to do the same for you."

"My wife's wish is my command."

"Eyes up here, buddy."

"*You're* the one not wearing a bra. *You* told me to douse you with water. Call and response I think your people call it. Though I thought you told me never to mess with a black woman's hair if I wanted to live?"

"I see you're back to normal. Thank God." And with that, they held each other until they reached some kind of equilibrium. It felt good.

"If you're done looking at my tits…"

"Nipples, to be exact," Raines corrected.

"Can we go?"

Raines bent to take hold of her breast with his mouth through her thin, damp shirt.

Sheila moaned in what seemed like a long forgotten pleasure. "This is *not* going."

"Going, coming, whatever," Raines muttered as he shifted to lay her across the back seat. And with God knew who watching, he ravished her. She didn't mind a bit.

One block over, Hotep observed her from his parked car. He had hoped that the separation would stick. But by the way they were coupling in the back seat for all the world to see, he threw that hope out the window.

He had gotten a glimpse up close of her power. One who could astral travel under stress and so quickly was not to be underestimated. He had anticipated crushing her quickly and continuing to play with her sister as long as he desired. Things were changing, though. He knew everything was about to get much more interesting.

She had called him by a name he hadn't heard in millennia. *Ha satan*. Yes, he had been known by that moniker long ago. She had recognized him, understood the game he was playing. He succeeded by remaining hidden, with his true motives and methods obscured. She had robbed him of that. He had still been able to wound her, but it hadn't been deep. She had actually turned it to her advantage. He hated those ones. But he would bring her to task, and see her go down into the pit of her own volition. He couldn't wait.

PART FIVE
FORWARD MOTION

CHAPTER TWENTY
CROSSING OVER

Sheila breathed free and easy for the first time in what seemed like forever. Back in her mother's shrine room, she felt ready. That should have scared her. She had been meditating, and it felt good to not be conflicted. In the past, her intolerance of confusion had led her to make some poor decisions, just for the sake of making a choice. But this choice felt right, like it would stick. And that centeredness freed her to work on repairing her relationship with God.

She supposed she had been the cheater in that relationship, replacing God with the seductive void of denial. Sheila had repented, but that didn't mean she and God were as close as they used to be. Lately, she had been too busy freaking out to devote much time to prayer, meditation, or study. Her dealings with God had been more functional than personal, and she missed the intimacy she had enjoyed before all of this. It would forever be different now, she knew. It was as if God had been this incredible secret she and her mother had shared. Now that her mother was gone, with whom could she share that secret?

Raines was coming along. She was still too unused to his newfound spirituality to trust it. But she thought, maybe one day, they could truly share that. In the meantime, she didn't have the luxury of someone else to lean on and look to in her relationship with God. She was it. Thinking back to her mother's words, she knew they were correct. She had relied on her mother as an intermediary with God. Ma had always been there, so much wiser and more committed. It had been an easy and warm habit to slide into.

Now, she had really let her mom go, and given her spirit permission to fly. It wasn't the most theologically sound motivation, but she knew that the only way she could be close to Ma now was to be close to God. That realization lit a fire under her. She had given up so much in accepting this new destiny; she was determined to be the best she could at it, even if it killed her. And she knew it would.

"I'm sorry." The voice rang out in the room's stillness, a concise, clear baritone. Sheila wondered for a moment how she would know if she were an interdimensional superhero or a sad schizophrenic.

"If I had a nickel for every time I heard you say that, I'd have a nickel." It still meant something to her that her grandfather, who, as far as she was concerned, was made of ice, acknowledged her loss. "Thank you…will she be my guide now?"

"It will be years before she can touch this world again, should she choose to. Perhaps one day. She will not be your mother anymore, though. I am not as I was."

"Guess we leave things as they are, then." She wasn't sure she could handle her mother if she were going to act as cold as he.

"Clever, leaving guards at the gate. You forget that all energy can be transformed, transmuted. It is dangerous to leave your power there. That is your craft, your creation. It knows your name and can lead others back to you. It is enough that you are attacked at the gate. You do not want to be hunted outside of it."

"Do you ever deliver good news?"

"I said you were clever."

"I'll take it. So, I can't leave traces of my power at the gate because it can be tracked back to me. I've used the same philosophy to trace a curse back to its owner. But what am I supposed to do, *live* at the gate?"

"In a way."

Sheila waited a full moment. "You seriously can not be done with that statement."

"I am not obtuse. I assumed you knew how to co-exist."

"I will be dead before I know how to do all of this."

Sheila tried to get a handle on her frustration and feelings of inadequacy. She hated feeling unprepared.

"I thought you were reading the relevant materials."

"I was a little distracted, what with my marriage falling apart and the accuser after me."

"Everything else is a distraction. If you don't master this job, it will kill you, or worse, and then others."

That robbed Sheila of a snappy retort.

"Prepare yourself to cross over. You take far too long."

Sheila had been in high-pressure situations before. She thrived on them. But her grandfather's grinding her down was something new. She had never had someone in her life like this, not that she couldn't afford to walk away from. Their every interaction left her wounded, feeling less than, yet she needed him. She didn't know how she was going to manage.

Tired of dwelling on how trapped she felt in this situation, she rose to retrieve the items she needed from the cabinet. An hour later, she had sweated through her clothes with the effort of speeding through her preparations, but she was ready. The circle had been cast, and she had marshaled her powers. All that was left was to cross over to the place where every energy wanted to annihilate her. She lay down in the circle and closed her eyes.

The scene was completely different from before. It appeared to her senses as if she were in a typical country landscape with trees and a brook. On one side, it ended abruptly with the appearance of a white wall and a plain wooden door. She was nervous about entering a door she couldn't see through. Before, an open archway had floated in midair and an invisible membrane had separated her from the chaos until she passed through. Now, she worried what might come flooding through the moment she cracked it open.

Suddenly, one of the panic attacks that plagued her in the real world visited her here, in a place where weakness could mean death. If she didn't do something quickly, she would faint here, losing her connection to her body back home. She dashed toward the brook, despite the vise that was tightening around her chest. With an abandon borne of desperation, she dove into the waters. She did not know why she did it. She was aware of the transitive properties of water and perhaps had hoped being in it would cleanse her of her fears.

The moment she was immersed in it, she realized her mistake. It was all a veil. She was already at the gate, and this appearance had been created to confuse and disarm her. Clawing at the water, the currents ripped at her with the viciousness of an ocean. She couldn't breathe. Sheila knew she was about to die.

If she couldn't breathe in, then she would breathe out. She exhaled as violently as she could, expelling from her all of her fear, resignation, anger, confusion, and every vestige of desperation. The waters boiled on contact and the shrieking began. She had guessed right. Something her mother had said about holding back the waters had tipped her off.

The waters had been energies hoping to ensnare her; the chaos monsters of old. She hated fighting fire with fire, unless there was no other option. She had thrown some chaos of her own into the waters, and the battle had begun. Chaos monsters were not strong on intent, they just liked mayhem. They would fight her chaos as happily as they fought her. She had been eager to give them an alternative.

Sheila clawed her way out of the stream before it boiled her alive. She lay panting on her side. That was one way to relieve her anxiety. The ground rumbled beneath her. In an instant, the stream turned to steam. If water was to be her enemy today, she would gladly counter it with earth. She envisioned a grounding chair beneath her. Together, she and it sank into the ground.

It took several moments to adjust herself to her new surroundings. It seemed she was to be queen of the mole men today. She sat on a throne in what she could only describe as an underground royal court. Torches burned bright and people, or *things* more accurately, milled about in old world palace finery. Everything and everyone was caked with dirt. Sheila almost screamed in frustration. Why did the universe have to run this way? Was all of this supposed to mean something? Why dress things up like this? What was going on?

"Gatekeeper, your petitioners are waiting." A man with a scepter trumpeted as he opened doors to an outer court. She saw a line that stretched out of sight moving towards her. A young girl in rags came before her, crying and groveling.

"My daughter," the woman sobbed, "I left my daughter behind. She has no one. I beg you to let me go back for her."

"What would you have me do?"

"I want my body back!" she cried. "You can give me that chance. I overdosed, but no one has discovered me yet. My daughter's in the next room. She's all alone. You have to let me back. I just need another chance."

Sheila sank back into her chair. She thought she would just have to beat up bad guys trying to pass through to her dimension for mayhem. But it was so much more. Spirits were coming to her like she was Solomon, ready to dispense wise and just decisions. A mother wanting to go back for her daughter. If only someone had been here to let *her* own mother back.

But that wasn't how things worked. There was life and there was death in her dimension. Could she change those rules just because she wanted to? People died all the time and left people behind. She was a testament to that. But, where would she have been if her mother had not found a way to pierce through to her dimension? She would probably have flung herself out that window. Sheila was the only one who could help this woman get back to her daughter. All she had to do was break all the rules.

Was she really prepared to bring a drug addict back to life? How could she know the daughter would be better off with this mother? For a moment, she wished she were back in the water battling the chaos monsters. Everything had been so much clearer back then.

"I can't send you back. Your choices brought you here, and I will not unbind you from them. I wish you had thought of your daughter before you overdosed, I truly do. I am sorry for you and sorry for her, but I cannot send you back."

The woman screamed like a wraith, clawing at the air. Terra cotta warriors dragged her away. The line of petitioners inched forward.

Next up was a sprite. She couldn't remember seeing one of them since her childhood. "I want to visit my friends in the forest." The sprite flitted around so erratically it almost made Sheila cross-eyed.

"Are there any of you left in my world?"

"So few," the sprite chirped. "Your toxins kill us. But, most of all, the disbelief. There is so little magic left."

"Why go?"

"I do not have hope in your world. But some of my friends are trying to redeem the time there. I want to visit my friends."

"Granted, and I pray for your hope." The sprite flew around the room, releasing a delightful laugh. Was it right to witness such joy on the heels of such despair?

The sprite came to land before her, and panic struck Sheila again. She realized she was supposed to *do* something. She couldn't just say 'granted,' she had to enable the spirit to pass through to her dimension. But looking around, she saw no door or passage.

And suddenly she realized. S*he* was the gateway. The gatekeeper was the way through. Sheila thought back to a book her mother had always seemed to have on hand: *I AM the Open Door*. She had only ever browsed through it, but now the truth was painfully obvious. The book's opening line was, "In the center of your being is a Great Light, and you are that Light." She had asked her grandfather if she was supposed to live at the gate and he had said 'in a way.' Of course.

Throughout her life, it seemed Sheila was always running from herself, yet without relief. All these years she had been running from the gate, from the fate that lay within her. But, however hard she tried, she had never found liberation. It was because the gate lay within her. There was no escaping her essence.

Rising from her seat, she descended the few steps to where the sprite flitted about. Sheila raised her arms and suddenly the robes she wore faded away. She stood naked before the entire court. "Pass through to your destination."

The sprite floated towards her…and right through her. It chilled her to the bone. She turned blue from the effort. Turning back and struggling to her chair, she realized as she collapsed into it she was still naked. The line continued to creep forward.

Sheila came to herself in the circle and lay there for hours, unable to move. After a mighty effort, she croaked, "Raines."

Raines peeked his head in the door. Sheila had resented his insistence on sleeping in the hallway when she spent her nights in the shrine room. But right now, she was nothing but grateful. When he saw her, he entered the room and shut the door behind him.

"What can I do?" he saw the strange circle she lay in

and honestly wanted nothing to do with it. But he couldn't ignore the fact that she looked like she had almost had the life wrung out of her.

"I…" Sheila couldn't summon the breath to get her sentence out. "Must get out." She swallowed the more detailed explanation she had planned.

"How?" Raines asked anxiously.

"Break the circle." Sheila fought for more air and the strength to keep her wits about her. "Use the broom." Raines nervously swept part of the circle away. "Great." Sheila managed a smile in his direction. "Now take me home," she pleaded. He hesitantly stepped into the circle and scooped her up in his arms. Despite the pain from the unseen spiritual injuries she had incurred, in his care, she could finally rest and let her guard down.

There was an enormous gaping hole in her middle where beings had passed through the "gate." They had taken little pieces of her and now she felt brittle and hollow. One more thing would break her completely.

"I hate this." Raines had gone from nervous anxiousness to a tightly controlled anger as soon as he left her mother's shrine room.

"But if I say, 'I will not remember him or speak anymore in his name,' Then in my heart it becomes like a burning fire shut up in my bones; and I am weary of holding it in, and I cannot endure it." Sheila mumbled, half asleep. "Ain't nothin' to it, but to do it."

"Crazy as ever." Raines shifted his hold as he prepared to walk down the stairs with her. "It's late. You just want to stay here?"

"Can't." Sheila did her best to stay awake a little longer. "Tomorrow's the first day of my consulting gig. Up and at 'em bright and early."

On her way home, Sheila drifted in and out of sleep, wondering how she would ever refill the hole that had been carved out of her. This job was going to kill her.

She clung to Raines like a second skin for the rest of the night. He didn't mind a bit.

CHAPTER TWENTY-ONE YOUR CHEATING HEART WILL TELL ON YOU

The morning light still had that weak quality that Raines had taught her to recognize, and the clouds were already doing interesting things in the sky. She had been enjoying some peaceful alone time gazing out the patio doors in the kitchen when her former coworker, Rick Sarensi, rang the bell at Sheila's front door at 7:30am. Answering a few moments later, Sheila did not look amused.

"You must be joking."

"I heard you're hanging your shingle out today." Rick swept past her, smelling of fine cologne, and into the foyer, where he took his coat off and handed it to her. "Just came to wish you well."

Sheila closed the door and sighed. There was no point in lecturing him on manners and propriety. He would always do whatever he wanted in the end. Her long-time coworker and friend, Rick, had seemed to just pop into her life and do what he wanted. It grieved and amused her. She couldn't decide which of those feelings won out right now.

Luckily, she had been up since 6:00, reviewing her agenda for the day and making sure everything was in place. She was expecting Gerry at 8:30, and Raines was fast asleep. He hated mornings. She supposed she had some time to spare for Rick.

"Coffee? Tea? The last of my patience?" Sheila leered at him half-heartedly.

"Well, since you asked, I'll take an explanation of what happened to you at the annual meeting."

"I cannot think of anything I want to talk about less."

"Nevertheless," he said absent-mindedly as he showed himself into the kitchen.

Sheila followed, preparing a cup of tea while Rick talked about life with her former company.

"You tell me what you know about New York, and I'll fill in my perspective." Sheila's steaming mug of tea warmed her hands.

"You didn't circulate much, but everyone saw you on the dais with the president, of course. Your department presentation came up and no one saw you anywhere until John called you out. Then you just got up from the back of the room and walked out. No one saw you after that." Rick paused for a long moment. "It occurs to me there are far more productive ways to handle your exiting the company."

"It occurs to me as well," Sheila sighed. She took a swallow of her tea and thought about how to explain what had happened at her company's annual conference in New York last month that she was trying to forget. "There is nothing more to tell really than what you described," she lied. "I wasn't as focused as I could have been when I attended, so I kept my activity to a minimum. You know I was not even in the office the week before, so of course I was excluded from the presentation; until there was an appropriate time to blame someone. He really disappoints me. I know that's life in corporate, but I always thought of John as more of a mentor to me." Sheila struggled to edit the actual reasons around the pivotal events in New York as she recounted the story to him.

"You look…" Rick considered her, "tired. And it's not like you not to call. A man would think you'd forgotten him." His mouth formed a wicked grin.

"Not in my home," Sheila said tersely. "My husband is upstairs."

Rick made his way around the kitchen island to approach her. His moves were slow and deliberate. "Come now," he muttered as he fingered the lapel of her silk blouse. "After all we've been to each other. All we've *done* to each other."

Sheila swatted his hand away. "Step back now," she

growled.

"I know you're with that husband of yours, but is it *him* who stays up with you all night before a presentation rubbing your feet? Does he suck your toes like I did?" Rick's eyes glinted.

Out of nowhere, Raines entered the room, punched Rick in the face, and pushed him onto the floor. "Get out of my home." He stood over Rick with murder in his eyes.

Rick, for once acting sensibly, got up and left quickly and in silence. Then Raines turned that deadly look on Sheila.

"It was before we married," she said apologetically.

"I have *never* liked him. And you always told me there was nothing to worry about. It's clear he has been disrespecting me from the beginning. And you let him. That he thinks he can come into *our* home and put his hands on you, speak that filth." He hurled her tea mug across the room.

"I…"

"And you can't tell me," Raines talked over her, "that what he did came from out of nowhere. You said 'not in my home,' as if it were acceptable elsewhere!"

"Thinking about it, that hotel manager in New York had looked at me strangely, as if I wasn't the one he was expecting. Who was he expecting, Sheila?" He stepped towards her, looking dangerous. "Who was he expecting?"

Sheila dropped her head to the floor. "Rick."

"You look me in the eye when you tell me you've been unfaithful," Raines exploded.

"I wasn't unfaithful!" Sheila snapped back. Then, more soberly and guiltily, she added, "Just stupid."

"We slept together when I first started there. Actually, I got him his job." Sheila's mind threatened to float to pleasant memories of the countless places where and ways in which they had pleased each other in the company's offices. "But, when you and I got exclusive, I cut it out with him…except, he had already done this dumb thing of telling the usual hotels we frequented he was my husband. And we kept up the tradition of him staying with me the night before big presentations on the road…separate beds," she quickly added.

"He always enjoyed rubbing my feet, and you hate rubbing my feet. So I figured, why not? Though clearly I see why not now." Sheila maintained eye contact. It was excruciating.

Raines took a long moment to collect his thoughts. "You gave the intimacy that was due me to your former lover, under my nose, and despite my misgivings about him."

The seriousness of what she had done weighed on her. She had hurt his pride, and that was a big deal to him. She was such a free spirit. It had almost seemed like a silly game to her to play with Rick. She played on his affection for her, teased him, and loved to think she had a hidden life—meaningless, but still something just for her.

It was selfish. She had always been aware of that in the back of her mind. She had chosen to ignore it. Now she had to face the fact that it was also hurtful and threatened their relationship.

And that was why she preferred being a free spirit above all else. Because then she had no higher calling than her own will and that of God's. But she had vowed vows with Raines. She had to think in terms of "we," not "me."

Being one flesh sucked; except when it was amazing, life giving, and joyous. Sheila had to grow up and embrace that truth with mindfulness and intention. She had always assumed instinct would be sufficient in guiding her actions. She had been wrong.

"I *was* unfaithful to you, not with my body, but with my attention. I focused on myself and what I enjoyed without considering you as much as my own preferences. Before we connected, I was a flake, with men anyway. It was never serious; I just did what I wanted because nothing was deep. It didn't matter. You *matter*. I fell in love with you and I wanted more, I wanted deep. I guess I thought everything I did would automatically conform to a committed life. But Rick stayed a fun game to me. I'm so sorry."

Raines paced the kitchen for a long time, ringing his hands through his hair in silent frustration. Sheila picked up the pieces of broken ceramic from the mug he had thrown and cleaned up the tea that had spilled. Finally, they came together at the kitchen island.

"Well," he sighed, "it certainly can't compare to my wrongs. But it still hurts. And it feels different because it was so casual to you. I'm glad you forgave me, but honestly, I expected better from you. I always expect you to be the better of us. I never thought you would hurt me on purpose."

"But," Sheila started before a wave of Raines' hand cut her off.

"On purpose, or without giving me a moment's thought, it is to the same effect. I don't mean to force my cultural expectations on you, but I think this one is fair—as my wife, you need to be above reproach. I can't think straight if you're not."

Sheila couldn't concentrate. She couldn't put one thought in front of the other because she was wrong and guilty. She was used to being pitiful and not enough, but she didn't enjoy being the bad guy. All of her chickens were coming home to roost, and it was quite a reckoning. She honestly had never thought of what she had with Rick as cheating, but when she had actually said it out loud, she sounded like a vamp or something. What had she been thinking?

Life was a series of choices, Sheila pondered. And she had chosen to not take things as serious as they deserved. She had played with her marriage and been caught red-handed. Not because she had meant to cheat, but because she hadn't meant *not* to cheat. She had assumed her vows were things that would take care of themselves, not things to be guarded.

She loved Raines, but maybe she hadn't really needed him until now. And that had made honoring what they had a little less of a priority. It had made it easier to pretend her marriage wasn't at the core of her being. She had played with fire as if it couldn't burn down everything they had built. She was guilty as sin, and the weight of it was crushing.

If the shoe was on the other foot…what was she thinking? The shoe *had* been on the other foot, and she knew the depth of the pain it had caused. How could she have done this to someone she loved? Sheila hadn't a leg to stand on. She had to change her ways; to be better than she had been. She loved Raines, and it was time to start, not just enjoying him, but also valuing him as she should.

"You come first, before anybody else in this world—your feelings, your needs, everything. I swear to be more intentional about us going forward."

"You swear? Then I know it's done."

"You forgive me? Just like that?" Sheila eyed him suspiciously. It seemed way too easy.

"Sometimes you wear your heart on your sleeve. I can see you get it and that you meant what you said. After the grace you've given me, who am I to be unforgiving? Plus, I really need to believe you right now, to believe what we have is worth saving."

"It is." Tears were in Sheila's eyes.

They shared a fierce hug. It was turning into more than a hug when the doorbell rang.

"I'm going to shoot them all," Raines growled.

"Come on," Sheila sighed as she pulled away from their embrace and fixed herself up. "Its Gerry. It's game on for my consulting today, remember?"

"Don't think I'm done trying to convert you into a housewife. I mean, considering all that you're doing now…" Raines let the thought hang in the air. He still didn't know what to call her new vocation. She hardly knew herself.

"Ma ran the Institute *and* watched the gate," Sheila

protested.

Raines just stared at her, and they shared the same understanding—she was not her mother.

CHAPTER TWENTY-TWO WORKING AGAIN

Sheila shook her head, as if the movement would actually put her brain back in working order. The last half hour had been a whirlwind of emotions and activity. Now she had to slide into her professional self, but was not sure she was up to it. She banished those thoughts and took time for a few deep breaths before she opened her front door.

"Hi, boss." Gerry stood outside looking cold. She had kept him waiting a long time.

"Hello. Come in, come in! Thank you so much for your patience." Sheila ushered him in, closing the door and taking his coat. "Can I get you some coffee or tea?"

"I'm used to asking you that kind of stuff. No, no. I'm fine, but thank you."

The conversation was stilted as they both navigated their new working relationship. Sheila still couldn't believe he had jumped off the cliff with her, following her from his position as her assistant at their old company into a life of consulting. They made themselves comfortable in her office.

"Today should be fun. That's what I want you to remember. No nerves. We know what we are doing, and this first gig is an excellent fit for us. The conflict level should be nice and low, which is what you want when you're coming into a new environment cold. We're just taking some intake statements and getting to know the players.

"Thanks for coming out here. I wanted us to drive into and out of the place together so that we could have some time to debrief immediately after, though it is a bit of a haul for you." Sheila realized she was being a bit too mothering and reminded herself that Gerry was a grown man, a capable assistant, and didn't need hand holding.

"No problem. I am pretty excited about starting our new venture, so the miles flew by."

"Well, I'll do the rest of the driving, and you can fill me in on the last few weeks as we go."

i

Sheila and Gerry pulled up to an unassuming four-story building in the industrial park area of Fairfax, Virginia, which held the wildlife conservancy company, Wildervancy, Inc. They had hired her and Gerry to perform the exit interviews with their Chief Financial Officer. It was a minor job, she admitted, but they had to start somewhere. Gerry had secured this work, so she wanted to show she valued his ability to get clients.

And she had bills to pay. Sheila knew Raines at least half-joking about making her a housewife, but she couldn't even wrap her head around not bringing a paycheck into the home. Although it was a small client, she saw this as a symbolic return to working.

It meant returning to something that was just for her. Her husband didn't intrude. Her grandfather had no purchase here. Hard work and calm efficiency reigned in her work life, and she needed that world of order to anchor her, especially now.

Sheila and Gerry sat on one side of an oval conference table and looked at Thomas Krone, CFO of Wildervancy, Inc. with open expressions. He had a very corporate energy around him and wondered how well he had fit in at the non-profit. His six-foot frame sat easily in the chair and he seemed ready to get down to business.

"We appreciate you taking time out of your busy schedule to meet with us. Tying up years of work can be a Herculean effort." Sheila spoke in a supportive tone.

Thomas gave a small nod of acknowledgement. Good, Sheila thought, it looked like she had someone who was sparing with his words.

"I like to start with open-ended questions. What is most on your mind about this organization as you prepare to leave it?"

Thomas steepled his hands together and appeared deep in thought for a moment; his gray eyes clouding over. "This organization has incredible potential. But I can't be a part of it anymore. I pride myself on being able to adapt to different environments as the situation requires. I never got used to how things worked here, though."

"How do things work here?" Sheila was intrigued. She had forgotten how much she loved the mystery of unraveling workplace dynamics.

"The President and CEO is..." Thomas searched for a word, "demanding."

"How so?"

"He wants your loyalty. And then some." Thomas cleared his throat and looked at the doors of the conference room.

Sheila knew better than to press, even though she wanted to. You had to give a fish on a hook some line. He was leading her down this path. He clearly had something he wanted to reveal. But she had to keep control of this meeting. She changed the subject to give things room to breathe.

"Let's talk about your role here." She registered his confusion at her not following up on his statement. "I would love for you to describe what your day-to-day role at the company looked like. What are the things I can't get a sense of from simply reading the job description?"

"The job is everything to the people here. That means we're always working. Our social lives get absorbed into the company. Even our significant others get pulled in. That's unfortunate." Thomas rubbed the base of his left ring finger and looked away. So, Sheila thought, this job had ruined a marriage.

"Some nonprofits can drive you harder than the corporate world."

"But you love it," Thomas explained. "It brings you life. The work is so important, and everyone is committed to it. What more could you want in a workplace?"

"You tell me." Sheila looked at Thomas seriously. What had he needed that Wildervancy hadn't provided?

"Protection! The CEO is a predator. And he makes you look like one by association, because you've had this man in your home, championed him to your friends, defended him to your own wife, even when the proof was staring you in the face."

So much for a simple exit interview. Sheila reeled. Simple was never easy, it seemed.

"Our statements from this conversation can be called upon later. Are you sure you want to continue?" Sheila offered him an out in case he would rather talk about this to a lawyer, which she thought was an excellent idea. If any of the buzzwords he had mentioned were actually based on reality, Thomas Krone was about to bring down an organization.

But it looked like he was finally free somehow, like a balloon that had been dying to be popped. She bet he would spill it all now that he had taken the first step. She noticed a bit of sweat along his salt and pepper hairline. He had been nervous, but he had gotten it out. His jaw was unclenched, showing relaxation. It was hard to be relaxed while insinuating what he had, not unless it was true.

Did she want to be in the middle of this? It didn't matter, because here she was.

"Why don't we start from the beginning?"

Ninety minutes later, Sheila and Gerry emerged from the building and got back into her car.

"OK, we are still looking perfectly fine and acting as if all is well," Sheila said through teeth clenched into a smile as she backed out of their parking space. It wasn't until she had exited the entire business park that she seemed to let out the breath she had been holding in.

"Gerry, Gerry, Gerry. Your first client, and you bring us something out of a John Grisham book?!"

"Sex trafficking," Gerry said, stunned. "He works for an actual villain. And I guess we do, too. His signature was on our deposit check!"

"No, sir! We work for the organization, not any one individual, and that is where our responsibility lies. Besides just being human beings, of course."

"So, what do we do now?"

"I have absolutely no idea. There was no expectation of privacy at our meeting. I think we need to call the FBI because there are minors involved in a crime. But I don't even know how to do that. It's not as if I can just dial 9-1-1 emergency services.

"In the meantime, we still owe a report—to the organization, not the president. I'll get that together, quickly, so I can get this foul taste out of my mouth. But we need to prepare for the possibility, perhaps even probable, that the organization is going to want to keep us on in some capacity. They'll want us to either help them weather the storm that is coming, or keep us tied up with conflicts of interests to reduce our credibility as potential witnesses.

"It all seems like a scenario out of a TV crime drama. It doesn't feel real. If they want to engage us and if I feel that they really want our help, would you want to continue being involved? This subject is not for everyone, and we'd be getting deeper into the matter before it got better. We'd be looking at something protracted; *if* the organization can even survive it."

Gerry looked ahead for a few long moments. "If we can help the organization heal itself after this, I think we should. Who better than you?"

"Who better than *us*?"

CHAPTER TWENTY-THREE
A NEW NORMAL?

Sheila saw Gerry off once they reached her house, then went inside her office for the rest of the afternoon. Her floor-to-ceiling bookcases greeted her, and the chair at her white desk was waiting for her to get to work. It turns out it was easy to find the number for the FBI, but hard to reach someone who could actually help you. She took the better part of an hour just trying to reach the right person. Then it took another hour to explain her situation and recount her experience.

She remembered thinking it was a good thing she wasn't in the mob, because she rolled on Thomas Krone like the Alabama Tide. She reminded herself that Thomas had wanted to get this secret out. He had walked into that meeting with the story almost bursting from him. She had just been a means for him to get it out. She refused to feel bad for the trouble she was unleashing upon his head.

Around 6:00pm, Sheila staggered out of her office, finally finished talking to the FBI and finishing up the first draft of her report to Wildervancy. She had already decided that, for everyone's protection, her report would be cc'd to the entire Leadership Team and the Board of Directors.

Was she being played, Sheila wondered? If Thomas' accusation was true and things were as deeply embedded in the organization as he said, why would they ever have agreed to bring in someone from the outside like her? None of this made sense.

But she had been over it a million times in her head, and there were no answers to be found at the moment. It was time to put the matter to rest, for now. She filled her lungs with air to the point of bursting, held for as long as she could, then had the satisfying feeling of all the air, tension, and concerns rush out of her.

Sheila headed to the kitchen, washed her hands, put an apron on over her work clothes, and pulled out some ingredients to make a quick stir-fry for dinner.

It had been too long since she had worked the professional part of her brain, Sheila thought. After a long day, she felt rusty and tired. She still had things to do, though, and knew sleep was a ways off. She ate her dinner, trying to be mindful of each bite, but it was more accurate to say she scarfed it down as she realized she hadn't had breakfast or lunch that day. No wonder she was worn out.

Finally, her belly felt full, and she could put her attention to other tasks. Sheila made a plate for Raines and put it in the fridge, writing a note on the dry erase board on the door: "Stir fry inside for the hungry man hard at work." She didn't want to be a homemaker, but she had to admit, she enjoyed providing the comforts of home to him. Especially when she had something to make up for, as she had today.

Sheila headed up to her shrine room. She had been neglecting it the last couple of weeks, as she had been spending so much time in her mother's shrine room with her grandfather. At some point, she was going to have to do something about that, she knew, but it would not be today.

She sprinkled herself with the Florida water bottle on the small table outside the door to her shrine room and ran her hands up and down her frame, sloughing off all the negative energy that had been dumped on her or generated from her over the course of the day. Taking a moment to enjoy being clean, she gave herself a pat on the back for making in through a tough day. She knew there were more days like this to come and that this wouldn't even be the worst of them, but she needed to give thanks for making it through each one.

Entering her shrine room and turning on the lights, she immediately felt tired again. So much to do. She had to clear the shrines of their offering plates and empty candles, clear their energies, and set up new offerings for each one.

She got to work.

It wasn't as daunting as she had feared it might be. She applied herself and within a half hour, everything was done. Anyone looking would see a well-attended shrine room, and she finally felt peace in her spirit as she sensed the low thrumming of positive energy throughout the room.

She looked at her ancestral shrine and pondered how she would have to change it. Was it time to include her mother yet? She knew there were a certain number of days after passing before a soul passed over into the ancestral plane, but she didn't know how many. That was yet another detail she had relied on her mother for.

Sheila took stock of the vodka next to her Buddhist shrine. The vodka was for the God of War. He was partial to strong spirits. She could see from the scant amount left Raines had been "communing" a lot in here with the God of War. She chuckled and thought about how much they had been through in the last months. It was a wonder Raines hadn't drunk the entire state dry.

He was becoming more spiritual, just as he had said he would. She had seen such the change in him. It still surprised her to see a grown man change. Her mother had told her that never happened and it was best just to accept people as they were, not who you hoped they would become.

As she poured some white jasmine rice into an ornate bowl and placed it before Quan Yin, the Goddess of Mercy, she wondered what their marriage would look like after all this. Who would they be together? Her grandfather had said they had the chance to become more than they were, but that she had to go through some pain to get to that point. When would she be done with the pain part—both experiencing it and causing it?

She winced as she thought about the events of the morning with Rick and Raines. That had not been her most shining moment. She wondered how she could have been so stupid. She grabbed a large white candle in its glass container, cleansed it with Florida water, and set it on her Buddhist shrine.

As she lit it, she realized it was finally time for her to grow up, to realize that what she did mattered. There would be no more hiding behind her mother's skirts or pretending that the rules of life didn't apply to her. She had lived too long as a pixie, and, while she didn't want to lose that joy, it was definitely time to lose the carelessness.

Sheila lit three sticks of incense and bowed before the shrine three times before sticking the incense in a small bowl filled with sand and leaving them to burn out. "God of War, give me strength. Goddess of Mercy, give me gentleness. Buddha, give me wisdom. Monkey God, give me craftiness." She certainly needed them in her corner.

She walked over to her bookshelf and saw that he had pulled her Bibles out and they lay on the floor. Men were so messy, she thought. She picked them up and put them in their places. Raines had been reading the Bible lately. It made sense that was the strongest pull for him, with his Catholic upbringing. Maybe she would get him a devotional Bible all his own. It would keep him from ransacking hers.

It occurred to Sheila that they should do some things together spiritually as well. She made a note to find a local mass they could attend. It would be comfortable for him, and short enough for her. That was one thing she would say about Catholics—they got you in and out of a service with stopwatch precision.

Sheila loved Jesus. She had just never liked to be tied down to one thing, and Christianity was a bit too exclusive for her. What exactly would her flavor of spirituality look like without her mother to shepherd her anymore? She couldn't imagine. It all was still too new.

Now that her shrine room was clean and glowing, Sheila felt like she could think straight again. She supposed she was done being mad at her grandfather. She should go over to her mother's shrine room and do her job.

Interdimensional gates didn't watch themselves, as Grandfather was quick to remind her.

On Sheila's drive to her mother's house, it was hard to see through her tears. She still missed her ma. Would it ever get any easier? She longed to take a full breath with no hitches of heartache in it. Her greatest desire was to be whole, not this broken shell of a motherless child.

"God, carry me through this pain. Make me better than I think I can be. Open the windows of heaven and pour out a blessing for me. I need your help—with everything. I know you're there. Please, just let me *feel* your comforting presence. Tell me I'm not alone in this."

She turned off her engine in front of her mother's house, lay her head on the steering wheel, and let out all the tears she had been holding back the last few days. It was the good cry she needed, but by the time she entered the shrine room, her eyes were red and puffy and her sinuses were stopped up. She made a poor excuse for a superhero, she thought.

She repeated the same process here as she had for her home shrine. Keeping up with two shrine rooms was getting old quick. The physical labor alone was tiring her out, and the spiritual focus and power needed was no small thing. By the time she finished preparing the room so that she was ready to talk to her grandfather, she was tuckered out.

She wanted to find a bed to crawl in, preferably with her husband in it, but she could feel the pull of her grandfather. He was demanding her presence. Sheila planted herself in front of the ancestral shrine and turned on the small Mr. Coffee beside it she had just refreshed. It started making comforting, percolating sounds. When it had finished, she poured a fresh cup. Then she lit a cigar and tried not to choke as she took a few puffs of it. That part hadn't gotten any easier.

Sheila bowed down and waited. Actually, she bowed down and fell asleep, but that was splitting hairs.

"What am I going to do with you?"

Sheila jerked up and took a moment to orient herself. "Hello, Grandfather."

"Why are you always falling apart when you come here?"

"Well, let's start with that question. Why exactly do I have to come here? If the reins have been handed over to me, why am I still in my mother's shrine room? I'm spending an hour and a half just traveling back and forth, not to mention the labor of maintaining two shrine rooms. Every time I cleanse these shrines, they confront me with the fact that I'm not her. It's hard."

"Get more rest."

"Not on the schedule you would prefer for me to keep. But that doesn't answer my first set of questions. I want to do this work from my shrine room. Let's make it happen."

"Your shrine room is not sufficient."

Sheila let her shoulders slump. Yet another way in which she was not up to snuff. But the challenges would not stop coming simply because she wanted them to. She lifted her head back up and plowed on. "Well, we need to make it sufficient. Tell me what needs to happen. and I'll do it."

"The current arrangement suits me."

"So you need me to watch the gate, but you won't do a thing to make it any easier for me? Thanks."

"We have work to do. Let us focus on that."

"I don't know what kind of relationship you had with my mother, but this is not working for me. I don't care that the current situation suits you. It doesn't suit me. And I seem to be the one doing the work, so my opinion matters. I won't have you sweep it aside like this."

"You are difficult."

"You are welcome, more than welcome, to find somebody else."

A long silence stretched out, and Sheila was fine with

that. She met her grandfather's demands, many times reluctantly, but still she met them. She was not about to give in to his preferences as well.

Sheila realized her grandfather was simply not going to answer her. She put out the cigar she had lit and left the coffee in front of the ancestral shrine before going home. One thing she knew how to do exceedingly well was to be stubborn.

Sheila found Raines asleep in their bed and was suddenly wide awake. Perhaps it had been the war of wills with her grandfather that had lit a fire in her and woken her up. She peeled off her layers and jumped into the shower. Ten minutes later, she emerged clean and refreshed, having washed the heaviness of the day off of her.

Sheila crawled into bed, and Raines moved to wrap around her, still half asleep.

"Where you been?" he asked sleepily.

"Ma's. Having a fight with Grandfather. A fight I will win."

"That's my girl." Raines kissed the back of her neck, which prompted her to turn around.

"I think you should take off all these clothes, sir."

Raines had taken to wearing a t-shirt and pajama bottoms since coming back from Las Lomas. It was a modesty she had thought the situation had called for. But now, his clothes were just getting in the way.

Sheila needed him. She needed to connect with him. They were married, after all. And more than that, they had chosen each other again, turning down the other options.

One thing was for sure, she didn't have to tell Raines to get naked twice. She blinked, and it seemed like he had instantaneously shed his clothes. She worked to get out of hers, laughing that she had just put them on a few minutes ago.

"Are you sure about this?"

"I absolutely want to consummate our reconciliation.

If that's alright with you, that is."

His mouth took hers, crushing down on it with an urgency. He rested his forehead against hers as his hand outlined her jaw. "I missed you."

"Show me."

Raines grabbed Sheila and pulled her so close that it knocked the breath out of her for a moment. She liked it. Sheila reached for his manhood, and he moaned. "No foreplay. Let's just get on with it."

Raines pinned her hands above her head. "I'm sorry, but you're not in charge right now." He had a wicked expression on his face.

For the next hour, Raines tortured her, feasting on different parts of her body, but not giving her what she really wanted. He definitely knew how to drive her crazy. When, for the umpteenth time, she was sure she couldn't take it anymore, suddenly he was on top of and inside her. Sheila let out a delighted gasp and held on for the ride.

Afterwards, they lay staring up at the ceiling in a companionable silence and comfortable haze of good feelings and exhaustion.

"Have I mentioned you're amazing lately?"

A smile spread across Raines' sleepy face. "No. I always love to hear it. It takes two, you know."

"I'll say. I think I pulled something." Sheila winced a bit as she stretched out her left calf.

Raines grasped her hand and brought it to his lips. "Sorry. Not sorry," he chuckled. "So, what got into you tonight?"

"Oh, stop pretending you don't know you're irresistible. I just had to have you, is all."

"I'm up for a repeat anytime you want, then."

"Great. Only not now; I'm exhausted."

"Thank God, because that was all talk."

They laughed together and dozed off, tangled up in their sheets.

CHAPTER TWENTY-FOUR
LATE

Sheila woke up and gave herself a nice, long stretch. She really was sore in places. She had the Lord on her mind and figured she would get up and spend some time in her shrine room. As she swung her legs over the side of the bed, her stomach revolted. She barely made it to the bathroom in time before she threw up the contents of last night's dinner.

Raines was up and by her side in a flash. "You ok?"

"Must have been something I ate." Sheila gargled with water and spit it out, then grabbed her toothbrush. Her mouth felt disgusting.

"I had the stir-fry you left me, and I'm fine."

"Your stomach could contain hazardous materials, and you'd be fine."

"It's weird that it would take so long. It's not like you to get morning sickness…" Raines heard the words as he spoke them and an expression of surprise registered on his face as he put his hand to his mouth.

"No. Now you stop it right there. This is not morning sickness. I mean yes, it is the morning, and I threw up, but it's not that. So don't even get started on that line of thought." Sheila spoke scoldingly, but inside was wondering the same thing. Then she started counting backwards. Technically, she was late, but she had assumed it was all the stress.

"Only one way to find out," Raines said in a sing-song voice. A huge smile covered his face.

"Yes, that will put an end to this rampant speculation. I'll get a pregnancy test, then you'll see." Sheila worried she was trying to convince herself.

"Don't move, just rest. I'll go get some. I'll be right back." Raines seemed beside himself as he ran around getting dressed.

"Raines, I'm not pregnant. I threw up; it's nothing to worry about. And it's certainly not worth getting excited over."

Raines stopped and gave her a kiss. "A guy can dream, can't he? I'll be right back."

While he was gone, Sheila took a shower and calculated that she was about two weeks late. It wasn't like her to forget her period, but she had been so busy with her grandfather's training she had barely had time to notice anything. And besides, he had said she wouldn't be able to have children as part of this job. She might be unhappy with many aspects of her relationship with her grandfather, but one thing he was not was a liar. So, it was simply an unrelated incident.

Raines came back home with a bag full of pregnancy tests a short while later.

"Did you buy out the entire store?" Sheila chuckled at him. She would be sorry to rain on his parade, but it had to be done. "You know there isn't enough pee in the world to take all these tests, right? Pick two, and I'll take them."

Raines made a big show of reading the backs of the tests.

"Oh, they're all the same!"

"I want to make sure I pick two good ones."

"Did you ask the pharmacist?"

"No, this is private."

"I'm pretty sure the person at the checkout knows all your business, dear."

"Here." He handed her two packages with pregnancy tests inside. "This one says it's 98.5% accurate, and this one says it's 99.9% accurate," he said solemnly.

She went into the downstairs bathroom and coaxed a urine sample out of herself. She stuck both sticks in the plastic container, making sure they got wet. Then she set them down and opened the door. Raines almost fell in. He had been leaning on the door in anticipation.

They both stared at the two small windows on the tests, waiting for results to show up.

"This is about as exciting as watching paint dry, you know." It was anything but boring, Sheila admitted to herself, but she had a stoic reputation to maintain.

A single line appeared on one panel, and two lines appeared on the other.

"Split decision," Sheila wondered aloud.

They both took turns reading the back of the packages again. She had been in such a hurry to get it over with that she hadn't bothered before.

Oh no. On the first test, no line meant not pregnant and one line meant pregnant. On the second, one line meant not pregnant and two lines meant pregnant. The tests agreed.

Sheila was stunned. She barely registered as Raines picked her up and spun her around in his excitement. He planted a big kiss on her and hugged her.

"You're going to be the mother of my children!"

"Uh-huh," Sheila muttered, still in a daze. "I think I need to sit down."

Raines scooped her up and carried her to the sofa off of the kitchen.

"Are you ok? You don't seem excited."

"I'm just confused. Grandfather…"

"Was wrong," Raines interjected. "And I couldn't be happier about it. I hope you can be happy, too."

"I," Sheila swallowed hard. "It will take some getting used to, but yes, it looks like we'll be a family soon." She smiled and touched Raines' cheek. "It will be our next glorious adventure."

Raines gathered her up and held her close. "Thank you, God, for this blessing."

CHAPTER TWENTY-FIVE
A PACKAGE WAS DELIVERED

It was a cold, sunny morning, and Sheila was having an early morning winter workout on the back porch. She enjoyed exercise, but hated being stuck in soulless gyms, preferring to be in the fresh air when she could. Trying to follow the dance workout video on her screen, she laughed to herself as she struggled to keep up with the choreography. She would never be the world's greatest dancer, but it wouldn't be for lack of trying.

As she toweled off inside after her workout, she noticed a package on the foyer table. How had she missed that yesterday? Picking it up, she saw there was no postage. What was Raines playing at? Opening it, she pulled out a chunky picture frame. In it was a picture of her sister, Jasmin, embracing Sheila's enemy, Hotep. Jasmin looked excited.

Sheila's blood ran cold. Hotep was showing he could get to her anytime, anywhere. And he was reminding her he had her sister. She cursed herself again. If only Sheila had maintained a better relationship with Jasmin recently, perhaps she could have separated her from him. She still couldn't believe Jasmin had stayed with him after she had revealed his true identity.

How was she supposed to interact with Jasmin now? Anything Sheila told her would be known to Hotep, *ha satan*, she corrected herself. She had to keep the fact that he was the eternal *accuser* at the front of her mind.

Sheila reminded herself there was only one divine remedy to the *accuser*—to confess. It was the shame over what you did wrong and your desire to hide it that got you into more trouble than the wrong. She had to be completely transparent. It was not human nature, and it certainly wasn't Sheila's nature to admit her flaws and faults so freely. But it was probably the only way to get her sister back and to free herself from Hotep's grasp.

Sheila picked up her phone and called Jasmin. The call went to voicemail, and she was preparing to leave a message when Jasmin called her back.

"Hi Jas," Sheila said cheerily.

"Greetings, my sistah," Hotep's warm voice came through.

"Hotep. Is my sister there?"

"Oh, she's here, but she's not available. In the shower, you see. We just got done with something, well, sticky." Hotep let out a rich laugh.

The thought of them together disgusted her, and she knew that was his point. She did the only thing she could do and not be ensnared—dive into the pain.

"Jasmin deserves love, and I'm glad she's found some happiness. I will not begrudge her life's joy."

"Mmm, a likely story."

Hotep was speaking with entirely too much sexuality in his voice for Shiela. She felt as if she were having some kind of illicit conversation.

"Hotep, why did you call me back?"

"I know you received my special delivery to you. That must be the *only* thing that would make you call your sister. You two honestly don't talk much these days."

Ouch; he would always know where to strike, she reminded herself. Again, she dove into the pain. "I haven't been a very good sister lately, but I want to be. She's my heart."

"Of course, of course. I just wanted you to have a picture of us to remind you we are together, and that I want us all to be one big, happy family."

"Let us speak the truth to one another, you and I."

"I don't think you can."

"I want you out of my life. It is not the time for my sifting, so you are unwelcome here. I know who you are. Let's not pretend. What do you want with me, *accuser*?"

"It's not time for your sifting? As if you would know of the seasons and times. You don't even know the number of your days. I am of an essence you can not even comprehend, yet you demand to know what I want with you? The only thing you need to know is that you will fail. You are not a worthy heir. You could never live up to your mother's expectations, much less her. I'm just here to remind you."

Tears stung Sheila's eyes. She had told herself she was ready to face Hotep, that she would teach him a lesson. Yet with a few words, he had undone her. But she couldn't fall back into that well of despair and self-hate she had been in before. She had to fight for the peace she had reached.

"I'm most definitely not a worthy heir, but I *am* the heir. I will do all I can do, the best that I can do, for as long as I can do it. Accuse me all you want, but I won't stop." Sheila didn't know where that strength had come from, but she would not look a gift horse in the mouth.

"Let's play again soon."

Sheila's phone flashed. "Call Ended."

He really burned her up. Just his existence bothered her, how much more his pursuit of her. He had been right, though. She *didn't* know the seasons and the times well. That had never been her focus in life, and she had always taken it for granted that her mother would keep her aligned with the flow of life, the spiritual and the supernatural.

Maybe it *was* her time of sifting. What timing, she groaned. It had the ring of truth to it now that she thought about it. God *would* pick when she was already in the crucible to let her be weighed and assessed by the *accuser*. It was the impossible situation life loved bringing to her door.

Only, this time, she couldn't muscle through it. Sheila had to submit, agreeing with her *accuser* quickly to free herself from him. She couldn't lie to him. She had to tell the truth: she *hadn't* been a loving sister lately, and she was a poor, poor substitute for her mom. The truth felt dangerous, but it was never as dangerous as the lie. In the long run, you always paid for denying reality. The only way to rob it of its power was to face it.

Sheila wondered how she was going to do that, then dropped to her knees in the foyer and went into prayer.

"God, you've got to fight my battles for me. Sometimes I feel as if a stiff wind will knock me down. Still, I know you have been with me. Let me resist the temptation to control things. Help me give you complete control of my life. Let me surrender to you. And get Hotep off of my back. He can only do what you permit, so revoke his access to me, God.

"Protect me from him, but protect Jasmin most of all. I don't want it, but I can take it if I have to. Let no hurt, harm, or danger come to her. You know I hate him in her life, but I love her happy. Bless Jasmin so that her latter is greater than her former. I just need a little more of your grace, Lord."

Sheila walked into the kitchen to make a cup of tea. She still didn't see how any of this was going to work out, but she had reminded herself that she didn't need to see it, only to know that God would work it out. She inhaled and exhaled slowly as she made a conscious effort to release all of her worry, confusion, and hurt. By the time the kettle boiled, she was free, mostly, of Hotep's snare to send her down a spiral of regret and self-recrimination. She loved how prayer changed things. If she could keep that in mind, she might just make it through this.

PART SIX
CHOICES

CHAPTER TWENTY-SIX
BAD NEWS

Sheila paced the kitchen, not knowing what to do with herself. She put her hands solemnly on her belly, as if she could feel something. Sheila even found a small squeal escaping her lips. She was terrified and overjoyed.

She was still awestruck by the situation, but by that evening, was slowly getting used to the reality that she was pregnant. How far they had come from mere weeks ago, she thought. They had been through so much—she supposed they were due some good news.

And it *was* good news, Sheila realized. Just because she couldn't imagine how it would go, it was still a blessing. She supposed her need to plan every aspect of her life was going to take a real beating when motherhood came into the picture.

She was going to try really hard to be a good mother. And she knew Raines would be a great father. His enthusiasm for the matter knew no bounds. She had had to banish him to his downstairs studio to get him out of her hair.

That afternoon, she had made an appointment with her doctor for later in the week to confirm the matter and get advice on how to move forward. She had to admit she had no idea how pregnancy actually worked. She would have to study up on the subject.

She tried not to burst into tears every time she wished her ma was there to share this news with and get advice from. It threatened to make her feel very lonely when she thought about it, but she countered that with the knowledge that her mother would be so proud of and happy for her.

She was motherless, but she wasn't alone or forsaken. She had Raines. And she had her grandfather, too, for what that was worth. She would wait until she got confirmation from the doctor to call her sisters and give them the news.

That brought the situation with Jasmin and Hotep back to the front of her mind. She couldn't believe Jasmin had chosen him over her, even once she had some idea of what he was. Sheila was now experiencing the results of having taken Jasmin for granted. Jasmin had been hurting, and Sheila had been too caught up in her own grief to be there for anyone but herself.

Going forward, she had to foster and sustain a spirit of togetherness and teamwork. There could be no more going it alone and doing what she wanted without considering the needs of others. She had seen where that had gotten her. She had almost wrecked her marriage and ruined her relationships with her sisters and friends.

She realized her mother had been the one that had kept her from going off the rails before, always counseling her to be kinder and more considerate. Now, she needed to be that voice in her head, encouraging her to stretch and grow in the directions she needed to. She had to if she wanted to keep her husband, sisters, and loved ones, let alone be a loving mom to her child.

Sheila blew out a breath and tried to take it all in. She was about to be a mom. She felt like she was just getting a handle on what it meant to be a responsible and loving adult! Well, life was coming for her, whether she was ready or not.

She clasped her hands together and bowed her head. "Lord, I know you know what you're doing. Please strengthen and equip me to handle this blessing. Make me better than I am. Help me mend things with my sisters and husband. Make me a good mom and let my child be healthy and happy. You can do anything but fail, so I place it all in your hands. Amen."

Sheila let Raines know she was going over to talk to her grandfather and, of course, he had insisted on coming with her. He had taken to keeping watch in the hallway outside her mother's shrine room ever since she had begun this work, and she had to admit, as much as she preferred to be independent, his presence had been a real comfort.

They drove over together and talked. She told Raines of her latest efforts to transition things to her own shrine room.

"That will save a lot of time, and wear and tear on your body, from going back and forth. I'm all for it."

"Grandfather seemed less than pleased with the idea, but now I will have to insist."

"Don't much care for his opinion on this matter, I can tell you. I'm just glad he was wrong about you not being able to get pregnant. It means he's not infallible."

"I won't lead with that line, but the same thing had occurred to me. I think there are very few absolutes about what can be, even from his dimension."

"So, have you told your sisters yet? Should we have a plan for how we tell people?"

"I haven't told them, and I need to talk to you about Jasmin. I guess I'll let them know after I see my doctor and get confirmation. But I think we're supposed to wait until after the first trimester or something like that before you let everybody know. I'm not sure."

"We'll have to buy books!"

Sheila knew Raines liked to read, but she had to laugh at how excited he was about reading. "Yes, we'll have plenty of time to figure out what's going on and how to handle it."

He leaned over and kissed her on the cheek.

"Keep your eyes on the road, mister," Sheila laughed.

"So, what did you want to tell me about Jasmin?"

Sheila's expression sobered. "So she's seeing Hotep, the man from your art exhibit in New York."

"I'm well aware of who he is."

"It wasn't until I saw him a second time that I fully realized he's not a man. He's an entity known as *ha satan*."

"Wait, Hotep is Satan?"

"It's complicated, but kind of. And she knows. At least, I tried to tell her she was with the a*ccuser*, and she doesn't care. She said he had been there for her when I had not. She is under his spell. I guess I can't blame her. I was almost fooled myself, at first. But it means that whatever I tell her, my enemy knows. And I'm just not sure I want him to know I'm with child, yet. But if I don't tell her, how do I try to mend the rift that's growing between us?"

"You mean the *actual* Satan that's in the Bible? How is that even possible?"

"Yes, the Satan that's in the Bible, but no, not the horned red devil that Christian tradition has made him out to be. He walks the earth looking for people to devour, and he seems to have settled on me."

"And you just happen to mention that Satan has his sights set on you in passing during a conversation about Jasmin?"

Sheila felt guilty for it not having occurred to her to talk to him about it before. "In my defense, a *lot* has been going on."

"Mmmm," Raines grumbled, barely accepting her excuse. "So he's after you. What does that mean, exactly?"

"No idea. I have to talk to Grandfather about it."

"You haven't told him about it?! While that makes me feel a little better about not being told until now, I'm very concerned about what in the world it is you think you're doing. This is the thing you need help with, isn't it?"

Sheila hung her head down. "Grandfather and I have been busy fighting since I got back. He is very difficult to work with."

"As are you."

Sheila raised an eyebrow at him.

"I mean, one could imagine," he backpedaled.

"Oh," Sheila gave up. "You're right. I'm no picnic, that's for sure. But with everything going on, my head has just been spinning like a top. I've not been at my best lately."

Raines turned into her mother's driveway and shut off the car.

"I need you to be at your best. You have more than yourself to worry about now."

"I know." Sheila kissed him and let her head rest on his shoulder for a minute. "No time like the present." They got out of the car and headed inside the house. She looked with pleasure, as always, at the custom doors that graced the home. The wood carvings were looking better over time, it turned out. She was glad she had them to remember Ma by.

As had become tradition, she and Raines did a sweep of the house to see if they could figure out where the stale smell that permeated was coming from. It was another fruitless attempt. They had already cleaned up everything in an already clean house. It was starting to take on the tone of a mausoleum. Sheila couldn't decide if she liked that.

A short time later, Sheila was before the ancestral shrine in her mother's house, calling on her grandfather. She drank the coffee and took a few puffs of the cigar. She had never expected that her spiritual life would turn her into a smoker. Technically, she didn't have to do this for him to come here, but it was an anchor here for him, calling him to this place and time, and to help him recall who he had been while he was on earth. He seemed demanding enough as it was, so she wasn't sure she wanted him conjured without the anchor to his life. He was liable to be even colder.

"You really should spend more time here," his voice intoned.

"Hello, Grandfather."

"Let us get to work."

"We need to talk first."

"Will you never obey me?"

"We need to talk first."

Sheila was met with silence. She plowed ahead. "I have to go to the doctor to confirm, but it seems I'm pregnant. Raines is ecstatic, and I am slowly getting used to the idea. We'll have to change the way we do some things."

"This job doesn't change for you; you change for the

job. I have been trying to explain that to you."

"Some things will have to change. For starters, we are going to have to move this operation to my shrine room. It's a bit of a trek for me to keep coming here and Raines insists on coming, too, so it's disrupting the whole family. It will be easier and I'll have more energy to do what I have to do if it can be in my home. That *is* my seat of power, you know."

"And this is where the existing connection is."

"I'm not bending on this. We have to adjust to this new reality. And you know this is something I wanted to do even before I knew about this little one." Sheila patted her stomach. "Baby first, or something like that."

"Or something like that?" Sheila could hear the ridicule dripping off of her grandfather's words. "You have no idea what you are doing."

"Well, not to put too fine a point on it—*you* said I couldn't get pregnant, yet here I am."

"I did not say you couldn't get pregnant. I said you could not carry a child to term. And I am not wrong about that. I am sorry."

Her grandfather's voice softened at the end, but Sheila could not take that in. She remembered her mother's miscarriages later in life, the ones she had known about, and cursed herself for confusing what her grandfather had said. She had simplistically assumed she would get pregnant and then have a baby. The possibility of losing the child inside her had never even occurred to her.

"But I'm young, young-ish anyway. Healthy."

"You can barely drag yourself out of here most nights, and we've mostly been training. Your husband had to break the circle for you once. The spiritual damage you incur shows up as physical damage, at least for a short while. A fetus can't survive that. I told you this. You should have taken precautions."

"I didn't feel the need to tell you about my family planning. And, near as I can figure, this happened before you told me."

Silence filled the room. Sheila thought about the bruises, pain, and exhaustion she had been experiencing in her work, and she hadn't really gotten started yet. She had only taken a few trips to the gate, and the work had been hard. She was sure she would get better at it, but the work would always pose a risk. It wasn't as if it were a desk job.

Sheila thought about Raines. He wanted children so badly. The memory of what telling him she couldn't have children had resulted in still ached within her. She wasn't eager to repeat such devastation. There had to be another way, but as desperate as she was to find it, nothing surfaced.

So Sheila simply made a decision and forged ahead. "No. I will carry this child and birth this baby inside me. God will just have to help me."

"So now you're even telling God how things will be?" Her grandfather's voice sounded partly amazed and partly afraid. "You know that's not how it works. I know this news is upsetting, but, Sheila, it's not as if you even want a child, not really."

"But it's here now! That changes everything. And I was coming around to wanting a child. It was just a slow process. It doesn't really matter what it seems to be, it only matters what God will decide on the matter. I am appealing to him. So I don't want to hear another contrary word from you. It is not in your hands, and I need your support. Please."

"Well, I agree with you that God will have the final say. But the farther you go with this, the worse it will be for you if things don't turn out the way you want."

"Not a contrary word. I can accept that you're never going to cheer me on in anything I do, it seems. But you will not stand in my way. Not concerning my child."

Silence followed her statement.

"Let me hear you agree to this."

"Not a contrary word. We are in agreement on this. I hope you win."

CHAPTER TWENTY-SEVEN THE CONVERSATION

It was after midnight when Sheila came out of the shrine room. She leaned against its door, weary with a bone deep exhaustion. Raines was in the hallway, sketching on a pad and mumbling to himself. The twin size air bed he was lying on looked like heaven.

She sat down beside him, and he wrapped an arm around her. She picked up his drawing pad, holding it this way and that as she pretended to critique it. "Still at it with the temple, I see."

"Just in my spare time. It bugs me that I can't get it right."

"I'd be frightened if you could. But how great would that be? This is *the* original tabernacle. To come up with a coherent version of that would send any believer into pure bliss."

"Speaking of that, what *do* you believe exactly?"

"What do you mean?"

"I know you believe in God and all, but what's going on now is so much more than that. What are we going to raise our child believing? Are you going to tell them all this stuff about interdimensional gateways and imps from the fifth dimension that leave pantyhose in the bed?"

Sheila let out a laugh at the mention of imps and pantyhose. He always remembered the strangest things about their conversations. The laugh also let out some of the tension of what was winding up to be a heavy-laden conversation. She took his hand in hers and thought about it.

"I've been thrust into all of this because my mother told me nothing about this part of her life. I don't want to hide things from my family, so I will tell our children about this side of things when we decide the time is right and they can handle it. As to what I believe, I've always been under my mother's wing, so no one's asked me that in a really long time.

"I believe in a God of many faces. And I see some of those faces in different religions and faith traditions that have love and peace as their core. I'm definitely a new-age weirdo on top of all that. I've been sincere in my efforts, but I've also been a dabbler, picking and choosing as if life is a dim sum restaurant. I need to go a lot deeper. How I define and express my faith might change. I'll just have to see what God requires of me now, and what the best way forward is. I hope that's ok for an answer." Sheila looked at Raines anxiously.

"It's fine. I'm not grading you or anything like that. It's just, reading the Bible, there's a lot of talk about idols. I'm no expert, but your shrine room seems full of them."

It felt like the oxygen left the room to Sheila. He was calling her to task on a very complicated manner. Well, maybe it wasn't all that complicated. Maybe she just didn't want to say it.

"What are you asking me?" Sheila thought she knew, but wanted to hear the words come out of his mouth.

"I'm not coming for you, I promise." Raines raised his hands in a conciliatory gesture. "But how is your shrine room, your mother's shrine room, not idol worship?"

"I'm *trying* not to take it personally, believe me. With you expanding spiritually, this was bound to come up." Sheila closed her eyes and took a deep breath. "I'm not worshiping other gods, if that's what you're asking. I think of the identities of the various shrines as aspects of God. One God of heaven and earth, multiple aspects.

"Yes, I have statues portraying those aspects of God. When I pray at the shrine, I'm not praying to the statues, I'm praying to the glory of God that I have invited to abide in that place. I know it can seem like a minor distinction. It may not even be a distinction I honor all the time, but it is the goal.

"If you're further embracing Christianity, and it seems you are, there's gonna be some," Sheila searched for the words, "creative tension."

"And how do you know these 'aspects' aren't other gods or beings you're worshiping?"

The strain of the conversation was causing Sheila to sweat, but she pressed on. "I commune with different aspects of God to get guidance and help on things. But my worship is for God alone, the culmination of all those aspects. I talk to the Goddess of Mercy, but I don't worship her. I pray to my ancestors for guidance and power, but I don't worship them. They are all just pieces of the whole. The One that cannot be measured. So I kind of cheat. I take God in bite-sized portions I can wrap my head around. But at no point do I think one of those portions is a God. *Of* God, yes. But not a replacement or competition."

Sheila blew out a breath. "And I hope that anything I just said makes any kind of sense at all, but I *think* I said what I wanted to say."

Raines sat silent, deep in thought. Sheila worked to manage her expectations. Was he about to call her an infidel, or worse, a sorceress? What would she have to say about all of this if she were in his shoes? She wished they could skip the uncomfortable negotiation that had to happen when different faiths encountered each other. But it had to happen if they were ever to fit together spiritually. She forced herself to take slow, deep breaths, waiting quietly while he thought.

"I don't know. I can see how it makes sense, but it doesn't. Let me think about it some more. Pray on it, too, I guess."

Sheila let out a breath. She guessed she would have to take what she could get.

"So, what did your grandfather say when you told him you were pregnant?" Raines was full of glee again and put his hand on her belly. It was a sweet but foreign gesture.

This conversation's intensity was not giving her a break, Sheila thought. "He said I had made a grave mistake. That getting pregnant is one thing, but carrying a child to term is another, and that I'll never birth this child." Sheila watched as the impact of her words spread across Raines' face.

"Well, you have to stop," Raines said.

"I can't stop. Some jobs have to be done."

"But he just said it will kill the child. You have to stop."

"That's what *he* says, but he's not in charge, God is. And I'm appealing to him."

"That's all well and good, meanwhile you endanger the life of our child with this work. I know the toll it takes on you, some of it at least. Now your grandfather says you'll never be able to do it and keep our child. You can't just say you're taking it to God and leave it at that. You have a choice to make."

"It's not that easy. It's not like I'm doing clerical work, it is something apparently only I can do right now. And the stability of our dimension depends on it. Can you have some understanding of the situation I'm in?"

"In a day, I've gone from dealing with the so-called fact that we couldn't have children to having a pregnant wife. This is a dream come true. And you want me to appreciate the position you're in? No, I don't see it. That is my seed in there, our child. I can't accommodate any position that doesn't put that child first."

"I'm not trying to not put the child first. I just need to do both things: have this baby *and* watch the gate."

"When there's a tie for first place, nobody wins. Think about that."

He was right, of course. Raines had the annoying habit of calling a spade a spade.

Sheila leaned back against the wall and stretched her legs. This wasn't the conversation she wanted to be having, but it was the one she had wound up with.

"This work is brutal, but I can make adjustments for that. There's a way to make this work."

"Why would you take the risk? I know you're not ecstatic, like I am, to be pregnant, but you have to take this seriously. You are responsible for another life now. You owe that life protection."

"I *do* value this life and believe me, I'm taking this seriously."

"Sounds like you want to have your cake and eat it, too."

"Do you honestly think guarding the gate is cake?! But if I walk away, there's no one to replace me. I think I can do both."

"Oh, have you been pregnant before? Do you know what it's going to be like?"

"Don't do this to me. Can we talk without the rhetorical questions?"

Raines stayed silent and crossed his arms. That meant he was done talking. He had made up his mind and was no longer in listening mode, if he ever had been.

"Be mad at me all you want, but this is a conversation we need to have." Sheila stuck her tongue out at him, which made Raines loosen up a bit.

"You really are impossible. Well, I will live to fight another day. Let's go home."

Sheila helped pull Raines up from the floor, and they headed out together.

CHAPTER TWENTY-EIGHT
BOTH

Sheila paced her kitchen as she waited for the electric kettle to boil. She would wear a groove into the tile at the rate she was going. She stopped when she finally realized she had restarted the kettle three times, each time not noticing when it boiled.

She didn't know what to do. Raines and she had been going back and forth on the matter all day and there was no end in sight. Raines could be as stubborn and impossible as she could.

It wasn't as if she enjoyed this life she had been thrown into. Interdimensional gatekeeping was one of those things that had to be done. Wasn't it? Sheila wasn't exactly sure what would happen if she lay down her role. When she had initially refused, she had been so blinded by her fear and grief; she had not given a single thought to the consequences.

Now she couldn't get around them. Just letting in *any* being in, from *any* dimension, was a bedlam that her mind could barely stand. Maybe she could…she hadn't a single idea with which to finish her thought. She felt well and truly stuck.

It wasn't as if Raines were being unreasonable. He was thinking of the life of the little one inside her. And if Grandfather were to be believed, this job of watching the gate would end that life. Anyone in their right mind would tell her she couldn't do both. There was no way to bear their child *and* keep the gate.

But none of them were her, and she was determined to find a way. Perhaps that meant she wasn't in her right mind, she mused. Well, folks had been telling her she was nuts for ages, but she was still here. It wasn't as if she even *wanted* to keep the gate. She had been an unwilling heir.

This was an impossible situation. She thought back to

their discussion of her faith. Maybe she *had* put Grandfather on the same level as God, instead of understanding him as merely an aspect of the Most High. Her grandfather didn't have the final say. She still had an all-powerful God she could appeal to. She *had* to find another way.

Sheila went into her shrine room and sat on a bench by the window. She sang hymns until she felt centered in the Spirit. She held herself, rocking back and forth, trying to get a prayer through to God. It was hard because her judgment was so clouded, her emotions were inflamed, and her mind felt overworked. It was like trying to still a raging storm. How would she overcome the evils of this world if she couldn't overcome herself?

Using the hymns to regulate her breathing, she pressed forward, bringing captive one thought, then another, until her mind started to feel some peace. Sheila sweat with the effort to spread herself out before God, to have God fix her. She couldn't get a prayer through in the usual ways, so instead, she had thrown her entire self on the altar and asked God to deal with it.

Finally, she felt that connection with the Divine that she had been searching for. She could feel herself held in the palm of God's hand.

"Lord, if I'm wrong, you need to tell me. Tell me what to do! I've tried to hear your voice and I can't make it out over my own pig-headedness. I want it all. Can you, this once, give me favor? Let the gate *and* my child be safe. I don't ask for me. If I were asking for me, you know what I would want. But bless this child. Give my child life!

"Am I wrong to say I can carry this child to term? Am I fooling myself? Just tell me what to do, God! I need to hear it from you, not my grandfather, not my own mind. Give me your grace and protection. I plead for your mercy. Let me know how it's going to be. I'm not willing to lose this baby. Show me what I have to do to protect my child. Just show me and I'll do it. Amen."

Sheila knew the answer before the amen passed her lips—it was up to her to make a decision and live with whatever the consequences might be. She believed life was sacred. Shouldn't she just avoid anything that posed a threat, especially keeping the gate? But the gate was about more than one life, one human being. She could preserve more lives and peace of mind by regulating the gate than the one life now within her. Could you even make a decision about life based on math?

This was a test. She had everything she needed to make a wise decision, and she would be judged for her choice. Sheila dropped her head into her hands. Why was it never easy?

She wanted a magic answer that would let her have the best of both worlds, but life usually came down to the choices you made, and it was time for her to decide. Somewhere along the way, she had begun to feel fiercely protective of the life inside her. After her initial shock over being pregnant in the first place had passed, she had become more and more used to the idea. She stood in front of the mirror, poking her belly out to imagine what she might look like when she began to show.

She surprised herself with the motherly feelings that seemed to be churning out of her. She wanted this child with an intensity she would have never thought possible. God loved playing tricks like this on her all the time, making her want the thing she had been trying to avoid or even running from.

But opposing her child was the thankless role of keeping the interdimensional gate. It had seemed to bring her nothing but pain and problems. Her guide was stoic and unrelenting, and her job was rough on her body, mind, and spirit. She was new in her role and wasn't even that attached to her work. The choice seemed obvious.

But Sheila knew destiny didn't consist of what you wanted to do, but what you were called to do. She knew she was called to watch the gate. How could the choice she was facing be so horrible?

Life versus duty. Sheila couldn't make a choice. She had to press forward with both paths: keeping the gate *and* having a baby. If one caused her to fail at the other, she would have to live with that for the rest of her life. She had to make sure not to fail.

Sheila went downstairs to find Raines at work in his studio. His canvas was painted jet black, and he was staring at it intensely. Pulling himself away, he stepped from the painting and turned to face her.

"Been thinking?" Raines knew she needed time on her own to process big decisions.

Sheila nodded. She walked forward and wrapped her arms around him. "I can't decide. It has to be both. It *has* to be both."

Raines pinned her with a serious look. "Do you swear to guard the life of our child as well as you guard the gate?"

"And then some."

Raines' body was still rigid as he spoke. "I don't like it, but I think I can live with it. How about you? Can you live with the consequences of this if things don't work out?"

"I just don't know. But just so you know, I've come quickly to loving and wanting this little fetus of ours. I want to be a mom. I'm going to be careful. I'm all in. This has to work."

Raines gave her a smile that didn't reach the uncertainty in his eyes. He closed his eyes as he held her and let out a brief prayer. "Please God, let this work."

CHAPTER TWENTY-NINE
WAITING

Sheila had done all she could do, and it was all over but the waiting. She had carried out her grandfather's instructions to his exacting standards, working for the better part of a week to make her shrine room "acceptable" by his measure. He was relentless in letting her know when her efforts were insufficient or incorrect.

Now, she sat before her ancestral shrine, having presented a cup of coffee and lit the cigar, waiting to see if he could show up. This was ridiculous, she thought. Her grandfather was a spirit. He could be anywhere he wanted. Why had she had to work so hard to get things just right for him? If only he spent any time trying to make things right for her, they might actually get somewhere.

Suddenly she could feel his presence, but still there was no voice. He did not make himself known. She drank his coffee and took a small puff of his cigar. That was fine. She swore before all that was holy, she would wait him out. She would not work herself to the bone and then beg him to speak.

She watched the sunset as its pink and golden light flooded in through the windows and knew she was in for a battle of wills. He might be implacable, but she was stubborn and mad. He was going to have to speak to her first if he wanted to have a conversation again. So she waited as the sky turned dark and gentle knocks on the door by her husband went unanswered.

She switched from sitting cross-legged to sitting on her heels to lying on her side. She was half-dozing when his surrender finally came.

"The thing that is your greatest asset makes you so hard to teach."

A slow smile crept across Sheila's face. "Good

evening, Grandfather."

"Your work seems to have been sufficient."

"Oh, damn me with faint praise why don't you?"

"My statement is accurate."

"But what about kind? Can you be kind?"

"Your mother and I were focused on getting the job done, not flowery words."

"I am not my mother, as I'm sure you are well aware, and I know you know it's not just flowery words. I don't want to work with a robot. Can't you be a little more human? What's the problem with being nice to me?"

"We don't have time for me to coddle you. And the ways of your dimension are far from me now."

"Are you saying there are no feelings or kindness in the great beyond? Because I know that to be a lie."

"I'm not saying that. It is just that I don't know what you need."

"I'm telling you! Don't treat me like I'm in your personal boot camp, not all the time. I can't take it."

There was a long silence.

"I remember one year at Christmas you always wanted to sit on my lap. We sang "Rudolph, the Red-Nosed Reindeer" over and over. You couldn't get enough. I still remember."

Sheila smiled. "That is a start. Let's talk about some other starts. I had a conversation recently that reminded me I am not my mother."

"This, we know."

"I'm not finished," Sheila said with aggravation in her tone. "So since I'm not her, *and* I'm having a baby, I figure it's time to bring in some help."

"I am your help."

"You help teach and guide me on how to guard the gate, but you can't help me actually guard the gate. I say we need some more gatekeepers."

"Would you like fries with that?"

"There's no need to be sarcastic. I know it's not as easy as that, but I'm thinking that I have two sisters, all from the same bloodline. This keeps it in the family."

"They can't do what you do."

"Only because they haven't learned. But if they had the chance to study, they would catch on, no problem."

"You don't understand. The anointing is on you. You have been chosen and sealed for this assignment."

"Why me?"

"You are the one. I don't know why. But just as I was chosen as the one among my siblings, and your mother was chosen instead of your aunt, you are chosen—imbued with what you need to do this job."

"I don't feel special."

"It is not an honor, it is a responsibility. Your shoulders have been broadened to carry the load."

"I can't carry the load alone. What are our options?"

"Stop treating this like an after-school activity you can shape however you like. There are no other options."

"Then we are about to make some. I was serious when I said there would have to be some changes."

"Speaking of guarding the gate, when are you actually going to do that?"

Sheila was embarrassed and rubbed the back of her neck while she made a study of the carpet. "Yikes. How often did Ma actually travel to the gate?"

"Almost every night."

Her neck snapped up. "Impossible. I know she didn't sleep in her shrine room every night."

"Cathy didn't need the shrine room. She could travel there from her dream state."

Sheila took in that information and, instead of feeling bad about her lack of ability, was proud of her mother's strength and talents.

"She was amazing. A workhorse. I thought I was doing alright at once or twice a week."

"The longer you leave it, the harder the work."

"If you don't know why I was chosen from my generation, perhaps there are some other things you don't know, such as if this job can be a shared one."

"It is impossible."

"Why? Simply because it hasn't been done before?"

"Exactly. The way things are is part of the order of the universe. Why must you try to change everything you lay eyes on?"

"The universe needs something of me, and I'm willing to pay, but I require something in return. I need my load lightened."

"This is all because of your…"

"Don't you cast a word of aspersion on my pregnancy," Sheila warned as she cut him off.

"This is all due to your insistence that the universe make room for you. You are alive. That's all the room you get."

"See, I can't believe that. I think that if I ask, I shall receive."

"That's a children's dream and you need to be prepared for when the answer is no, or there simply is no answer. 'Ask and you shall receive,' what a simplistic view of God."

Sheila didn't think her view of how God operated in the world was simplistic or naïve. So much for her grandfather being nice to her, she thought. "Do you want to tell me that 'nothing is impossible with God' is imaginary, too?"

"I didn't say you were wrong, just that your view was too simple. *Entreat* God to get what is yours; don't just ask for it."

"What do you mean?"

"You need to show God how much it means to you. What you would do with your request, how it aligns with God's desire."

How could she entreat God for her child's life? How could she show God what that life would mean for her? She lapsed into silent reflection.

"If you carry your child to term, you would be the first gatekeeper ever to do so. It would be a miracle."

"Where would I be without the miracles I've already received? Maybe God's got one more for me."

"Sometimes the miracle never comes, and, the more you depend on it, the harder the fall. I don't want that for you."

"Then agree with me I won't fail. Believe in God for it with me. Be useful."

Her grandfather let out a rich laugh, and it shocked Sheila. It felt like honey to her ears. She hadn't heard joy in his voice for so long. She could barely remember the life of her grandfather. He had died when she was so young, but she remembered his laugh. It always seemed to fill whatever space he was in to bursting with joy. She had wanted to have his laugh when she was a little girl. Sheila remembered practicing with a tape recorder and playing it back to see if it sounded like his.

"I always loved your laugh. It was the definition of joy for me for so long."

"I was just remembering how stubborn you are, in a good way. If God is going to do something for someone, it might as well be you."

Sheila was elated to have him on her side on this. She could feel a ball of anxiety within her relax.

"It's good when we are of one accord. I hope we can have more of this."

"If you do what I say, we will."

"I knew there was a catch."

CHAPTER THIRTY
SERIOUS CHARGES

The next night, Sheila had prepared her first traveling circle in her own shrine room. It was a lot smaller because of the room's size. She would have to sit up cross-legged instead of lying down. It was also trickier to make, as her shrine room was carpeted. As she had laid down a coat of sulfur until it formed a circle, she could already see lots of vacuuming in her future.

It was different, and it was difficult, but it was done. She stopped to give herself a pat on the back.

"Good job," her grandfather said.

"Don't patronize me," Sheila said, dusting off her hands and putting the sulfur away. She'd had to move another shelving unit in to hold all the tools and materials required for gatekeeping.

"I mean it. You're getting better at it. It's becoming more natural for you. The stronger your circle, the easier the journey is on your body and spirit."

"Well, it's good that I'm getting better at it. It usually takes so much concentration that I feel exhausted before I even travel to the gate. But, now that you mention it, I am less tired than usual. That is a nice benefit, for me *and* baby."

"You've gotten more excited about this pregnancy than I expected. You spent so long not being a fan of the idea that the reversal is glaring."

"I don't know how to explain it," Sheila spoke as she straightened up her shelves of materials. "Almost as soon as I knew, everything changed. *Almost* as soon as I knew. First, I had to have a freak out. But, while I'm definitely not a fan of the morning sickness, I'm actually very excited about what is coming. Raines has ordered books for us. We're having a read-in next weekend," she added excitedly.

"Let's get to work, then. Let me not keep you from

your plans."

"Unfair, Grandfather." Sheila cocked her head in annoyance even as she entered the circle. She cleared her mind and set her intention. Before a word came out of her mouth, it was essential to set the intention. If not, your energy would scatter anywhere.

She formed a mental picture of where she wanted to be and *how* she wanted to be, telling God what her agenda for the time was. Her chanting wasn't magic utterances, simply a tool to help her stay focused and strengthen her intention. Sheila wrote her name on a piece of parchment, folded it, then placed it beneath her bra strap near her heart. It was scratchy and felt foreign. She was about to leave her body and enter the astral plane. That piece of paper would help her find her way home.

As she sat in the circle, she tried to get settled into a position she could maintain comfortably for an extended period. It wouldn't do for her unattended body to go falling outside of the circle just because she hadn't balanced things right. Finally, she was centered, with a blazing intention, and a stable core. She felt her spirit separating from her body and slipping onto another plane.

In the astral plane, one could travel anywhere in the blink of an eye, be a silent witness to any conversation, or just relax and enjoy the cosmos. It was also a door that led to other doors, including the only one she was interested in right now. Her spirit walked down a corridor of doors. She still found it funny that her spirit took on her physical form and mimicked physical behaviors like walking. She was spirit in this realm; she could be completely non-corporeal, or at *least* float.

She stopped in front of the door whose handle was literally sizzling, it was so hot. This door, otherwise identical to every other, was the one she wanted. Sheila's spirit mimicked taking a deep breath, then turned the handle and went in.

Sheila's two guards that she had left to watch the gate dissolved on either side of her as she entered. A cacophony of color and sound assaulted her. As it had been the other times she had come, the scenario was different and arresting. She came to stand in the witness box of a courtroom as bright lights shone down on her and obscured her vision.

"I accuse." A voice from beyond the lights spoke out.

The energies in the galley rumbled and chittered.

"What are the charges?" Sheila was irritated. This was her domain now. She should reign supreme. Who dared bring charges against her? If only she could see past the blinding lights.

"Gross negligence. You ignore the gate. You are a doorway, not a wall, and we must be permitted to pass through."

"Says who?"

The galley erupted with noise, and the floor seemed to undulate a little.

"You dare question the laws of the cosmos? They were set in place by the Maker!"

"I mean, who is it that accuses me? I would know your name."

"Your sister's lover sent me. He sends his greetings."

Sheila's worlds were colliding, and it left her in a tailspin. She not only had to deal with *ha satan* in the real world but also here at the gate? His reach went everywhere, it seemed.

"I have evidence that will condemn you. There is no escape."

Sheila knew that she had been lax in her visits to the gate, but to be brought up on charges? She was embarrassed by and ashamed of her absence. The *accuser* always went to the exact spot where you were tender.

And what kind of punishment could a "court" such as this administer? "Escape from what? This is *my* space. I rule here."

"We have ways that can break you, and we will do it."

Sheila's spirit crossed her arms. "No, you don't. If you did, you would have broken through the gate long ago. Don't lie to me."

"We will hurt you!"

"Yes, but how? I see no authority that would even give you the right."

Something reached out to Sheila, and she took a knee to the ground with a sudden and blinding headache.

"Is that enough authority for you?" The voice was almost gleeful.

"Yep." Sheila got back to her feet and willed the pain away. She wondered if she would still feel it when she returned to her body. "I get the idea that you can hurt me, but by whose authority is this charge being levied? Who has given you the right to charge me?"

"I needn't say who, only that authority has been given to me. Though, if you put your mind to it, I'm sure you can figure it out."

Sheila bit her lip. If it really was her time of sifting, then that would mean God had given permission. This court really might make a ruling she would be bound by.

"And who will judge me?"

"Oh, but that is the best part," the voice said delightedly. "You judge yourself, but you must promise to be fair. You will be duty-bound to render an honest decision, so help you, God."

Sheila's jaw dropped as she registered her predicament. She always judged herself harsher than anyone else. This could go badly. She still wasn't sure of what was on the line, should she find herself guilty, but she knew it was bad. The memory of that blistering headache the voice had given her was still fresh in her mind.

"What happens if I am found, if I find myself guilty?"

"We devour you, my dear." The voice sounded

hungry.

"But what exactly does that mean?"

"We start taking things away."

Sheila thought about the life of her unborn child. God did not allow the A*ccuser* to take life. But would that apply to her unborn fetus? She should have studied and looked more into this situation when she discovered who Hotep was, but she had neglected to…there went that word, neglect. She already seemed to be finding herself guilty.

She knew the *Accuser* in broad strokes, mostly from Christian and metaphysical sources. The instances in the Bible were Job and the disciple, Peter. Those were scary stories, ones she had no desire to compete with. She thought of the scripture about quickly agreeing with your adversary, who was taking you to court, before it was too late. Maybe she had a way out of this.

"I would like to ask the court for leniency."

"You appeal for leniency during sentencing, not now."

"I plead guilty. And I appeal to the court for leniency, and seeing that I'm the judge, I know I have a lot of leniency."

The voice made a sputtering sound and that let Sheila know she had done the right thing. She had thrown the *Accuser* for a loop. He saw where she was going with this. Hopefully, she had a clear path out of this mess.

"You plead guilty? Leniency? What are you doing?"

"You already know. I propose restitution. I admit I have been a bad gatekeeper. I pledge to be better and to be present more often. My future behavior will be my litmus test; if it ever fails, my leniency can be revoked. I pledge my life to my ability to be a better gatekeeper."

"And let me guess, since you're the judge, you will allow it. You are making a farce of this!"

"This *is* a farce! You may have God's permission, but you wasted it with this ridiculousness. This is my God-given role. I'm here on orders, and my duty will not be stripped from me by *you*, whoever *you* are.

"You have no right to judge me. *I* have no right to judge me. Only God. You almost tricked me into yoking myself to error thinking. I can *always* go to my Father instead of the court."

"Your father." The voice spat. "Oh yes, I'm well acquainted with your father. Your biological father didn't help you when he was alive, and he certainly won't help you now. We have him."

The voice got her attention. They *had* him? Why would they even bother to mention her biological father? It's not as if she thought about him. Well, hardly ever.

"Why bring him up?"

"My, my, you really didn't love anyone outside of your mother, did you? One wonders, if you care so little for others, how much can you care about your job as gatekeeper?" Sheila heard the voice suck its teeth.

She tried to stomp down her fury. "None of this moves me. I appeal to my Heavenly Father. I won't let you make me forget who I am."

"You think you're so clever. Well, you're not. We will have our day."

"I thought today was our day?" Sheila tried not to smirk, but she couldn't help getting a dig in at the voice.

"Careful of that arrogance, dear. It will be your undoing."

As Sheila was thinking about how true the voice's last words were, the voice and the lights disappeared. She was still standing in the witness box in a courtroom. She turned and cast a withering look over the spirits and energies in the gallery.

"You were all so quick to see me disposed of." Her heart softened. "But you just wanted improvements in the way the gate is maintained. *Most* of you. I will improve and things will be better."

Sheila left the witness box and sat in the judge's chair. "Let's begin. Who's first?" Pops of sound and color went off around her. Everyone said they were first. She closed her eyes and focused on peace and quiet, then she pushed that energy out from her into the surrounding area, stilling the noise and visual chaos.

She noticed a quiet energy that did not seem to be calling for attention. "You there. Why do you want to pass?"

"I died too soon, and I miss my ma."

Sheila's heart broke. Would this be her own child one day, ripped from life too soon because of this gatekeeping? "What happened?"

"I was born sick, but I was getting stronger. I don't know what happened, but I didn't last very long."

"Little one, you haven't had your forty-two days of transition to move from the earthly realm to your divine home. I can't let you come back into this dimension, or you might never complete your transformation."

"That's ok, I like my mom. I want to stay with her. I don't care if I transition."

"I know, but I can't fill my dimension with spirits that won't leave. Your life in that body, in that reality, is over. It's time to move on."

"I don't want to."

Sheila took a deep breath and tried to see beyond the tragedy of this situation. "Why do you want to be with your mom?"

"She really loved me. It felt good, not like here. It's cold here, and I'm alone."

"You've spent so much energy trying to get back where you were that you've never thought about where you're going. This is not the end. Your Heavenly Father wants to welcome you to your forever home. He loves you, too. It will feel great there, I promise. Will you go?"

"I want my Mommy!!!"

The child spirit's sweet visage turned into a gaping

maw, and its piercing scream sent the entire space into chaos. The spirit flew towards Sheila, intending to force its way through.

Sheila had been afraid of this. The young had such unregulated emotions. With so much intensity, it was easy for them to become corrupted. Through no fault of its own, this little baby had turned into a wraith.

Sheila put her right hand in front of her, making a stopping gesture. She poured love, but also steel, into a beam directed towards the wraith. "Shhhh. Shhhh." Sheila tried to both soothe the spirit and block its passage back to her dimension. The spirit fell at her feet and made a desperate whimpering sound.

"I promise things will get better." Sheila wiped the tears from her eyes. "But not until you stop being angry. I want you to transition to one of the heavenly realms, but you have to let go of earth first."

The wraith turned back into a baby, and Sheila took it into her arms, rocking it until it finally settled down and stopped crying. Finally, the child fell asleep. Sheila turned her head upward and closed her eyes. "Father, into your hands, I commend this spirit. Be the mommy she needs." The baby's form dissolved into tiny particles of light that floated upward. "Thank you, God."

She let out a long breath and looked around her. "Who's next?"

CHAPTER THIRTY-ONE
HONESTY

The pre-dawn light was streaming in the windows of her shrine room when Sheila opened her eyes inside her traveling circle. She dragged herself through clearing the circle, running her cordless vacuum over the carpet for anything she may have missed.

By the time Sheila opened the door of her shrine room to leave, she was, as usual, exhausted. She hadn't noticed any bruises on her body when she had come back to herself this time, which was great in her book. Not paying attention as she opened the door, it startled her to see it did not open fully. Looking down to see what was blocking it, she saw Raines asleep on the floor.

He really was in this with her, Sheila thought. He didn't know quite what to do, but he was there for her. 'Thank you, God, for giving me a real partner,' she said in her spirit.

Sheila knelt down and gave his sleeping lips a kiss. He woke and kissed her back. They wound up making quite a jumbled mess on the floor.

"I say we sleep in this morning."

"Very alright with me."

As they walked down the hall, Raines raked over her with his eyes.

"You don't look too bad."

"Gee, thanks." Sheila elbowed him playfully, but her voice was a bit brittle. "The ache is on the inside this time." Sheila thought about the little child and tried not to cry.

Raines stopped and caressed her face. "I'm sorry." Sheila turned to him for a hug. Finally, in a safe space, where she didn't have to put on a brave face and pretend she knew everything, she let her tears flow.

"It's getting better," Sheila said through her tears.

"But tonight was just hard."

"You made it. All that matters is you made it. Let's go to bed. You need rest."

"Yeah." Sheila wiped her tears away. "Sorry to fall apart on you."

"I wish I could do more. But I can at least give you support when you need it. Let me put you to bed."

They went to bed and Raines held her until she went to sleep. He stayed up a long time thinking about how he couldn't take much more of this. Getting up without waking Sheila, he went to her shrine room and opened the door. He saw the candles on the shrine lighting the room with a flickered glow that made himself feel like it was holy ground. Standing on the threshold, he addressed Sheila's grandfather.

"I don't know if you can hear me or not, but you need to do better. She's getting beat up on *your* watch. Get your act together. I will tear this shrine room apart with no regrets if you don't start doing something." Raines stood there for another minute, feeling only slightly foolish for talking to the air, before closing the door.

At the ancestral shrine, Sheila's grandfather was surprised that Raines had been able to summon him. That was usually reserved for blood relatives who knew what they were doing. Raines must have been overflowing with emotion to have called him to this dimension.

The truth was that the gate was wearing Sheila out more than he had expected, even before they knew she was pregnant. She had a great deal of strength, but, for some reason, she wasn't using it. Instead, she was muscling her way through everything. Why hadn't she had a breakthrough and begun reaching her full potential?

He *did* need to do something, but he did not know what. Sheila was more sensitive than his own daughter, Cathy, had been. He didn't know how to deal with her most times, but perhaps they had started to come together and develop a better working relationship.

He barely remembered his time on earth, but when he focused, he could remember the joy he felt whenever he had been with Sheila. When she was a little girl, she could have stolen his heart with a kiss. Perhaps if he tried to remember and act out of those emotions and memories, he would have better success.

He had not wanted to tell Sheila that she wasn't doing a good enough job, but maybe it was time for them to have a talk about where she was in her development and how to jumpstart her progress. He didn't think Raines was the type to make idle threats. Raines might actually dismantle the shrine room if he deemed it necessary to protect his wife. There would be no one to watch the gate if Sheila didn't rise to the occasion soon. As he ascended back to his dimension, he prayed for guidance. He *did* need to do better.

Sheila was searching for a way out of her dream. She had tried waking herself but had had no success. As she ran up the stairs; they disintegrated behind her. She felt like she had been doing this forever. It felt like fate was catching up with her as the crumbling stairs came closer with each passing step.

Sheila was annoyed. Not only did she have to watch the gate, but she was also plagued with nightmares on the nights she wasn't in the shrine room. She, mostly, could control her dreams, and they didn't bring her much trouble, not anymore. But the dreams where someone or something seemed to chase her were hard to banish.

There was no need to figure out what the dreams meant. With *ha satan* sifting her and so many spirits at the gate mad at her judgements, she could take her pick which being was tormenting her sleep. Why did she owe them anything? How could they so easily penetrate her dreams?

The step under her foot gave way as she pushed off to climb higher. She was running out of time. Changing the limitations of the dream, she began to float upward, no longer dependent on solid ground to support her. Why hadn't she thought of that before?

Lately, she seemed a little slow on the uptake in her estimation. At a time when she should be growing, it seemed like she sometimes forgot even the basics of her spiritual practice. It was not encouraging to know that her grandfather was correct—she *wasn't* doing well enough. Keeping the gate would eat her alive, and her child, if she didn't wise up and make a change. She had to get better.

Sheila tried not to fall into despair as she watched the setting of her dream turn to ash and blow away. The universe had given her this role of gatekeeper. She had to redeem herself and do a better job, or it would be the end of her. At her last visit to the gate, she had wiggled her way out of being condemned by swearing to do better. But how, when she was barely maintaining herself as it was?

Sheila wasn't used to failing, but it seemed like lately she was getting a masterclass in it. She kept asking God for another chance, and another, and another. At some point, she had to make good on the grace she had been given.

Sheila thought about her mom's conviction that to whom much was given, much was required. She had been given a lot, and she wasn't living up to her promise. She had ability, and she had had an excellent teacher in her mother, but she was barely treading water, and each approaching wave threatened to overtake her. Why wasn't she doing better? She wished she could point to some definitive thing, some simple reason she wasn't thriving as a gatekeeper.

Sheila didn't know whether she needed redemption, deliverance, or salvation, but she knew she needed *something*.

PART SEVEN
POORLY LAID PLANS

CHAPTER THIRTY-TWO
THE FEDS

Sheila woke up with her mind racing. Too much was changing. It was more than her mind, which loved having a place for everything and having everything in its place, could handle. First, her mother had passed. Then, she had quit her job and become an interdimensional gatekeeper. Next, she had somehow managed to get pregnant. Now she was about to let go of her nascent consulting business.

In nine months, eight, she corrected herself, there would be a living, breathing baby. *If* she could manage her gatekeeping responsibilities without damage to her body too much. The odds were against her on that, but she was determined to do it. Sheila prayed God was on her side in that fight.

She got out of bed and went down to the basement to run on the treadmill and burn off some of the frenetic energy coursing through her. She put the machine's speed high enough so that she couldn't think, just run. Still, she could feel her thoughts nibbling at the edges of her mind, testing the barrier.

Going into her shrine room, she sat, hugging her knees to her chest and trying to think her way through to some kind of solution, some realization or approach that would bring her peace. She finally reminded herself that she could not think herself into peace.

"God, please fix my mind. You see, I'm all discombobulated. Settle my spirit and help me deal with everything that's going on. Give me…"

The persistent ringing of her doorbell interrupted Sheila's prayer. She looked at her watch: 8:15am. Raines, who could sleep through the apocalypse, wouldn't be any help. Sheila got up and went downstairs, peering out to the porch through the sheer curtains by her door.

Several men in mediocre suits were standing there, looking official. She looked at their shoes, all in good shape, which meant they weren't Mormons. They must be some kind of law enforcement, Sheila surmised. Opening the door and placing her body between them and the inside of the house, she greeted them.

"Gentlemen," Sheila said wearily.

One man displayed a badge and spoke. "FBI, ma'am. May we come in and speak with you?"

"What is this regarding?"

"You left a message regarding the activities of the Wildervancy organization. We are here to talk to you about that."

Sheila had forgotten that she had jumped straight into a hornet's nest with her first consulting gig.

"And you need five people to show up at my door unannounced to talk with me?" Sheila did not know how things like this worked, but it all seemed like overkill to her.

"We are all part of the Bureau's sex trafficking division, and we are treating this seriously. May we come in and speak to you about this matter?"

Sheila agreed, opening the door wide and stepping out of the way. They were all middle-aged except for the older man who entered last, looking gnarled but experienced. She showed them into her office so that she would have access to her files. She grabbed a folder from her desk.

"Here is a write-up of my recollections of my experience and the recording from my interview with Thomas Krone."

The man who had spoken at the door moved forward to take the folder and looked through it.

"This is impressive. I must say, the folks we usually speak with are not nearly as prepared and thorough as this."

"I did call *you* to report what I thought was a crime. I just wanted to get it all down while it was fresh in my mind."

"We have been tracking Wildervancy for years. If we

can get Krone to testify to what he told you in court, we might be able to put away some very bad people."

"Why are you talking to me?"

"We find it quite irregular that Mr. Krone told you what he did. Why would he incriminate himself as a party to such heinous activities?"

"People are often compelled, you might say, to tell me the truth. It happens often enough. But I would say that he walked into that meeting looking for an opportunity to get this off of his chest. As you will see from the recording, he was almost eager to share, which makes me suspicious, but that's an issue for you to deal with, not me."

Sheila noticed the older man looking at her in an assessing manner that made her uncomfortable. She focused on the man standing in front of her.

"We'd like to conduct an interview on the event in question, if you don't mind."

"Of course." Sheila wondered why it took five agents to conduct an interview.

For the better part of an hour, Agent Menck questioned her and examined her recollections. Everyone seemed to take notes except the older man. Sheila knew they could get the same information from the write-up she had given them, but she supposed they didn't know that, so she went along. And perhaps they were noting down other things—her believability, her viability as a witness, some little detail she had noticed but dismissed, or if they even thought she was telling the truth.

"So what happens now?" Sheila asked after Menck had put away his notepad and tape recorder.

"Next we talk to Thomas Krone and everyone at Wildervancy. For once, things seem fairly straightforward." Agent Menck stood and his colleagues followed. "Thank you for your time and for contacting us. I'll leave my card and ask that you call me if you have any other contact with that organization."

The men headed toward the front door except for the older gentleman, who seemed to dawdle. Menck looked at him, then shook his head.

"We'll see ourselves out, ma'am."

As the agents left, the older man stood in the middle of her foyer without making a move to leave. Sheila closed the door behind the other agents and turned to face the man, hands on her hips. She just stared at him, not willing to ask what in the world he was still doing there.

"Cathy Orly was quite a woman. We tried to bring her on at the Bureau for years, but she refused, saying that she had a different calling."

Sheila knew this, but never thought she would meet an agent who had actually known her mother.

"She never did cotton to guns," the man continued, "and said she wouldn't wear one just to use her gift. I see you have something of her talents." Reaching into his suit pocket, he produced a business card. "I hope you would consider calling me when you're ready to make a real difference in the world, as I know you could. Good day, ma'am." With that, he saw himself out of her home.

Sheila looked at the card in her hand. "James Horden, Paranormal Division Chief." What a morning, she thought.

She vaguely remembered when men in suits used to come visit her mother while she was young. She tried to recall their faces to see if she could identify Horden, but had little success.

Her mother had told her later in life that the FBI had wanted to hire her to use her psychic powers to catch murderers and kidnappers. She had said it was too high a price to pay. Sheila hadn't understood her mother's choice. If you could help solve crimes, why wouldn't you?

Now Sheila had begun to understand the price her mother had spoken of. She paid a high price with every visit she made to the gate. She couldn't imagine her mother doing that, running the Institute, *and* solving crimes. Although she knew her mother could do anything she set her mind to, that was not the same as doing *everything* she could have.

Sheila walked back to her office and put Horden's and Manck's cards in her desk drawer. She turned off her desk light and put the matter to rest. If it was too high a price for her mother, then it would be completely out of the question for Sheila.

CHAPTER THIRTY-THREE
AND BABY MAKES THREE

Sheila was on pins and needles. She was watching the clock furiously, calculating what time it was in Paris and whether it was late enough in the evening for her sister, Corrine, to be done with work yet. There was no point in trying to guess whether her sister, Jasmin, was free; her schedule was so unpredictable. Finally, at 2:30pm she sent the text to them that had been running through her mind all day. 'I'm totally pregNancy,' she wrote, referencing what their great grandfather used to say when someone was with child.

Less than a minute later, a video call from her sisters was popping up on her phone. Answering the call, it seemed as if they all started screaming in unison. Raines came running up from his basement studio with a look of alarm on his face. Sheila mouthed her apologies to him and beckoned him over. As soon as he came into the picture, Sheila said, "This husband of mine got me knocked up!"

Raines relaxed, now convinced there was no threat, and joined in on the screaming. "We're telling people? I thought we have to wait more trimesters or something."

"Yeah, but not for sisters. I just couldn't keep it a secret any longer."

"Our family is about to have an awesome addition!" Raines was positively giddy as he smiled into the screen.

For a few minutes, they all talked at once, asking questions, laughing, and squealing congratulations.

"Okay, it's time for sister talk, Raines. You can go back downstairs."

Raines kissed her and bid Corrine and Jasmin goodbye. He whispered, "You're still sexy," in Sheila's ear and had her blushing before he left.

"I need a prayer team. Grandfather says I won't be

able to carry this child to term. I need that not to be true. I'm asking God for all the grace I can get."

"Is that why Momma had all those miscarriages?!" Corrine had a stunned look on her face.

"What miscarriages?" Jasmin asked.

Corrine and Sheila looked at each other. It was a truth that they had kept from their little sister. Everything came to light eventually, Sheila thought.

"Yes, that's why. So I need your help to get this baby born the right way."

They all spent a moment looking at each other, thinking the same thing.

"I know, if it didn't work for Momma, then why would it work for me? But here's the deal; it *has* to work. It's not like I planned this, but now that it's happening, it has to work. I don't know what I'll do if I lose it." Tears gathered at the corners of Sheila's eyes.

"Then we'll stand in the breach for you. We won't let you fall." Corrine had a steely glint in her eye.

Sheila let out a breath she hadn't realized she was holding in.

"How is the gate?" Jasmin asked. Sheila saw a chocolate complexion arm wrap around Jasmin's shoulder and tried not to be furious that Hotep was a witness to this conversation. She reminded herself that he no doubt knew all of this already, so there was no need for her to be particularly upset.

Sheila forced herself to tell the truth. "I'm barely holding on. And your beau is not helping things, either."

Jasmin just shrugged her shoulders. "He's not there to make it easy."

"Wait, what?" Corrine said in a bewildered tone.

"Oh, Jasmin didn't tell you? Her man is none other than *ha satan* himself." Sheila felt the childish pleasure of telling on her little sister fill her as if they were still kids pulling each other's braids. "And I'm in the middle of being sifted by him. The hits just keep on coming."

"That doesn't seem very loyal," Corrine said in a disapproving tone. "I know you're mad at her, but this is ridiculous."

"So says you, the sister Sheila *didn't* use her powers against. I earned my disloyalty at her hands." Jasmin's voice was defiant.

"I'm sorry about that! I thought it was water under the bridge. You said you forgave me."

"I did. I forgave you because that's what I was supposed to do. But it still hurts. I'm never putting myself in that position again. So I don't care who my boyfriend is in relation to you. I'll see who I want."

"I didn't even know you felt this way. What can I do? How can I make it right?"

Corrine snorted. "Only you could think everything was fine after you psychically assaulted your sister. You're as thick as a brick sometimes."

Sheila burned with shame and embarrassment. She had to work hard not to lash out in self-defense. There was no defense for what she had done. She had apologized, and Jasmin had accepted her apology. But, of course, Corrine was right, such things weren't swept away with just a conversation.

"I can look at your face and tell you're sorry. And that you're ashamed of yourself, which you definitely should be. I don't bear you any ill will, but it will be a while before I can be on your side again."

Corrine rolled her eyes. "Jasmin, you don't have a leg to stand on. You are with *ha satan* while he is sifting our sister! And somehow that mystical mind of yours thinks that is ok. Well, I guess we know what the quickest way to get you to stop thinking is."

"Oh, Corrine, stop being a big sister," Jasmin complained. "You're too far away to pinch me, thank God."

"You two need some sense talked into you, and that's

my job since Momma's gone."

"Oh, and you just appointed yourself our leader?"

"I don't see anybody else stepping up to the plate. I *am* the eldest. Tradition is on my side. And I'm never too far to pinch you."

Corrine put her thumb and forefinger together in front of her face to remind us of her legendary pinching prowess. Jasmin and Sheila involuntarily shuddered as they remembered the last time they had been on the receiving end of one of her pinches.

"I don't know who Jasmin thinks raised her, but I remember who raised me, so I will *always* put family first, even when they've messed up. The two of you need to grow up and stop expecting perfection. Sometimes life is messy, and you just have to deal with it as it is."

And with that, Jasmin and Corrine were transported back to childhood, where every word from their big sister was the gospel truth.

"Yeah, ok," Sheila muttered.

"Ok, I guess," said Jasmin. They both had begrudging expressions.

Corinne saw through their half-meant apologies easily enough. "Well, don't have *me* make you love each other, for heaven's sake! I'm handing it over to God."

Sheila relented. "I am sorry, and I do love you, Jasmin…I'm just having trouble with the consequences, is all."

Jasmin looked at Sheila with dispassionate eyes. "I think you deserve to be sifted. Maybe you'll learn something from it."

Both Corinne and Sheila looked stunned.

"This is a breach. We have to correct this immediately. Jasmin, what can we do to reconcile you with Sheila? We can't have such discord between us. Nothing good will come of it."

"She *attacked* me. I don't have to forgive her."

"What do you mean, you don't have to forgive her? You are literally commanded to forgive others."

"She is supposed to be a pacifist. What a hypocrite. I can't believe I'm the one on the defense here. She should be the one explaining herself." Jasmin's lips stuck out in a pouty expression that hadn't changed since childhood.

"*She* is right here, you know." Sheila reinserted herself into the conversation, seeing as they had forgotten she was there. "I'm sorry. There is nothing to explain because I have no defense. When I lashed out at you, Jasmin, I messed up. All I can do is beg for your forgiveness. If I need to keep begging, I will, but I need you to know I *am* sorry."

"Yes, but *why* did you attack me? You have apologized, but you haven't explained. How can I ever trust you again if I don't even know why you did what you did? Do *you* even know?"

"Yes," Sheila said sullenly. Jasmin and Corinne both looked at her expectantly. Sheila pressed her thumb and forefingers to the bridge of her nose, trying to keep the tears in. "I'm just such a failure at everything Ma tried to teach me, and now she's not here to fix me! And every time someone says what I should do and how I should act, it's like they're twisting the knife. I *know* I should be better, I know! I'm trying!" Sheila broke down in tears.

This time, it was Jasmin's turn to look stunned. "I had no idea you felt this way. What do you mean you're a failure? Momma didn't make no junk, so you can't be that. I'm not gonna apologize for telling you how you should act, but I don't do it to twist a knife in you. I'm trying to remind you that you should do better because you *can* do better. You can do better than you've been doing, so be better."

Sheila wiped her face and took a few deep breaths. "Yeah, I'll do better." Sheila thought about how that was like asking for blood from a stone.

"Well," Jasmin considered, "maybe I'm getting closer to really forgiving you. I'll try. I just hope you dealt with

Massad with even half the vigor you used against me."

Was that not twisting the knife, Sheila thought.

"Massad's taken care of, for now."

"Still seems too good for him, if you ask me," Corinne snorted. "Cursing him with love. I want to see him suffer."

"That *is* suffering for him. Overwhelming enemies with love is like pouring burning coals on their heads. Plus, I was rusty when I did it, so I wasn't sure an all out battle would go my way."

"I guess you got the job done. I just wish I could enjoy it more."

"Seeing people get their just desserts is never as satisfying as you think it will be. You know that."

"I have an ax to grind for all the trouble he caused Momma."

"We don't know that for sure. She was restraining his evil, keeping it from spreading in the world. Perhaps that was her spiritual assignment. She never shared it with us, so the odds are it was really easy or really hard. None of us had a clue, so I like to imagine it was just another day at the office for her."

They lapsed into silence as they walked through their memories of Momma and how strong she was. Sheila remembered one time they had gone on an all-day hike, only to find out afterwards that Ma had been fasting for a week. Momma would surprise her with things like that all the time. Sheila tried not to compare herself to her mother, but it was hard. Every aspect of Ma seemed to call out her lack of ability. She shook herself out of that dangerous line of thinking.

"Well dearies, Lawd willin' and de creek don't rise, y'all will be aunties in eight months. Get started on those baby blankets, or whatever you're supposed to do for kids."

"Whatever you're supposed to do for kids?" Jasmin laughed. "You have no idea what you're doing, do you?"

Raines, who had been at the door to the basement quietly observing the conversation between the sisters as they had traversed more sensitive topics, spoke up. "Hey, we've ordered books! We're gonna get the hang of this."

"*We*, huh?" Sheila looked at him teasingly. "*I'm* the one that's preggers. You've just got to get me ice cream in the middle of the night and rub my feet when they hurt." Sheila realized only after she said the words that the last thing she should have mentioned was feet. The image of him decking Rick was still pretty fresh in both of their minds.

A brief cloud passed over Raines' face before he became jocular again. "Whatever you need, babe."

"So let's set up a prayer rotation schedule by text and work out the details. We are going to cover you in prayer. Yes, that means you, Jasmin," Corinne said pointedly.

"I know, I get it," Jasmin relented.

"Let me know if there's anything I can do to help," Raines offered.

They had all forgotten he was a more spiritual being now, Sheila included, so their faces registered surprise at his statement.

"Well," Corinne said, clearly taking the measure of him, "I guess we'll have to include you in the chat. Sheila, for heaven's sake, teach the man how to pray. Help him level up."

"Yes boss," Sheila made an only slightly mocking salute as she answered. Raines looked pleased to be included in their plans.

"And Hotep," Sheila addressed the chocolate arm that had been wrapped around Jasmin for most of their conversation, "no coming for my child."

He laughed, and his face came into frame. "You know I can't take life. But I'm coming for everything else." His smiling face concealed his evil intent, or perhaps revealed his delight in the plans.

Raines' frame stiffened as he saw Hotep for the first

time since that night at the gallery.

"Raines," Hotep said in greeting. Raines responded with a barely audible grumbling. "How kind of you to forgive your wife's infidelity, though your behavior was certainly nothing to write home about either."

"Alright. Show's over," Sheila announced. "I'll talk to my sisters later, and, Hotep, hopefully never."

CHAPTER THIRTY-FOUR
A NEW GAME PLAN

Sheila had spent the morning crafting the perfect email to the president of her former company. He liked Sheila, and she wanted to capitalize on that. She was asking for one of those, it'll be good for you in the long-run, favors. It was day two of her looking for a landing spot for her assistant, Gerry.

The day before had included a half dozen carefully worded inquiries to colleagues she liked in the business of corporate ombudsmanship. This morning and afternoon had yielded no positive results from yesterday. Most responses to her talked about how times were tight. She knew that already. That's why she was asking, after all.

She hadn't wanted to go back to her old company. Gerry had quit there to follow her on her independent consultancy journey. A return there would be tricky. But she had leverage with the company president that she didn't have with her other colleagues.

'It happens to so many people. A baby makes you reassess your priorities! I will take you into my confidence and say this pregnancy could be difficult, and I want to rest as much as I can to ensure its success. Gerry, my former assistant at the company, took a huge chance in following me into my consulting career. I need to get him set up in a situation that will apprentice him so that he can become the ombudsman he wants to be.

'Can you help? I know times are tough all over, but you are the most powerful person I know, so I'm hoping you are tougher than the times.'

Sheila went over the email, revising and adding touches here and there. She wanted to make it clear that she was relying completely on his mercy, and hint that she was open to throwing some of her own labor in as part of any bargain they might reach.

'Please tell your lovely wife I will be in touch soon, and apologize for me telling you the news first.' She rounded out the email with her regular invitation to host him whenever she was in the area. She knew he would never accept. It was certainly not the climate for the male head of a company to stay with a junior female employee. They both knew that, but it was part of the dance of hospitality that meant a lot and was actually a meaningful gesture.

Maybe now that she was no longer working for him, they might actually become friends, not just the nearly friends that you can be with people you work for. But, more than likely, they would simply drift in different directions. Before that drifting began, however, Sheila wanted to leverage her relationship with him one more time.

By late morning, Sheila had sent her email and was moving on to other things. She wrote up her notes from the FBI's visit to her. She still thought that it was strange that so many agents had come to see her, only to stand around doing nothing. It didn't add up to her. Maybe it had all been an excuse for Horden to see her, to assess her, she corrected herself. He knew she had some of her mother's abilities, but he would be sorely disappointed to know how little she had actually inherited and honed.

Around noon, Raines forced her to stop working and eat a sandwich. He piled it high with the butter lettuce she liked. They sat at the now repaired kitchen table and joked about their days so far.

"We'll never be done with email, will we?" Sheila wiped her mouth and luxuriated in a pleasant stretch.

"You know I hardly touch the stuff. That's for my assistant." Raines wiped a smudge of mustard off her face she had missed.

"That's what I need, just an assistant with life to keep me from losing my marbles."

"I would get you one if I thought you would actually

use the help. You'd probably wind up working twice as hard to optimize your aide's time."

Sheila looked guilty. "You're not wrong. Stuff I do tends to have a lot of steps. Maybe I need to simplify. Not sure I know how, though. Argh, life is hard! But we're pretty blessed."

"That we are." Raines put a hand on Sheila's belly. "And the best is yet to come."

"Anything's got to be better than throwing up most mornings," Sheila commented grouchily. "It's a good thing I sleep closest to the bathroom. Ma never had morning sickness. I sure wish I knew that secret."

"My grandmother ate a root that came from the mountains. Maybe I could ask her to send some."

"Couldn't hurt. Your grandmother may be the only member of your family that doesn't hate me. I wouldn't mind seeing her one of these days."

"Which leads me to my question: when are we telling people about the baby? You told your sisters, but the book says you're supposed to wait until the end of the first trimester."

"See, stuff like this drives me crazy, rules and traditions. I guess we should wait, Raines. I'm just so afraid of losing this child. I guess telling people was my way of making things more irrevocable."

They both lapsed into silence for a bit. Their nervousness and fear seemed to hang in the air around them.

"Can't help but notice you don't seem interested in any of the books we got." Raines picked up a book, *So You're Going to Have a Baby*, from the table that looked like the spine had never been cracked.

Sheila ran her hands over her face in frustration. "That's because none of these books can teach me how to be a better gatekeeper, which is the essential thing I need to keep this baby safe. I need to kick into another gear or something, but I can't seem to get there." She drew her knees up to her chest. "It seems like I'm running in molasses."

Raines rubbed her back to comfort her. "You'll think of something, because you have to."

Sheila knew if they lost this child, it would be entirely her fault. Her stupid pig headedness would be to blame. She would never be able to forgive herself. That was why things had to be ok, because there was no way to live with the consequences if she failed.

"Yeah, I'll figure it out," Sheila responded. But right now, she had nothing—no ideas, no strategy, no agenda. What in the world was she going to do?

She thought back to her earlier idea, to get others to help her watch the gate, that her grandfather had swatted down. It seemed perfectly reasonable to her. And even if it had to stay in the bloodline, she had two sisters. Her recent conversation had showed her she couldn't rely on Jasmin to help her, though. Jasmin seemed content to let her squirm at the moment. Sheila couldn't say she blamed her, but it gave her one less avenue for help.

Why should she bear all the risk for her entire dimension? Why couldn't Grandfather see she needed help? The entire situation seemed pitted against her, and she had only a dogged determination to win. That didn't count for much sometimes.

Sheila stood up and shook off her frustration. Dwelling on negative thoughts would not help her. She trotted up to her shrine room, found the Bible she wanted, and sat down to read. Normally, she steered well clear of the book of Revelation, but today she remembered a passage she wanted to meditate on. After a bit of searching, she found it and read aloud.

"I know your works. Look, I have set before you an open door, which no one can shut. I know that you have but little power, and yet you have kept my word and have not denied my name."

Sheila put the Bible down and clasped her hands

together. “Have I kept your word, Lord? Because I need you now. Open the door for this child that no one can shut. I swear I’ll be so careful to give you all the glory. Just make me able and give me grace. You can do anything but fail. Help me trust in you, but I need you to show up right this moment. Make a way for me right here and right now, Lord. We need you so much. Just let us touch the hem of your garment. Why did you place this life inside me if it couldn’t be born?! I just don’t understand you sometimes. But I know you can have mercy on your servant if you choose. Choose me, Lord. Choose to open the door to this life. Please don’t break our hearts.”

Sheila wiped the tears from her eyes and took a deep breath. That prayer had gotten a bit more intense than she had planned. She stayed where she was for a few minutes. Often, when she was in such dire need, God would answer her right away. This time, however, she didn’t feel the electrifying jolt of guidance or clarity.

Standing up, Sheila noticed she had been sitting on something. Retrieving it, she found a picture of one of her best friends, Naima. It must have dropped out of her Bible, where she kept pictures of those she was praying for.

She put the picture back and looked up. “Message received, Lord.”

They hugged for a long time, as dear friends that hadn’t seen each other for a while are bound to do. Sheila breathed in Naima’s musky patchouli scent.

“I’m so glad you called,” Naima said, “But I know I did not show up early, so where are the rest of the girls? You know we come as a box set.”

“You are powerful together, but this is more of a one-on-one conversation.” Sheila guided her to the living room, where she had tea set out.

"Ooh, like I'm a real guest and everything," Naima teased. "Tea in the parlor," she said in an awful English accent.

Both Naima and Sheila weren't much for needless words, so they spent a few minutes just enjoying the tea. This was what Sheila had thought she wanted in a marriage, two like souls ascending to higher planes of existence and knowledge. Instead, she had gotten Raines. He was loud, loved routine, and would protect her against the gates of Hell without a second thought. Sometimes God did the right thing by not giving her what she wanted.

Naima was her sister-wife, though. They were very much peas in a pod. Given that, one would have thought Sheila would lean on her more in her time of grief. But the tears and the sadness were things she kept to herself. Sheila wasn't normally that way, but her mother's passing had been too seismic of an event for things to go on as they had before.

Some chasms were so wide, there was no point trying to describe them to others. The mind cannot comprehend. That's how Sheila felt about her grief. It was too huge, always clawing for her time and attention.

Then, there were the people who knew you so well, they could see all the pain you tried so hard to disguise. Sheila almost didn't want to be around Naima; she had nowhere to hide under that loving gaze.

"You know I want to do better," Sheila started with an apology.

"So you say. Two is better than one, you know. I heard they have a good return for their labor." Naima smiled over the rim of her tea mug.

"See, it's impossible for someone to just say what they want to say around you. Stop preempting me!" They laughed together. "I am sorry for being out of touch. I wish I could do better."

"You are. Here's to tonight." Naima raised her teacup

in a toasting gesture. "I've been under the weight you're trying to carry alone.

"My grandmother meant the world to me. I was with her for the summer on the Res', when she had the nerve to die on me. I knew the Choctaw tradition was for her next of kin to carry her body over the threshold. My grandmother was an enormous woman. How was I supposed to do the impossible?

"The tradition said I had to carry her. It didn't say I had to carry her alone, though. I had made that last part up all on my own. It feels too big to share, I know, but that's the only way you'll get through it."

Sheila hung her head and worked to get a handle on her emotions. "Thank you. I know everything you said is true. Saying it and doing it are just two different things. I'm trying."

"It hurts me to see you in this pain. And it's as if you're fighting to keep it. I know you think you're protecting me by keeping me out, but it is heartbreaking. Let me in."

Sheila shook. She thought she had had a handle, for the moment, on her grief, and here came Naima, rattling pots and pans together, pulling everything out of the cupboards. "I wasn't really prepared to go into all of this."

"I'm not a meeting that you have to strategize and prepare for. I'm just saying, I'm here. Make use of me, because I know I'm gonna make use of you when the time comes."

"When the time comes," Sheila rubbed her hands against her thighs. "Yes, I suppose the time comes for all of us. It's helpful to remind myself I'm not the only one going through this. I didn't know about your grandmother. So you can relate to me having had to carry my mother's dead body."

Naima reached out and grabbed Sheila's arm in sympathy as she heard details of her mother's passing she hadn't known.

"Because I did." Sheila wiped the tears from her eyes. "Had to carry her up a fricking hill, and then down the road to the car. I had to sit in the car at the ranger station until the ambulance came, with her sitting next to me like we were in the middle of a conversation. Like she was just resting her eyes."

Sheila dissolved into tears, and Naima just held her. Eventually, she sat up and blew her nose. The spell had passed.

"Thank you for being here for me."

"You did the hard work of letting me in."

"I'm about to let you in a whole lot more than that."

"Do we have enough tissues?"

"This one is going to be tougher on you than it is on me."

"OK. I'm intrigued."

Sheila took a few deep breaths and convinced herself she could do this.

"My mother held a special role arbitrating travel to this dimension. I didn't know this until after she died, when my *dead* grandfather told me. He told me I needed to take her place, that *only* I could take her place. I said no and ran in the opposite direction, but you know how that goes.

"Now I'm trying, but it just feels like I'm fighting a losing battle sometimes. I need help, especially now…especially now that I'm pregnant. I'm asking for your help."

Sheila had the agony of seeing a host of reactions cross Naima's face. Laughter, disbelief, wonder, and, most of all confusion, were all present. Naima stared at her for a long time.

"So, this is…are you serious? No, of course you're serious." Naima let out a big whoosh of air to clear her head. She downed the rest of the tea in her mug. "This is crazy! You know this is crazy." She looked at Sheila with a look of resolve finally. "What do you need?"

"Well, you do body and energy work. Both take a beating in the work I do. I need this body to be in good enough shape to keep this baby alive."

"The work is that damaging?"

"Odds are against me keeping this pregnancy. I'm trying to beat those odds and need help. Can you give me a body and energy session three times a week? I can pay, but it's gonna be hard on you. I don't need the average Reiki session all the yoga moms want. I need the real deal."

"Then the real deal you shall have." Naima drew closer and placed her hands on Sheila's neck, just below her ears. They both closed their eyes and focused. Naima's head cocked in curiosity as she did an internal check of Sheila's energy flow. "Alright, you're a wreck. You need help now. Lay out here on one of these oversized couches you insist on putting everywhere."

"Don't think this gives you carte blanche to crack on my decor." Sheila slipped off her shoes and lay down. She stared at the ceiling and tried to relax. Naima ran her hands along an outline of Sheila's frame, stopping occasionally to make energy adjustments.

"Start having a real aesthetic, and I just might stop making jokes. But have you even been doing regular chakra alignments?"

Sheila was glad she was staring at the ceiling. It saved her from having to look away. "Life has been a little crazy, and maybe I've put myself last."

"That has to stop. You've got to reflect your priorities. Congratulations on being pregnant, by the way. Didn't see that one coming."

"Yeah, me neither, but it's welcome. You wouldn't believe how much I love this little zygote inside me."

Naima laughed. "Is that what it is, a zygote?"

"I don't know. There are books I have to read, but it's *something,* and I'm glad about it. I just have to protect it. I can't be the one to end this baby's life. I just can't."

"Shhh, shhh. Don't think about that now. Positive thoughts, positive intentions." She continued to run her hands along Sheila, lightly touching at times.

"Right. Positive thoughts. Positive thoughts." Sheila closed her eyes, but all she could see was the pain of losing a child. She was desperate to avoid that.

Naima had a light sheen of sweat on her as she worked to restore Sheila's energy flow. "You didn't lie. You need help, alright. You can't let things get this bad again."

"That's why I need you!"

"This is about more than needing me. Some things you have to do yourself, and taking care of the essentials of your body is one of them. You shouldn't be in this state. Don't make me work harder than I have to again."

"Yes, ma'am," Sheila responded sheepishly. "So that means you accept, right? You'll help me?"

"*If* you take better care of yourself. That's your part of the bargain you have to keep up."

"I will, I will, I promise."

"I'm serious." Naima stopped what she was doing and looked at Sheila. "This isn't a competing priority. Take good care of yourself—body, mind, and spirit."

"I know that's my only option. I won't lie and say it will be easy for me, but I can do it. This is important to me. I'm a vessel now in so many ways."

"What do you mean?"

Not knowing how much she should share about her gatekeeping duties, Sheila deflected. "Oh nothing. Shouldn't you get back to putting Humpty Dumpty back together again?" Sheila lay herself back down and stuck her tongue out playfully at Naima.

"You're gonna be the death of me," Naima said with chagrin.

"Positive thoughts. Positive intentions," Sheila said as they both broke into laughter. "Oh, I missed you, girl."

"I know," Naima said. "I'm easy to love."

CHAPTER THIRTY-FIVE
FALLOUT

"You don't just go around *telling* people!" Grandfather's voice was stern and unforgiving.

The shrine room felt way too hot, even though the house was temperature controlled. Discordant energies, like the ones that cluster when having an argument, raised body temperatures and agitated the spirit. Sheila opened a window to get some circulating air to escort those energies out of the room.

"I think we both know by now I take your feedback under advisement, not as gospel. I told you I have an agenda—to keep this child. Telling Naima is a part of that plan."

"What else does this 'plan' include?"

There was a long pause. "Calling it a plan might be premature. It's forming as I do it."

"In other words, you have no idea what you're doing."

"In other words, I'm letting God lead me."

"Did God tell you to share your destiny with this woman?"

There was more silence.

"I see," he said. "So you're just doing this on your own and you couldn't care less what anybody else thinks."

"I'm desperate. I can't lose this child."

"Desperation does not lead to good decisions. And even though you didn't ask me *why* you shouldn't tell anybody else, I will tell you. This work is a solitary business because it *has* to be. When you share your identity as a gatekeeper with anyone, you become yoked with them. Their fate becomes yours and vice versa.

"No one knew what I did, not my wife and not my children, even though I raised Cathy to replace me, because I didn't want to share the costs of this job with them. I chose not to put them at risk. Your mother did the same thing. And every other gatekeeper before us has done likewise. But here you are with what you think is a better idea. Heaven help us."

"Heaven *will* help us because we need it. You know as well as I do things are not going well. I can't do this on my own, not as I am. And as wonderful as you are," she said sarcastically, "you are not enough. I'm asking, so I know I will receive."

"Your understanding of how faith works is insufficient."

"What is wrong now?!"

"You ask God to do something for you, but then you try to go out and do it on your own without even asking God about your decision. That's not how it works."

"I move in the Spirit and I felt like my actions were an extension of the God within me."

"And have you been feeling particularly connected to the God within you lately?"

Sheila hung her head. "I don't need you *and* Naima getting on my case about this. I have not been doing what I should do with my spiritual life. In my defense, I've been very busy with the gate."

"You can do this the hard way, or you can do this with God. Didn't think I would have to remind you of that."

"When am I supposed to find the time? I'm supposed to be a good wife, guard the gate, keep this child, *and* maintain my spiritual practice? There was barely enough time in the day to get my agenda done *before* all of this."

"You know better than that. Being with God *regulates* time, not vice versa. You have gotten so confused. Just start with God, the rest will sort itself out."

"Easy for you to say. I was almost found guilty of dereliction of duty the last time I was at the gate. Things aren't just falling into place."

"That happens *after* you go to God, not before. The

difficulty you're having is evidence that your way is not working. But instead of going to God, you went out and roped somebody else into this endeavor. I know you're on your own spiritually since your mother passed. But we can't afford for you to be lost right now."

"So that's your advice, huh? I should just let God expand time for me and present the solution. Well, it doesn't suck, as advice goes. Sure wish you had told me this before is all."

"I didn't think it needed to be said."

"Well, you know me." Sheila knocked on her skull to indicate how hard-headed she was. She let out a long sigh and stretched. "So you're saying I should cut Naima loose?"

"It's too late for that. Your words have power. You've involved her in this, and there is no going back. If she is weak, you will be weakened. If she is strong, you will be strengthened. She'll bear your scars along with you now. I hope you chose wisely."

"Wait a minute. I told Raines, too. I haven't noticed him having any effects from my work at the gate."

"I need you to understand a couple of things. First, what you do at the gate is not your work, it is your life. You're still trying to treat it like a very demanding part-time job, and that's not going to work. Second, Raines is strong, and he's still bearing the protection of your sisters from when they exorcized him. The effects of the gate will show on him over time. You've yoked two people inexorably to your experiences, for better or worse, with the gate. Please stop doing that."

'Well, I've certainly been told,' Sheila thought to herself. "Grandfather, how do I let God expand my time?" She hated that she had to ask. She had always thought of herself as spiritually strong. But something had gone wrong lately, and she had clearly lost her way. She needed help.

"Just delight in the Lord. You used to have such a spirit of joy as a child. That's how I remember you. Now you always present yourself before me, weighed down by burdens. Find your joy in God again."

"It sounds so easy. I remember it *being* so easy. I don't know what's happened to me."

"You miss your mother. She was your guide. Now you have to lead yourself. It's not the easiest transition."

"How did you handle your mother dying and you having to become the gatekeeper, Grandfather?"

"Those memories are far from me now."

Sheila hung her head, sad that they couldn't bond over this, but she couldn't fault him for reality.

"I remember waiting the 42 days for my mother to transition to the land of ancestors. I didn't know then that it was an African and Buddhist tradition. It was just something we did. Then I set up my ancestor shrine. I had never had a shrine before. I took parts of what was my mother's to make mine and added some things from her to it. I took the cake mold her grandmother had given her. She and that Bundt pan had been joined at the hip.

"I remember having to fight my sisters for it. But I felt like it was the one thing I had to have. I had seen mysterious things and knew there were other levels to life, but I didn't realize how much my mother had prepared for me for what was to come. As soon as she contacted me at the shrine, I got to work. I devoted my life to finishing her work. It felt like an honor. I had no I idea what a responsibility it was until I started.

"I almost died my first time at the gate. I thought I was prepared. I was looking forward to it. My sister, Ruth, found me passed out, bruised and battered in a traveling circle two days later. She broke the circle and prayed over me until I came to. Never said a word about it to me, knew it wasn't her business. After that, I took my preparation more seriously.

"But Mother didn't talk to me like I talk to you. It was all through guidance and nudging. It's a wonder I didn't think I was going crazy. So I can't quite blame you for saying no to the call initially. It is a lot to take in."

Sheila was in a stunned and rapt silence. Grandfather never talked that much at one time, much less about himself. She had so few memories of him as a child and his manner was so harsh now; it was hard to remember he had ever been a human being. But here he was, reliving his time on earth and helping her feel like she wasn't alone.

It also brought home the dangers of the work. He had almost died from it. It gave his harsh and demanding nature some context. He was intimately acquainted with the risks and was trying to guide her as best he could. She appreciated his help, but wished it could have been her mother guiding her as it had been for him.

But mother hadn't been able to release the gate. She hadn't been able to stop looking after Sheila in order to make her transition to becoming an ancestor. Sheila remembered how her mother used to talk about becoming an ancestor with stars in her eyes. She had wanted it so badly.

But this world had trapped her, Sheila had trapped her, without even knowing it. If her mother had had more faith in her, perhaps she could have transitioned. But Sheila might very well also be dead if her mother hadn't appeared to her in that hotel room and stopped her from jumping in that fraught moment that now seemed a lifetime ago.

Sheila's life had been bought for a price. She had to make it matter. She had to do better.

PART EIGHT
LIVE WITH IT

CHAPTER THIRTY-SIX
THE RELAUNCH

"So you're just *telling* people now? I thought this was a secret?"

"Raines, are you going to pile on me, too? It was, is, a secret, but I needed, I wanted, her help. I thought it would make things easier for the baby. I didn't ask Grandfather about it, and it turns out I should have. Now everyone I've told, you and Naima, are joined to me and my life with the gate in a way that can't be undone. So since she's in it, she might as well be in it."

"Well, I'm already joined to you in life. We're supposed to be one flesh, so it's no biggie for me. How are you going to explain this to Naima, though?"

"Is it no biggie for you? As the protection of my sisters fades from their work on you when they exorcized that *thing* from Massad," Sheila still could not think on the matter without becoming disgusted with her mother's former assistant, "you'll start feeling the effects more strongly. We're going to have to build you up."

"I am a Montoya," Raines was doing his best inhabiting of an Old World conquistador. "I can handle it. Though I love learning, if you've got something to teach me so I can manage better, I'm here for it."

"Let's just get through tonight and take it from there. Naima will be here any moment." Sheila was nervously arranging and rearranging a vase of flowers. She had thought it would calm her down, but her anxiety was too high to be tempered. She stopped fussing with the flowers, placed her hands on the counter, and took a deep breath. Then another. After a few more, she was settling down.

"You good?" Raines asked when Sheila finally opened her eyes.

"Yes. I'm good." But Sheila knew she wasn't at one

with the Lord. Now that she was aware of it, she couldn't help but notice it. It was like there was a subtle discord, an unrest, underneath everything she did. But the trains had to run on time, and life had to move forward. There was no time to deal with that now.

That thought struck Sheila and stopped her in her tracks. She was letting time be more important than God.

"No. I'm *not* good. Can you do me a favor and keep Naima company? I've got to get back into rhythm with God. I've been putting the cart before the horse."

"You spend so much time meditating, and praying, and in your shrine room, how could you be out of rhythm with God? I just read a few chapters a day and I feel more than full with the Lord."

"Sometimes, being busy, even with the Lord's business, can keep you from delighting in the Lord."

"Hmm. How long do you need?"

"Maybe an hour?"

"Well, apparently, Naima and I are in this with you in a special way. We might as well get to know each other better." Raines gave her an assured smile. He did such a wonderful job of going with the flow, Sheila thought.

Even as the doorbell was ringing its little melody through the house, Sheila was closing the door to her shrine room and settling down to enter a little one-on-one time with the Lord. She lay down in the middle of the room, put her hands behind her head, and looked up at the ceiling. Then she became aware of the sound of muffled voices. She let go of those sounds and let go of the ceiling.

Sheila invited God into her being. A yellow warmth began to envelop her, like a sun rising on the horizon. She couldn't help but smile. She had been away for what seemed like so long, yet, at the first invitation, the glory of God filled her again. Sheila felt so lucky and wiped tears from her eyes. Life felt almost too perfect to stand at moments like this. It reminded Sheila to never underestimate God. He always came through.

She spent some time communing with God. No agenda, no requests, just time enjoying each other's company. Sheila always seemed to forget how restorative being with the Lord was for her. It seemed there was nothing God could not do. She cried through her frustration and fear of possibly losing her child. God comforted her, and somehow, the fear lessened.

Sheila fell on her sword. At least she felt that way. Whatever the gate demanded of her, she had to comply. It was a thankless job and what she had always been afraid of. She loved and adored her mother, but she had never wanted her life. God and other people were too much at the center. Sheila had wanted some space for herself.

Her mother's work had always seemed relentless. She was always helping someone, always working for the higher understanding and healing of others. Sheila had known she hadn't had it in her to be that selfless. Her mother had seemed to have joy *despite* her work, not because of it.

Sheila, as long as she was being honest with herself, was interested in having God at the center of her life, but not God's work as her own. It hurt to admit that she wasn't the child of light her mother wanted her to be, merely a self-interested, carnal being. She had skills and abilities, but she had mainly used them for her own enlightenment and blessing.

Now she was stuck in a job whose purpose was to ensure the safety of the collective. It took and never gave. It was the very definition of selfless. Was that why it seemed to drain her so deeply? Oh, how the universe was laughing and winking at her.

But there was no hope of escape. Sheila would never "win" at the gate. It would never be complete, and there were no benchmarks for her to pursue. It was simply her station in life.

For the first time, Sheila saw how much she resented

the gate and its duties that fate had foisted on her. *She* wanted to determine the course of her life. She was taken aback when she realized the implications of her statement. Not God? Didn't she want *God* to direct her life?

Sheila saw she had spent so much of her life merely playing with godliness. She thought of herself as enlightened, but when push came to shove, she was into a deep and meaningful spiritual life for the benefits, not the costs.

Sheila shook herself out of her self-condemnation. She hated looking at herself when the results were so unsavory. But you had to see yourself for what you truly were in order to move forward.

She wanted to move forward. Stewing in her resentment for one moment longer seemed unacceptable, now that she had finally figured out that's what she had been doing. But how could she make herself happy with her situation? How did she overcome the bone-deep weariness that keeping the gate left her with?

"Lord, please stop me from wanting a way out of my situation. I guess it's for this hour I have come. Let me enjoy the work of serving others. Let me not simply do your will, but draw joy from it as well. Make me over, Lord. Just fix me.

"I'm sorry for not getting it, that it was never about me. It was always about all of us. Please help me do what I can. And then help me do more than that. Give me your power, not so I might be great, but so I might serve. Thank you for helping me see. Amen."

Sheila lay quietly for a while as she felt the Spirit of God swirl about in her. She felt as if she were being changed right then and there. She tried to open herself to the experience, offering all that she was to the transformation. "Please make me over," she whispered.

She needed a fresh start to overcome her bad programming and try again. How could she have been so blind? She wrested her thoughts from self-loathing and steered them toward constructive brainstorming. How could she be better, more faithful to her purpose here on earth?

For one, she could stop running around like a cowboy, not listening to any counsel but her own. She had to stop resenting Grandfather for his part in this, and even for his coldness, and value him as the incredible gift and resource that he was. Sheila resolved to adhere to his advice more often. His advice to spend more time with God had turned out alright; she smiled.

God never left her without a way forward, even when she was the very thing blocking her progress. If she could stay in God's grace, she and her child might make it through all of this.

"Teach me how to like my job, Lord, my identity. Let me do better at it. I want You to guide me instead of my fears. Let me not run on a parallel track with You, but actually go with You in all my ways. Give me grace."

Sheila had missed this kind of ongoing prayer in her life. It felt like it had been a while since she had last let her guard down around the Lord. It was a liberating feeling to come as she was and spend time with God because she wanted to, not because there was a dire need.

It seemed like lately there was always a dire need brewing, but that didn't have to be the only reason she came into the presence of God. She could choose to abide in God as she was doing now, to be refreshed. It was amazing to see how the answer was always God. Every time she went searching high and low for deliverance and guidance, it was always with the God within her. She needn't have searched all over.

Sheila had told herself time and time again to seek God first, but that advice had such a hard time sticking. She thought she had done it, but every time she reached one level of trust and reliance, there was always higher to go, a deeper level of intimacy with God available to her. She loved how God always had something more to show her, even when it was her own mistakes.

Sheila finally sat up and took a moment to orient herself. She felt like she had flown somewhere far, far away to be with the Lord. Now that she was back, things didn't quite fit. She wanted to go back to where she had been, back with God. She reminded herself that God was always with her. Just because there were fewer fireworks in her daily life, that didn't make it any less spirit-filled.

"Thank you, God."

Sheila looked around the room. In a little while, she would be casting her traveling circle in here and going to the gate. Now, for the first time, she knew her travels and gate experiences affected others. Naima, Raines, and she were all inexorably bound up in this, not to mention her unborn child. How could what she did affect others so deeply? She was still going to do her best, only now her best had to be better, cleaner, complete. It had to be, for all their sakes.

Sheila came downstairs and found Naima and Raines at the kitchen table, eating and laughing together. Raines had made good on his promise to push on without her and was busy being a good host. He should be convicted for being so charming, Sheila thought. She planted a kiss on his forehead as she sat on his lap. Raines squeezed her and they spent a moment in quiet connection.

"Naima!" Sheila stood up and went to embrace her. "Always so good to see you. Sorry I wasn't here to greet you. I had something I had to do."

"Well, whatever it was, keep doing it. Look at you with your aura all bright and bouncy." Naima held Sheila's face and beamed at her. "Much better. Good to see my work wasn't in vain."

"I'm trying my best to maintain a steady connection with the Divine, eat my Wheaties, and do whatever else I'm supposed to be doing."

"I called Zincai this afternoon. He's going to put a homeopathic regimen together for all the nutrients the baby needs and send me the supplements. That's gonna be recurring on your card, hon. Thanks." Sheila winked at Naima and smiled at Raines.

A silence grew between the three of them.

"So, Naima, I have to tell you something. Just by telling you what I did, I have involved you in this. I have yoked you to me, to my successes, my failures. It seems there's no way to get you out of it…for now. I am going to continue to look for a way to release you. I know it is not what you signed up for, and I'm sorry."

"I can't say I'm surprised. When you called me to invite me over before, I knew there was going to be an ask. I had resolved to say yes to whatever it was. I should have figured that it would come at a price." Naima explored her own thoughts for a while before looking back up. "Well then, I had better make sure you win." She flashed the dazzling smile everyone loved her for.

"I don't deserve you, but I'll take as much help as I can get, so thank you. Tonight will be the first time I go to the gate with a little help. I hope to have stellar results." Sheila tried not to be nervous. If this didn't work, she had no other ideas on tap.

"So, where is the gate?" Naima's face showed excited curiosity. "Where are we going?"

"The gate doesn't really have a physical location. It's in a space in between dimensions that I reach by casting a traveling circle. It was recently impressed upon me that I am not at the gate enough and I have pledged to correct that. Naima, I'm hoping you can put me in tip-top energy shape before I go and be there to help me better recover afterwards. Let's see how it goes working together and how we can improve things."

"That's a little less exciting," Naima said, almost pouting, "but I guess it will have to do. Let's get you sorted out, then." Naima gestured toward the living room and they went in, and Sheila sat while Naima adjusted her energy.

"You're in better shape than earlier this week. This is good; it means your body wants to maintain the positive changes. That will be good going forward. We can compound some of your strengths."

"I always knew you were the right person to help me." Sheila was doing her mirror light visualization. It was one of her favorites. She emanated light from within while being covered with countless mirrors that deflected energy from the outside away from her. It was a great practice for building up your personal power and energy while being immune to negativity.

Working with Naima, Sheila felt a boost to her visualization she couldn't quite articulate. Everything seemed sharper and more concentrated. Sheila was sorry she had yoked Raines and Naima to her gatekeeping, but she wasn't sorry that she wasn't alone and had help. Even though she had her grandfather, the gate was still solitary work. Just knowing that they were rooting for her made a big difference, not to mention the actual assets they brought to the work. Two was better than one, because when one fell, the other could help pick them up.

"Thank you." Sheila opened her eyes at the end of the energy treatment Naima had given her. She felt readier than she had in a long time. She didn't feel like she was half dragging herself to duty, but that she actually had enough strength and energy for the task at hand.

"Ok, I'm going to do my thing. See you in a few to several hours." Sheila looked at them, apologetic for tying them up in this, then climbed the stairs to her shrine room. Once inside, she gathered her materials for casting her traveling circle, trying to take a softer and more appreciative tone to her preparations. She noted she was running low on several items. It was time to stock up at her local botanica. She made a mental note to do so.

About 45 minutes later—she was getting faster—her circle was established, and she was ready to travel.

"You've done this thing," her grandfather's voice rang out. "We'll see how it goes."

"I tried to delight in the Lord. I think I did. Thanks for that advice." Sheila settled herself in a comfortable, seated position in the middle of her circle. She said her prayers and affirmations of protection, then she let her consciousness slip from her body like casting off a comfortable robe.

Sheila went to the rainbow palace first, as she often did when she astral traveled. She always hoped she would get a glimpse of her mother. She knew it was ridiculous. Her mother's spirit wouldn't be here, in a dimension so tied to the physical world. Still, she wished she could communicate with her mom the way she did with her grandfather. Why couldn't *she* be Sheila's guide through all of this? Sheila knew that she herself was the reason, but it didn't stop her from wishing things were different.

After finding the rainbow palace empty and stagnant, Sheila let herself be drawn to the less traveled dimensions, until she identified the familiar pull to the gate. From her dimension, the gate was perceptible to only her. Her spirit was attuned to it in a special way so that it was always calling to her. She had already experienced the pull getting stronger in the little while she had been watching the gate.

It was as if it were imprinting on her. Sheila knew they were becoming one. She couldn't blame her grandfather for not telling her about it. It was something that couldn't be described. She knew there was an unknown spiritual alchemy at work. She and the gate were being fused together. Any remaining bonds tying her mother to the gate were falling away while she steadily made it her own.

Sheila had been right when she had said things weren't going well, but at least they were going. She hadn't had a breach of the gate. She was getting more comfortable with the feeling of beings using her as a means of passage. And she hadn't quit. They were at least avoiding disaster, and her growth, while too slow, was still progressing.

She came to the place where she could pass to the gate and encountered a resistance, as if something were pushing back at her. Sheila reminded herself that she was formless, so matter and its rules were irrelevant. She announced to the universe that she had authority to be here. Then she passed through what had previously been a squishy barrier without difficulty.

Sheila had been deposited on the edge of a forest with a column doorway in sight. She walked towards it, pondering on how the travel to a gate that was on no map had so many steps. It seemed to her it should be easier, more direct. But what did she know? It took as many steps as it took.

She walked through the doorway and encountered a feeling as if she was going from one side of the looking glass to the other. Things reversed and went topsy-turvy in weird ways. She got turned around and almost ended up walking back out of the gate. She blamed that on the chaos creatures trying to disorient her. The longer she stayed away from the gate, the more time they had to build up their strength and increase their numbers.

Sheila stopped short before she passed through the membrane between dimensions. 'Not today, chaos monsters,' she thought.

She turned around and took stock of the situation. It looked like a mob was about to rush at the barrier. They were here to test her. She had told them she would do better. They were her to see if she could.

Sheila relaxed her arms at her side and closed her eyes. She summoned all her power. It was puny. She was puny. Then she asked God for help. Her light became so dazzling that the other energies shied away.

It had always been this simple. She had just had to realize it. It was never about her or her worth; it had always been about her willingness to serve God's purposes. She had made this road so hard when it could be, not easy, but so much easier. It was never about how tough the road ahead was, but how strong the one who had sent her was.

Sheila turned her attention to the energies before her. They seemed less intimidating now. She sorted through them, weighing each of their intentions in her heart. She could see their plans, innately knew their requests. It was as if she had been given x-ray vision to see through their pleas to the heart of the matter.

She said no to all but thirteen spirits. The rest, she *finally* had the strength to disperse, instead of hoping they left of their own accord. She transported each of them back to the gateways of their own dimensions, even those that were assigned to different levels of Hell. It was the first time she had gone anywhere near the Hell levels and it was uncomfortable.

Even though she knew Hell didn't have literal flames, she still felt her temperature spike when she neared those dark gateways. But she returned all the spirits that would not be passing through her to their homes, announcing to the dimensions that she was "on the job" and up to the task. There wouldn't be another case that put her on trial if she could help it.

Then there were only thirteen spirits left. Up to now, she had only had as many as a handful pass through her in one night. Sheila remembered to ask God for help, and her fear dissipated.

She opened her mouth and allowed it to stretch and expand until it became its own doorway. The energies began to pass through her, out of the interdimensional waiting room and into her dimension, the *I* dimension. Each energy that passed through her felt as if it were frantically squeezing her heart, then releasing it. Thirteen mini-heart attacks later, the gate was clear and her work was done, for now.

Sheila had not been able to clear the gate since she had started. She felt lightheaded from the realization. She had done it. She felt horrible, but she had felt like that before. For the first time, she had never done her job well.

"Alright, God. It's you and me from now on," Sheila pledged.

She collected herself, turning to the columned doorway and preparing to pass through.

"Don't think we're done here." Hotep's voice rang in her ears.

Sheila turned back to find him facing her, a cold sneer taking over his expression. She broke out in a smile.

"You must be worried. I'm finding my way back to God."

"You are so full of yourself. You have one good night and think victory is yours. Life is long and relentless. I will have my victory." He spoke with a tone of absolute certainty.

"Let my sister go. Release her from the hold you have on her, I beg you."

"What?" Hotep looked uncomfortable and surprised.

"I understand you have to sift me, but *what* are you doing with her? That girl is pure. Let her go."

"That is the problem with all of you. No one is pure! I'm having quite the time with her, turning her hurt from what you did to her into hate. You'll see just how pure she isn't when I'm done with her."

Sheila's heart added ache to the pain and soreness she was experiencing.

"Yes, that's right," Hotep said and laughed. "My victory won't be that I will harm her. Instead, I will turn her. It was always her fate. All that innocence, so easy to misdirect and turn sour."

Sheila's lightheadedness intensified, and she saw stars.

"Go back to your dimension. You're not the only one who wields power here." Hotep made a brushing motion with his hand and she blinked out existence.

Sheila opened her eyes with a start, clutching at her heart. The pain was so great it was blinding. She almost fell over and out of her circle from the disorientation. She leaned forward and forced herself to take slow, deep breaths until the bands that squeezed her heart eased a little.

Sitting upright, she rubbed at her chest. It felt like someone had punched her heart a few times. Usually the pain after she traveled was an all over ache or intense head pain. This one was new. It kept taking her breath away and making it hard to have any rhythm to her inhale and exhale. She didn't like it.

Sheila finally opened her eyes and found the door to her shrine room open, with Raines and Naima standing at the threshold. They looked at her with expressions of concern and worry.

"We felt you having a hard time." They raised their hands in unison to show the bright red markings of fresh bruises on their wrists.

Sheila, again, felt the deep regret of them having no choice about being involved in this predicament. "I'm sorry," she squeaked. She couldn't seem to get enough air for her normal voice. She felt like her pain wouldn't go away until she put a cold compress directly on her heart. Who knew when the regret might leave her?

"You should put something on that," Sheila commented about their wrists. They gave a nervous laugh, thinking how much worse off she seemed than them.

"Seriously. I have to clean up in here. You all should go take care of yourselves, and I'll join you when I'm done." Sheila honestly didn't know if she had the strength to stand at the moment. But, as she had experienced from other nights after coming back from the gate, she could always crawl. She could, in fact, remove her traveling circle on her hands and knees. The only thing that required standing was the brief vacuuming at the end, and by then she had usually moved enough to be up to it.

After more insistence that she would be fine, Raines and Naima closed the door and went downstairs to put ice on their bruises. Still rubbing at her chest, Sheila asked

Grandfather, "When does it get any easier?"

There was a long pause. "It doesn't. The height of the challenge always matches as much as you can endure. That's not to say you won't have good nights where things go well, but it will always be almost too much."

"Right then." Sheila took a moment to absorb that hard truth before cleaning up her circle. She burned the folded piece of parchment with her name written on it. She had found her way back to her body and no longer needed it. While sitting on her heels, she did as much as she could, then transitioned to shuffling around on her hands and knees to sweep up the remains of her circle.

Finally, she stood up, taking a moment to steady herself before a quick vacuum of the carpet. She had a separate vacuum for her shrine room to handle the more sensitive things she had to discard. Given how weak she was after the gate, maybe she should spring for a handheld one she didn't have to stand to use.

Sheila eased herself down the stairs and found Raines and Naima in the kitchen with gel ice packs covered with kitchen towels and wrapped around their wrists.

"'We happy few, we band of brothers,' isn't that how it goes?" Sheila gave a wry smile.

Raines got up and guided her to a chair, which she gladly accepted. She felt like a sack of potatoes as she sank into the chair.

Naima rose, took off her ice pack and started running her hands over Sheila. Her face blanched. "If I hadn't seen it, I would have said it was impossible for someone to lose as much energy in one night as you have."

Sheila moaned with her eyes closed and gave herself the indulgence of a comforting rocking motion. "Don't say those things out loud, you'll make Raines worry. It's always better by morning. I'm almost all better by then. Your bruises should be gone in the morning, too, if it's anything like what happens to me. I hope they don't hurt too bad." Sheila caught herself babbling as she tended to when she was exhausted and made herself shut up. No one ever wanted to hear a sleepy person talk.

She felt energy pouring into her. She opened her eyes, suddenly wide awake.

"Leave some for yourself, Nai."

"You let me worry about me."

"I don't mean for you to give me what's yours," Sheila insisted.

"I just want to see if it will work," Naima snapped. "Now let me work."

There was no point in even talking to her when she was like this, Sheila knew, so she shut up. She was absorbing the energy Naima was pulsing into her and was almost at the point of feeling giddy. She felt like laughing; she felt so good.

Slowly, she felt the energy coming into her lessen and then stop. Naima took a seat and looked exhausted. Sheila reached out and touched her cheek. "Oh, dear heart, I never meant for any of this."

"Well, apparently God did, because here we are." Naima grabbed a magazine from the table and fanned herself with it. "Just wanted to see what I could do, is all."

Sheila stood up and took a deep breath. "You can do a lot! I knew you were a light worker, but I honestly didn't know the depth of your ability. This is fantastic."

"I didn't know it went that deep, either. That was a first. It seems I've been holding back." Naima chuckled.

"That's because it hurts you, doesn't it?" Sheila could see the discomfort on Naima's face.

"Maybe a little," Naima said with her eyes closed.

"Why did you do it? I don't need to feel this good."

"Something compelled me. I felt something outside of myself pushing me to make you whole again."

Sheila stilled. "That must be the yoking to me. It wants to see me restored. It doesn't realize we are a team, and we all have to function." She had distress in her voice.

"Stop talking like I'm dead. There's nothing wrong with me. I'm right here. It just took a bit more out of me than I expected. Something tells me you know all about that."

Sheila held up her hands in surrender. "All right, all right, I relent. Live your best life, Nai. Just know that you don't have to. God always restores me."

"And I am part of that restoration," Naima said, impassioned. "Let me do what I have to do."

"This is not what I wanted, to have you 'pledged' to me. You're not a knight in my service or anything."

Naima sat silent for a while. "It doesn't matter what you wanted, this is what's happening. My life is yours now. It's been decided."

"By who?!"

"You needed help; you got help. Don't look a gift horse in the mouth."

"But you're my best friend, not my vassal!"

"It looks like I'm going to have to be both." Naima finally opened her eyes. "Everything's changed now. Something's happened, I don't know what, but I *have* to make sure you're alright. It's fine. I told you when I said yes that I knew things would change. Surprise, surprise, things are changing."

Sheila felt like the world was spinning out of control. The act of asking Naima for help had literally rewritten her destiny. Her purpose now was to ensure Sheila succeeded above all else. It seemed unfair and too small a thing for Naima.

Sheila had barely come to understand and accept her own destiny, so she refused to be at the center of anyone else's. She would ask Grandfather, but this seemed like something that wasn't easily undone. She had messed with matters she shouldn't have, and these were the consequences—wounds on her friend and her husband, and she was now her best friend's liege.

Why could the universe not leave well enough alone? She had no one to blame but herself.

CHAPTER THIRTY-SEVEN REBALANCED

Later that morning, Naima had gone home and Raines and Sheila were enjoying some coffee and tea in the kitchen.

Raines put down his coffee. "I didn't ask her to be yoked to you, but I've got to tell you the truth—I feel a lot better knowing that she is. I feel guilty about it, but that's the truth."

Sheila put her face in her hands. "It's so much worse than I ever could have imagined. I feel like this is a page out of an epic quest or something. I'm not trying to collect disciples."

"Maybe this is what you need. You asked for help. It certainly looks like help to me."

"But the cost! I just changed her life. I've deprived her of something because I was foolhardy and asked her for help without knowing the implications."

"You always say, 'What will be will be.' Maybe this was written in the stars."

"What a poetic way to say I may have ruined her life."

"You said the gate *has* to have a watcher, and it can only be you. Well, maybe the watcher needs an aide, and it has to be her this time around. You don't like the cost. I don't enjoy putting our child in danger, but we all have got to just deal with it. I'm sorry, but I'm not sorry."

Raines was right, some things just had to be accepted. She had seen that look on Naima's face before, that look of devotion. It had been on the face of many of her mother's followers. It seemed almost like worship, and it made her uncomfortable.

"Did you see her face?"

"Yep. She would go to Hell and back for you. So would I. You can be uncomfortable with it, but accept the help. If she wants to heal you, *let* her!"

"You saw what it took from her. Would you have me let her harm herself to help me?"

"Don't get squeamish now because you don't like the implications. This is your doing, and I think it's for the best. Live with it."

"Well, no need to come at me like that. I'm not trying to fight."

"You're fighting this *blessing*, don't you think?"

"Am I about to get a spiritual talking-to from my husband?" Sheila arched an eyebrow, and they both laughed, letting some of the tension out of the conversation.

"Alright, alright, I get it, but I'm just saying; you got what you asked for. *Accept* it. This all seems to be on purpose. Go with it."

Sheila stuck out her lips and crossed her arms as she tried to refute the truth of that statement.

"Maybe you have a point, Raines. But I'm still gonna look for a way to release her bond with me."

He wrapped his arms around her, and she slipped hers around him in return. "What about me? When will *I* ever be free?"

"Oh, you? I'm never letting you go. I'm not even sorry I'm not sorry." Sheila kissed him. "Be a shame to waste all this extra energy I've been given, don't you think?"

Raines responded by kissing her with a fierceness that caught her off-guard. He pulled her against him and devoured her. Standing her before him, he sat and kissed at her waist as he pulled down her pajama bottoms. He aimed his kisses lower and heard her gasp. He feasted on her as she moaned.

He pulled down his sweatpants and boxers and sat her on top of him. They moved in rhythm with each other.

"All this," Sheila said as she tried to catch her breath, "before breakfast."

Raines leaned forward and claimed her lips, taking whatever air she had left. They finished together, and Sheila sat wrapped around him for a long while.

"Good morning," she said, happy and exhausted.

"Mmm. All I need now are some eggs."

"You *would* think of food at a time like this." Sheila stood up slowly and they both put themselves back together. "Over-easy hard or scramble?" She went to the refrigerator to grab butter and a few eggs.

"This is all I wanted, to make love to my wife and get a meal out of it." Raines laughed and clapped his hands, even when Sheila sprayed water on him from the sink. "Not taking it back," Raines laughed as he got drenched.

Sheila had finally had enough fun spraying Raines and turned off the water.

"Over-easy hard, thanks."

"You'd better be lucky you deserve these."

"Yeah, but don't I always deserve them?" Raines asked with an innocent smile.

"Maybe," Sheila admitted, shaking her head.

"Thank you for ordering the prenatal supplements. I saw you had read none of the books. I was afraid you weren't excited about our child. But as usual, you're just doing things your way."

"I will read *som*e books. You bought so many, just give me the short list. But yes, I'm happy and excited and totally into this baby. Part of me has not wanted to get attached, but it's no use. I just love this child, even though it's barely a fetus yet."

"Music to my ears," Raines purred.

"Order up," Sheila shouted as she turned the stove off and slid three eggs from the frying pan to a plate.

"Have I mentioned that you're the best?"

"That was easy." She put the plate down in front of him.

"Not just the eggs, or even before. You are the best, and I thought maybe it's been a while since someone told you how awesome you are."

Sheila was so touched she felt tears coming to her eyes. "Thank you, honey. That means a lot. You're pretty OK yourself."

"Oh, don't kill me with all this praise!" They shared a laugh.

"But let me be serious. You're amazing. You've been there every step of the way on this crazy journey. I'm so blessed. Thank you."

"I do not know where any of this is going, but I'm with you."

"As long as God's got us, we'll be fine."

"But do you think…"

"Don't doubt it," Sheila interrupted. "We are having this child."

"Amen." Raines didn't share his thoughts that any God who would let his child die wasn't worth worshiping. But it occurred to him that God the Father had let his only begotten son die for humanity. What hope did his own child have in the face of that?

"What's wrong? You look unhappy."

"God let his own son die. Is he going to let our child live?"

"Oh no. No, no, no, that's not how it is. Jesus died to *give* our child eternal life. God loves us. Loves us more than we deserve, and everything flows from that."

"Maybe it makes you slower at your job, and God doesn't like that."

"Where is all of this coming from?" Sheila wore a bewildered look.

"I just don't know why any of this is happening. So far, your grandfather has been right. Are we trying to change something that can't be changed?"

"God hasn't told me no, so I'm going to keep pressing. I'm putting my appeal in front of him every day, every hour, until I hear his response. We have to believe in God's mercy. Can I guarantee life will turn out the way I want it? No, but what I will do is make sure God knows how much I want this, how much it means to me. I pray without ceasing that He will grant my request. With God, everything can be changed. Everything."

"I'm trying to have faith. It's just hard. I have no idea what God is doing, and it's hard to trust him to do what's best for my child."

"Without God, you could be sterile, or some other woman could be carrying your child. This baby is a gift. There are no accidents. God knows what he's doing."

"I guess that's true."

"It's natural to doubt and be confused or upset with what God is or isn't doing. Just take it to God when you have those feelings. Don't keep them bottled up inside. They turn sour."

"What am I supposed to do, argue with God?"

"It beats giving him the silent treatment or faking it. I yell at God all the time. We've had some tremendous fights, but I never stop talking to him, and we always get through it together."

"Maybe I'll try that." Raines wiped the moisture from his cheeks and took a big breath. "Thanks. You always calm me down. You come get me when I'm going to a dark place."

Sheila took Raines' hand in hers. "We're a team."

"We are. I never thought I could have this with anyone. We really rely on each other. Thank you for needing me."

"Do you not think I needed you before?"

"Well, we were both content doing our own things, just together. Now it's different. We need each other to move forward. It feels like my presence really matters, and it's nice to be needed, is all."

"It *is* different now. Thank you for being there for me."

As they sat enjoying each other's presence, Sheila's thoughts wandered. What if Raines was yoked to her in the same way that Naima was? Was he was being what she needed simply because he was compelled to? She couldn't quite trust the relationships around her to be free of influence. She closed her eyes and willed herself to "live with it."

CHAPTER THIRTY-EIGHT
SISTERS

The top landing of Sheila's stairs to the second floor was one of her favorite places to hang out. She did not know how she had gotten into it, but she would sit there and talk on the phone, play games, even bring out her planner and work. It was a very functional space.

This morning, she sat there trying to craft the perfect text to Jasmin. She gave up on trying to relay the hilarious joke she had heard when she found out the comedian that made it had been canceled. She would have to figure out something else to say.

Sheila was having an affair with her sister Jasmin's phone. She would call and try to leave loving messages, reminding her of something funny from their childhood that had crossed her mind, and similar pleasantries. She always ended by telling Jasmin that she loved her and would do better.

Sheila wasn't sure it was having any effect. She wasn't even sure her sister was listening to the messages. Since she had found out how wounded Jasmin remained from Sheila's actions, she had been relentless in trying to repair the breach, but not quite knowing how. So, she was trying everything.

She had offered to take a trip out there or to fly Jasmin to her, but that text had never been returned. She had to find out how Jasmin was through her older sister, Corinne. Sheila was reduced to voicemail, hoping that some of her energy was reaching Jasmin.

Sheila called Jasmin and waited patiently for the ringing to roll over to voicemail.

"Hello?"

"Oh, hi! I actually reached you."

"Yeah, I've been getting your messages." Jasmin's

voice was flat and almost cold.

"Oh, good." Sheila took a big breath and plowed ahead. "I just want to tell you I'm sorry and I love you and I'll do whatever it takes to repair our relationship."

"I know."

Sheila paused and took a moment to remind herself it was ridiculous to feel awkward with her own sister. "So, how are you?"

"Have you ever thought that what's happening to you now is karma for what you did to me?"

It hit Sheila like a ton of bricks. She saw stars and felt light-headed. It appeared there wouldn't be any small talk.

"I haven't thought of it that way. I've been sorry and wanted to make things right with you, but I haven't thought about what I needed to do to make it right with God and the universe." Now that she said it, she couldn't believe she hadn't thought of it before. Of course, the universe would demand its pound of flesh from her. She had psychically attacked her own sister.

Jasmin might not be with Hotep at all if Sheila hadn't put her in such a state of hurt and vulnerability. Her shoulders slumped. She could see how this was all her fault. Sheila thought about her mother's teaching that it wasn't about what happened to you in life, but about how you responded.

How should Sheila respond now? She took a deep, cleansing breath and worked to release her guilt.

"Thank you for that. Sometimes I need to be reminded of the obvious. I don't think it's the sole reason the accuser is sifting me now, but it certainly can't be helping. And I'll ask *you* something. Do you need to see me suffer to be satisfied?"

"Come on, Sheila."

"Hey, we're being honest here. Maybe it didn't come out perfect, but you know what I mean. I know I may deserve everything that's happening to me right now, but what do you need to make us right again?"

"I need to know that you will *never* do that to any light-bearer again, and especially not to me. I don't know what will prove that to me, but I feel like I will know it when I see it."

"I suppose that's fair enough. For what it's worth, I would never do that today. I've changed. I want to show you. I'll do what I need to in order to prove it to you."

"I hope we get there."

"We will. I love you."

Sheila waited with bated breath. She had never wanted so badly to hear an 'I love you' in return. There was no response.

"I had thought things went well when I visited you before, when Raines and I were having difficulty. We were just sisters, and it seemed like there was no barrier between us. Things seem to have gotten worse since then. What happened?"

There was another long pause.

"Hotep suggested you should prove you have changed, that I shouldn't just forgive you because I wanted to."

"I wish you would listen to yourself more than you would listen to him," Sheila spoke between gritted teeth. Then she blew out a breath and tried to let go of her anger with Hotep. "But I understand that ship has sailed. You have my pledge that I am different. You know that I'm sorry. I can't blame you for wanting proof, no matter who put it in your mind. I'll do what I need to do to get back in your good graces. I miss us."

"I do too, but every time I try to go back to the way things were, I can't. I didn't know that it would be this hard. I need you to do some of the work."

"I will. I am. I just wish I knew what I need to be doing to reassure you it won't happen again."

"How's your relationship with the Lord?"

Sheila was grateful to have the conversation turn away from her guilt and atonement.

"It's going well right now. Grandfather reminded me to delight in the Lord, so God and I have been spending some quality time together. I had been focusing on the gate so much that everything else was falling to the wayside. It's so easy to forget how good God is, so I've been enjoying being close to him again."

"That's good. I've had trouble getting close to God lately. I don't know what it is."

'You're dating the accuser!' Sheila yelled in her mind. She gripped her phone and stayed silent until she was sure she had a grip on her tongue.

"I'm sorry to hear that. I hope and pray it gets better for you."

"I'm sure it will. Sometimes I have low times when God seems far away, but we always come back together. This time it's lasting longer than usual, though."

Sheila struggled not to curse Hotep out in her mind. That anger would profit them nothing. She had to remind herself he wouldn't have such a hold over Jasmin if Sheila hadn't given him the opportunity through her dangerous actions.

"Why do you think that is?"

"I know why *you* think that is, but I just don't know. I'm just trying to meditate and pray through it."

"That will get you back on track, I'm sure." 'If you would just drop your loser boyfriend, then it would be fine,' she wanted to add, but held her tongue.

"Thanks. And thanks for not making this about him."

"I'm trying." Sheila gave a small, wry laugh. The effort not to mention Hotep and lay the blame at his feet was making her sweat.

"I'm glad I picked up. This was nice."

"Yes, it was," Sheila said warmly. She was grateful to have finally connected with Jasmin, even if it wasn't the grand reconciliation she had fantasized about. She would have to put the work in. And perhaps that was the way it had to and should be. Some amends had no shortcuts to them, you just had to go step-by-step. "I look forward to talking again."

"Yes. Me too. Be well, Sheila." There was a pause, and Sheila wasn't sure if the conversation was over. "I really do believe you'll make it through your sifting and come out as pure gold. I wouldn't have let him do it if I weren't so sure of your victory. You never met anything you couldn't overcome."

Sheila was stunned again. She couldn't believe her sister's naiveté in believing that she could have prevented *ha satan* from doing exactly as he pleased. But it also spoke to Jasmin's unmistakable faith in her. Did she believe in herself as much as Jasmin did?

"I love you and thank you for believing in me. From your lips to God's ears. I'm doing my best."

"It will all be fine. Talk to you later."

"Bye, Jas." Sheila hung up the phone and stared at the screen.

She wished for the millionth time that Jasmin would come to her senses and detach herself from Hotep, but she knew that was something she couldn't affect. Sheila thought about the time she herself had fallen for her first bad boy in college. Her mother had obviously hated him, but had been careful not to say a bad word about him, knowing that it would drive Sheila deeper into his arms. It was only later, when they had talked as adults, that Ma revealed how hard she had cried and prayed for Sheila to see the light.

Sheila had been so angry with Hotep about how he was using her sister that it was hard to even see straight. She should spend more time praying for her sister than worrying about her or even being angry with Hotep. Every time Sheila tried to pray for her, she got caught up in her anger with him. If only he weren't a part of the equation, everything would be fine. But she knew that wasn't exactly true. He hadn't caused her to lash out at Jasmin with her power. That had been all Sheila.

She had to stop blaming him and do her part to rectify her wrongs with Jasmin and with God.

"Are you still pleased with me, Lord? What can I do? Please make me better and help me reconcile with Jasmin. Let me use the good sense you gave me to release my anger and focus on the task at hand."

Sheila felt resistance as she prayed. It seemed she was having a great deal of trouble letting go of her anger with Hotep. She had to admit it was almost blinding. She had already learned the hard way what damage she could do when she acted out of anger and desperation.

Sheila set down her phone and worked her way through one of her forgiveness exercises. If she didn't free herself of this anger, it would consume her and taint whatever she tried to do. She visualized him and herself, seeing the ties connecting them. She saw the ties dissolving in her mental image, one by one. When the cords entangling them had all been cleared, she bathed them both in light and love.

She recited one of the forgiveness mantras her mother had taught her as a teenager. *"I willingly release the thoughts and things that clutter my life. I forgive myself and others. I am free from all misjudgment, bitterness, injustice, intolerance, and revenge. All misunderstanding and bitterness is now eliminated from my mind, body, and world."* She repeated it over and over until it felt real, until she could apply it to Hotep. It took a long time, but finally she felt a loosening in her chest as her anger with him dissolved and released her from its hold.

Sheila opened her eyes and took a deep breath. It wasn't done, but she had made an important start. Maybe she could think more clearly now. She thought back to her conversation with Jasmin. She decided that what she most wanted to take from their talk was Jasmin's belief that she would come through this process of sifting.

"My sister believes in me," she said to no one in particular. Now all she needed to do was believe in herself.

PART NINE
INDEBTED

CHAPTER THIRTY-NINE
CHAFFING

Sheila waddled into the kitchen, one hand on her enormous belly. It was August and the dog days of Summer were upon them. Naima was sitting at the table in her robe, reading.

"You're up early," Naima said cheerfully.

"I used to be a morning person," Sheila responded groggily. "I don't know what happened."

"Being eight months pregnant will mess with your habits, I hear. Don't worry, when you give birth to that little bean, you'll be up all the time." Naima let out a wicked laugh.

"Can't wait," Sheila said with sarcasm.

"Want some breakfast? I can whip up something." Naima put down her book and got up.

"No, no. Please sit back down. You know I hate it when you wait on me."

"I'm here to make your life easier. Let me fix you something to eat and I won't tell Raines you came down here. You know full well you are supposed to be on bed rest. Dr. Klein was not pleased with you on your last visit. You know…"

"Fine, fine, just spare me the lecture. I'm allowed to stretch my legs, aren't I? A woman's got a right to walk around her own house."

Sheila and Naima stared each other down.

"You are impossible, but so am I," Naima pronounced, with iron in her voice. "Sit down," she said in a gentler voice. "Let's get something in you."

"Well, if you insist, I would just love a cheesy egg. Thanks, love."

"I live to serve," Naima said with mock humility.

Sheila kept her mouth shut. Since Naima had moved

in four months ago, against her strenuous protests, but with Raines' blessing, Sheila had been trying to get used to having her so close and eager to please. It still felt uncomfortable and chaffed her that Naima had become so devoted to her. But she had to admit it hadn't worked out so badly. Sheila had become slower and more tired as her pregnancy had developed. She could really use the help.

The pregnancy hadn't been easy. The last months had proved that it was more than a notion to be "with child." Sheila remembered her mother telling her she hadn't had a day of morning sickness with any of her kids. Her situation was anything but that smooth. She still had difficulty keeping food down, and Raines and Naima had teamed up to feed her religiously. She felt like she was being force-fed, but she knew she needed it.

"Raines still sleeping? He was still working downstairs when I called it a night."

"Yup, he's really driving himself to get this collection complete. I've never seen him hurry like this before. It's driving me nuts. He won't let me see! He's actually started covering his canvases when he's not working on them. And now that I'm supposedly on bed rest," Sheila stopped to stick her tongue out at Naima, who seemed mad she had said 'supposedly.' "He won't even let me in the basement. I'm *not* an invalid. If anything, I am the reason his tabernacle series came into being. I'm not saying I'm the reason he got religion, but…"

"But you're saying, if you do say so yourself." Naima laughed as she placed a small plate of scrambled eggs with cheddar in front of Sheila.

"Well, I'm just saying I should be the first one to see his work, not his darn agent. It's not fair."

"Are you actually pouting?"

"No. Maybe. I'm just saying." They looked at each other and started laughing. "Am I being ridiculous?"

"No, you're being pregnant. Hormones, dear. But I

know it must be hard not to be up close and personal with his work like you are used to. Sorry he's cut you off from the basement. If it's any consolation, I have no idea what's going on down there, either."

"Nope, that doesn't help." Sheila struggled to get her eggs down. She was already anticipating them coming back up, but she pressed forward, willing her stomach to settle.

"Slow breaths," Naima said calmly. It seemed everyone knew when she was feeling nauseous.

Sheila forced the last bite and put the forked down, pushing the plate away in disgust. She closed her eyes and took a few deep breaths. Finally, her stomach settled, and she believed she wouldn't have to part with her eggs anytime soon.

"OK. I've got it; I'm fine. That was close. I'm gonna go to my shrine room now."

Naima stood up. "Are you working? I'll go with you."

"Hold your horses. I'm just going to spend some time in prayer and commune with the Lord. *While* laying down, I promise." Sheila responded to Naima's objection before she had a chance to voice it. Heaving herself up out of her chair, she walked out of the kitchen. She felt like a whale.

"Take your phone so you can call when you need help getting up."

"I'm not an invalid!"

"But we are trying to make sure you have a nice, healthy baby. You're going to have to put up with us fussing over you until that happens."

Sheila started crying and covered her face. "I know! You think I don't know that I'm underweight and my child is underdeveloped for this stage of the pregnancy? I'm trying."

"You don't have to carry this weight on your own. That's why you came to me, and it's why God bound us all together in this effort. I'm not trying to make things harder for you. You know that, right?"

"I know." Sheila wiped the tears from her face, grabbing a napkin to blow her nose. "Well, at least I've had my first cry of the day. Only seven more to go." She tried to put a smile on her face. "Yes, I'll take my phone. And thanks for breakfast. I love you."

"Love you, too."

Naima watched her walk out and climb the stairs. It took a long time. She blew out a breath. It had been an arduous pregnancy, and they still had a month to go. She had felt compelled to move in months ago when she saw how much difficulty Sheila was having. Sheila was a strong black woman, so that meant she wasn't good at accepting help. She had tried to bear as much of the load as she could, unable to stop herself from shouldering all the responsibilities.

Naima and Raines had concocted the plan for her to move in. They had double-teamed Sheila and overrode her objections and misgivings. There was a lot for Naima to do in this new arrangement. She gave Sheila a body energy treatment daily, sometimes coming in dragging from her day job, only to have to turn around and have a whole 'nother job to do.

She also stayed up every other night when Sheila went to watch the gate so she could give her a treatment after she returned. Naima found her skills and power had grown since they had been working together. But it still seemed like Sheila needed every drop of effort to refill her. It was hard on Naima, and she could barely keep up.

The last few weeks since Sheila's doctor had put her on bed rest had been even more of a challenge. There was more to do involving the everyday care and feeding of Sheila, who was a barely cooperative patient. Raines and Naima had split the duties and were doing the best they could.

It was hard to see her best friend struggle through her pregnancy. She saw how much her gatekeeping responsibilities took out of her and how much carrying the child was costing her. Over the months, they had watched her grow thinner and thinner until they had started to force liquid nutritional supplements on her, hoping some would actually stay down and provide food for her body and child. Naima was afraid they would lose the little bean, as she called the child.

Naima got up and put Sheila's plate in the dishwasher. At least she had gotten two eggs in her this morning. With any luck, Sheila could keep them down. She took out her phone and opened the shared note that she and Raines used to log her meals. She tapped in "two eggs with cheese" and added a surprised face emoji. They would continue taking it one day at a time.

CHAPTER FORTY
PRAYER

Sheila closed the shrine room door behind her and slumped against it. If anyone had been around, she would have insisted that a simple walk from the kitchen to her shrine room upstairs was no big deal, but since she was alone, she didn't have to pretend. She worked to regulate her breaths, knowing that quick breathing often inflamed her nausea. Maybe she would relent and take the anti-nausea medicine her doctor had prescribed. She far preferred homeopathic remedies over Western medicine, but nothing had seemed to work, and she had to admit things were getting dire.

When she got her breath back, she went to the center of the room and slowly lay down on the carpeted floor, grabbing a nearby blanket and pillow to make herself more comfortable. She preferred the hard floor with only a little cushioning from the carpet to her bed, or really anywhere else. They were all far too soft, and she never felt like she got enough support. She joked God was making her uncomfortable to get her to talk to him more.

The light from the windows came in, reminding her of how much time had passed since she woke up restless, yet still tired, at five am. She had thought to sneak down to the kitchen and putter around on her own while Raines and Naima were sleeping. It seemed Naima never slept, though. Between Naima and Raines, Sheila felt like a sardine in a can with no room to move or just be.

They were constantly hovering—surveilling her. It was hard to take. But she had to admit she might have already lost her child if it hadn't been for their care and attention. She constantly had to remind herself of that fact, as their behavior was often grating.

She felt like she had lost nearly all of her

independence and freedom to make her own decisions since Naima had moved in. She loved her best friend and knew she meant well. The same went for Raines. But Sheila was unused to needing help, and it felt like her wings were being clipped. This was what it would take to birth this child, she reminded herself.

She tried to grin and bear it, but her hormones betrayed her constantly, causing her to be snippy, burst into tears, or even yell sometimes. It hadn't been easy on any of them. Sheila knew full well she was a bit of a terror in the house right now, but she couldn't seem to control herself.

She again regretted that she had unknowingly bound Naima to her in service. Sheila had watched as she had slowly become the most important thing in Naima's life. She had paused her services to other clients and, outside of the weekday hours she spent out of the house at work, devoted herself to whatever Sheila needed. It felt like Naima was her indentured servant and it caused her heart to ache, even more so because she knew she would be lost without her.

Sheila closed her eyes and gently rolled over to her side, adjusting her pillow to be more comfortable. She needed the Lord to fix her, to make sense of all the emotions coursing through her right now. Using her phone to control her sound system, she played some Gregorian chants in the room. She let the rich voices soothe her and bring her to a place of peace.

Opening her eyes, Sheila realized she had dozed off, and the sun was much higher in the sky. She didn't know if she had communed with God or not. She couldn't remember.

"Did you fix me, Jesus?" She waited for some kind of response and received none. She had better try again, she thought.

Sheila went within herself and searched her heart until she found the place where God abided. She spread herself out before him and listed her every woe and concern, including her complaints against herself. She sang an old negro spiritual her grandmother had loved, "The Old Account Was Settled Long Ago." Encouraged by remembering scriptures from various sacred texts that promised God would draw near to aid those who drew near to God, she pressed on.

She was having a high time in the Lord when she heard a knock on the door.

"Occupied," she said and chuckled.

"Can I come in?"

"The more the merrier!"

Raines opened the door and smiled. "You're supposed to be on bed rest," he said in a sing-song voice.

Sheila groaned and sat up to throw her pillow at him. "I'm two doors away from my bed. I didn't go run a foot race."

"Naima said you were downstairs for breakfast."

"She's a filthy traitor. And I took my time; I was careful. But yes, I went downstairs. It's my house!" She watched Raines give her a stern look. "*Our* house. It's our house, that's what I said." She gave him an innocent smile.

Raines sat down beside her and kissed her nose. "You know I don't mind taking you anywhere you want to go. Let me. I promise I won't crowd you."

"I know. Sometimes I just want to remember I'm a grown woman and can do what I want, just a little."

"The stairs make me nervous. Can you just agree to be a grown, independent woman on *this* floor?"

"I feel so bad with you all taking care of me. I just wanted to fix myself a cheesy egg."

"I know it must be hard for you. I'm sorry. You know what you have to do."

"Take my butt back to bed?"

"Absolutely."

"Well, help me up." Sheila and Raines did the practiced dance of getting her from laying to standing. "Thanks, honey."

Raines gave her his arm, and they walked to their bedroom as if they were at a cotillion. Once settled back in bed, Sheila could finally admit to herself she was tired and had probably had her fill of adventure for the day.

Raines left their bedroom to let Sheila rest. He texted Naima. 'You let her in her shrine room.'

'I thought if we gave Sheila her fill, she might relent on going to the gate this week.'

'We talk about decisions like this together. You don't just decide on your own.'

'She makes her own decisions, Raines. We are on the edge of controlling her life.'

Raines set his phone down in frustration. They were so close. But the closer they came to the delivery date, the more precarious things seemed to become. He had shut out of his mind the fact that Sheila was planning to travel to the gate this week, and Naima's texts were an unwelcomed reminder.

What would he do when that night came? Every time she did her gatekeeping, it put their child at risk. Now, even though their doctor had put her on bedrest, she still insisted. Was it now when he had to take a stand? He trusted Sheila, but he had to protect his child. Was he exaggerating things? He had to admit to himself he had gotten incredibly protective of Sheila and watched her every move. Maybe Naima was right. Sheila had never been controllable. The more they tried to counter her will, the more she would resist and not listen to anything they had to say.

Raines picked up his phone and replied to Naima, 'It's hard to keep things in perspective.'

'Just breath. We'll talk after work.'

Raines focused on returning to his painting, where he could escape almost any trouble. Still, it gnawed at him.

Sheila lay in her dream state and walked around in her consciousness. Her body slept while her mind and soul were wide awake. She had been practicing controlling her dream state ever since Grandfather had told her that was how her mother had watched the gate every night. She had succeeded in sliding between dimensions and she had traveled *to* the gate, but not *through* it to where she regulated its passage.

Sheila planned to tell her grandfather what she could do and try to watch the gate from her dream state tonight. She didn't know why she hadn't told him what she had been working on. Although their relationship had gotten better over the months, she still feared his censure and often hid things from him to avoid getting on his harsher side. Would he be proud that she had come this far?

Whatever his response, she knew it had to be this way, at least for a while. Her doctor had put her on bed rest for the last month of her pregnancy. That was too long to leave the gate unguarded. She hoped this method would be easier on her and her baby.

It had not been an easy pregnancy. Her fortitude and hardiness had been dwindling month by month. She had to admit that she was not doing well. Her grandfather hadn't lied. It was hard to be with child and watch the gate.

Her body was perpetually low on the nutrients she needed and no amount of supplements and homeopathic remedies seemed able to fix it. Her condition had been stumping her doctor, and they had all watched with increasing concern as she got thinner and thinner.

At least her body was prioritizing the child inside of her. Despite all of her health concerns, the baby seemed to be doing pretty well. That, Naima, Raines, and prayer were the only things propping her up. If she could just make it a few more weeks, she could prove her grandfather wrong and deliver a reasonably healthy child.

Now, even as her body got the rest it sorely needed,

she was still working on her calling, trying to find a less trying way to go about it. She ignored the voice inside her that said if her mother couldn't do it, why on earth did she think she could? She ignored the fact that she had been reduced to drinking liquid supplements for most meals because it was the only thing she seemed able to keep down. And she ignored the fact that God had not yet given her an answer to her prayers.

She usually heard from God clearly when they communed. God told her what to do, showed her how to stay calm in the midst of the storm, and directed her path. Although she had worked hard over the months to recover and strengthen her relationship with God, she had heard not a peep of instruction or assurance in return.

She had been trying to think of this period of her life as a kind of spiritual boot camp. If she could just knuckle down and get through it, she would receive power, and her relationship with God would be restored. So, she gritted her teeth and bore it. She worked on having hope that God would let her keep her child instead of fearing that He wouldn't. Faith was hard.

Most days lately, she had had to fill her consciousness with uplifting affirmations to keep the negative thoughts at bay. She and God had certainly been spending a lot of time together. She was glad of it and had discovered a new level of intimacy with him.

Then why could God not answer her? She was desperate for His instructions and guidance, but still she heard nothing. Was this how most people lived their lives, with only a vague sense of the divine at work? It was almost unbearable. All she could do was focus on her objectives and move forward.

Tonight would be a challenge. She fully expected she would have to battle Raines and Naima in order to travel to the gate. She had told them she planned on going. Perhaps they were hoping she would forget.

Unlike her, they did not have a judgment hanging over their heads. When she had been tried in the spiritual People's Court, as she called it, she had sworn on herself to do a better job regulating the gate. If she didn't live up to that promise, she would have to find herself guilty. Her job might be stripped from her, putting the entire dimension at risk. She thought of the chaos she regularly experienced at the gate being visited on her world and shuddered at the thought.

Grandfather had been right—watching the gate had become her identity. She couldn't imagine herself without this part of her. The thought that the gate would be unguarded and that the wrong spirits and energies could pass unchecked into her dimension almost hurt. The universe wanted order, and it had set her in place to help provide it.

She just needed a few more weeks, then everything would be fine. She calculated the minimum number of times she could guard the gate and manage the load was twice a week. Just six more visits to keep the gate and she could birth the child inside her and escape her fate.

Sheila needed Raines and Naima on board, but she doubted she would have that. It surprised her they were as mild with her as they had been when they had found her out of her room today. It made her suspect they had something up their sleeves. But it didn't matter. She would do what she had to and pray she could live with the consequences.

'God, it's not too late for You to tell me something, to talk to me again. I could use some help. Please don't make this a choice between doing what You called me to do and having a child. Give me both, Lord. Give me both. And just so You know, if You don't say anything I will take it that You agree with me! Amen.'

She let out her silent prayer as she prepared to reunite with her sleeping frame. Tonight, she would do it all for real.

CHAPTER FORTY-ONE
IN PIECES

That evening, Sheila set her resolve in place and called her husband to their bedroom. Her fists grabbed and released the covers over and over in nervous energy. She didn't want to have this conversation.

"You rang?" Raines popped into the room almost cheerfully.

"What's put a pep in your step?" Sheila inquired.

"Just listening to some music from home. It's giving me life right now." Raines danced over to the bed where she lay. "How are you?"

"I'm good. Refreshed. Ready." Sheila could see Raines' body stiffen, though he worked not to change his face. "Like I said I would be. But it may be a lot less stressful this time. I want to try something new, something that my mother did."

Raines paused for a long moment then asked, "You have something that can make this easier? I'm all ears."

"My mother accessed the gate through her dream state. I've been working on being able to do the same. Casting the traveling circle takes a lot out of me; this could eliminate all that. I just have to run it by Grandfather."

"Run it by him? Do you need his approval?"

"No. Yes. I don't know. I just am learning the trouble that can come from not consulting him before I do things. I need all the help I can get. It's only six more trips. I just need a little more grace."

"When does our child get put first?"

The question hit Sheila like a blow, but it wasn't unexpected. She hung her head.

"I know the gate is important, maybe even more important than what happens to us as individuals. Naima is working on helping me see that. But is the welfare of our baby *never* to come first? Are you going to do whatever you want to do and simply hope your pregnancy works out?"

Sheila worked hard not to either cry and jump down Raines' throat. She took a few deep breaths, cursing the hair trigger emotions that her hormones had unleashed on her. "I don't think that's fair. I'm not doing whatever I want to do. I'm caught up in something bigger than me here. I'm just trying to hold on for the ride."

"But you enjoy it, don't you? You get a sense of fulfillment from your work. So don't act like it's some huge hardship for you."

"What is going on right now? Did I miss something? How long has this been brewing?"

"It's really clear that our child does not come first for you, and I'm begging you to change your priorities. Six more trips? How about *no* more trips? That's what would suit me and be best for our baby."

"I have two priorities, Raines. They are both first for me. I can't choose."

"That's the wrong answer."

"I'm sorry, but it's the truth. They both mean everything to me and they go together. Do you want me bringing a child into a dimension where evil and all manner of other things can flow in and out at will? I'm doing it in part *for* our child! They're not at cross-purposes."

"Tell that to your doctor who put you on bed rest. It seems to me this work is trying to kill our child. How is that part of the plan? You told me to put my trust in God. Well, I've been trusting, but all I see are things getting worse. You were a healthy woman, now you're on bed rest!"

"I know things aren't going well."

"Aren't going well? This is a life that hangs in the balance. I shouldn't even have to ask you as the mother of this child where you stand. Yet here I am, pleading. Put your baby first. Case closed." Raines stopped talking ,and his face looked like it was set in stone.

Sheila massaged her temples. Life was hard. As she did, she prayed. "Lord God, you see me down here in distress. Why is it so hard for you to just answer me? Am I out of order? Am I doing something I shouldn't be? Answer me, I'm begging you. Show me what to do. Why would you place me in this position? I don't understand. Tell me what you want from me. What do I have to do?"

Tears sprang up, and she cried. Raines hugged her and tried to console her.

"Just because I'm hugging you doesn't mean I agree with you, but I'm still here."

"Thank you." Sheila scrubbed her tear-stained face and tried to pull herself together. "God hasn't released me from my responsibilities at the gate. What am I supposed to do?"

"What good is a God that won't let our child live? Surely you see that."

"God is still God, even if we don't get what we want."

"I'm not mad because they ran out of rocky road ice cream at the store. We're talking about life. This is not a tantrum. I have to take a stand."

Sheila lay back in their bed. She was in an impossible situation—obey God or preserve life. God was giving her no guidance now. That usually meant she was supposed to stay faithful to the instructions she had already received. But here was her husband, the father of her child, making the most compelling argument that her priority should be her unborn child. Was her child more important than obedience to God? She *must* be missing something. There had to be a way out of this predicament that she had yet to uncover.

Sheila tried to swallow the lump in her throat and press on. "I'm not your average believer, I *really* believe. I believe God always knows best. I'm going to be obedient, even if it costs us our child."

"You don't get to make that decision!" Raines

exploded. "There are three of us here. Our child and I outnumber you. Don't do this. I'm begging you, Sheila."

"It's not like I *want* to. I never asked for any of this, but I have to deal with what's been put before me. I can't shirk the work of the Lord, even for life. You're right, of course, our child should be my highest priority. But God trumps my priorities. I have to believe God will preserve the life within me. God doesn't make mistakes. So even if I lose this child, it was always a part of his plan for me."

"Then there's nothing left to say." Raines got up and quietly left the room.

A moment later, she heard a crash. Getting to her feet and entering the hallway, she found the noise was coming from her shrine room. Rushing over, she stood still with her mouth agape. Raines stood over her upturned ancestral shrine, stomping on its contents. Finally, looking up from his destruction, he saw her.

His lips made a thin line. "I won't let you." Raines walked out of the room, past her, and downstairs as if nothing had happened.

Sheila looked at her shrine. The wood of its case was splintered. Her glass coffee pot lay shattered and black coffee seeped into the carpet. It looked like a hurricane had hit it. The energy in the room was violent and edgy.

Sheila felt like she had gone into shock. She had worked so hard to get this room ready for her grandfather's spirit. She had hoped one day to even welcome her mother's spirit to that shrine. Now it lay destroyed at her feet. At the hands of her husband. No, not her husband, the father of their child.

Tears ran down her face. It wasn't Grandfather's fault that they were in this situation. Why take it out on him? Sheila and her grandfather had grown closer—not close, but closer—over the months. She felt like she had betrayed his trust by letting this happen. She was in so little control that her husband had gone on a mini rampage.

Had that just been the end of her marriage? The question thudded dully in her mind, not hurting only because she was so numb. Sheila cast her eyes about the room, looking for something to latch onto. She felt so violated. Locking onto the Goddess of Mercy's statue, she remembered to pay attention to her breath. She forced herself to take slow, deep breaths to calm and ground herself.

For all Sheila knew, Raines had grabbed his keys and left home forever. The destruction in the room was worthy of leaving-home-forever energy. She finally released her gaze and found Naima standing on the room's threshold. Sheila gestured towards the remains of her ancestral shrine sadly.

"I think he's left me," Sheila said solemnly.

"This is tough on him," Naima responded.

"I didn't say it wasn't. Did you know it had gone this far?"

"I suspected. I couldn't have imagined it would take this form."

"He must have been dying to do that all this time."

"He had to do something."

Sheila turned away from the remains of her shrine and focused on Naima. "Do you and I need to have a conversation?"

Naima remained silent.

"Because I'm sensing something's on your mind."

"I think you should go back to bed." Naima almost spat out the words.

Sheila stood, assessing Naima as if seeing her for the first time. Sheila didn't like her own odds in this fight. Raines had already rendered her numb, and, the truth was, she was tired.

"Ok, then." Sheila walked out of her shrine room as if she didn't need to be in there, salvaging everything she could. She went back to her bed and got in, bunching the covers around her to feel safer, like she had done since childhood. She looked at the bedroom door and was relieved to see she and Naima would not be having their big showdown yet. Sheila let out a breath she hadn't realized she was holding.

An icy feeling spread through her. Sheila felt disconnected from the events that had just happened. Her mind could not make sense of them. This had to be what it felt like when life crumbled around you. She worked on breathing in and out, wiggling her toes to make sure she was still there.

Where was her husband? Had he left? For good? Why was Naima spoiling for a conflict with her? It looked like everyone was against her. She lay somewhat helpless in her bed, trying to wake up her flummoxed mind. Raines was right—there had been nothing left to say, only an act of violence and destruction to perform.

She had never imagined it could come to this. She had naively assumed they were more or less on the same team, but the team had turned against her. Sheila felt alone and besieged.

She closed her eyes and rummaged through her spirit, desperate for some bit of peace to hold on to. Sheila gathered up the shards she found and tried to bind them together. She was not going to cry again.

CHAPTER FORTY-TWO
GATE OF DREAMS

Sheila kept finding her mind return to a particular snatch of scripture: "But none of these things move me, neither count I my life dear unto myself, so that I might finish my course with joy." Her life was shattered, and she *still* had work to do. Raines might never come back, and she had to go on. It might cost her child's life, and her duty remained.

How could God ask this of her? She thought of Isaac and how the Lord had told him to sacrifice his son. Isaac would have done it, but the Lord sent an angel at the last minute to tell him not to. Maybe God would do the same for her. It seemed to Sheila that the Lord loved sweeping in at the last possible moment to change everything.

"This is that moment, Lord. Tell me something! I said I would serve you, but don't make me pay this price." Sheila bit her tongue as she fought a silent battle to keep the tears at bay.

She lay in the bed, utterly exhausted. Beside her in bed was a tray of food leftover from earlier. She looked at the supplement shake and almost gagged. Where was she supposed to find the strength? She wanted to go after Raines, but she had seen that look before. There was no talking to him right now. He'd probably be even more mad that she had walked down the stairs. She *was* on bed rest. And right now, she understood why she needed to be. She wasn't sure she could make it down the stairs and back if she tried.

Who was Sheila trying to fool? What gate was she able to guard in her condition? Sure, she had talked a big game, but when push came to shove, could she even do what she had paid so dear a price for?

Sheila felt guilty for feeling a greater sense of loss over that realization than anything else that had happened that night. She understood really and truly what her grandfather had told her. She was the gatekeeper. It was the axis around which her life now revolved. She had said she understood, but she really did not know what she was getting into when she had said yes.

It hadn't just changed what she did; it had changed who she was. And now she was someone her husband couldn't abide.

"Is this what you need from me, Lord? Is my child's life the proof of my loyalty? I never thought you would go this Old Testament on me. You don't even care what it costs me, that I *can't* do this."

It infuriated her that God had put her in this position, but really, it had been Sheila that had done this. She must have missed something, some way out of this mess. She just hadn't seen it. What had she missed? Now she had lost everything by taking a stand on something she couldn't actually do. She could see the irony, even though she couldn't appreciate it.

"I'm sorry."

Sheila's head snapped up as she registered whose voice it was.

"You can talk to me anywhere," Sheila spat. "And to think of how hard I worked to move your presence from one shrine to another. What else have you been making me do that's completely unnecessary?"

"It's costing me to be here, but I had to be. I'm sorry."

Sheila lay her head back and all of her bravado evaporated. "Thanks."

"I know your thoughts, child. Take a night off. You're too weak and spent."

"It's not going to get any better. The doctor put me on bed rest! Weeks. I was so close to doing a halfway decent job. I've messed everything up. When you said this wouldn't work out, I didn't believe you."

"I wish I had been wrong."

"Me too."

A feeling of defeat hung thick in the air.

"I was going to surprise you tonight. I know how to access the gate in my dream state. I finally figured it out. Oh well."

"I don't like surprises, but congratulations."

"I must be beyond pitiful for you to feel sorry enough to give me my props." Sheila let out a wry chuckle. "I'll take it."

"You think too poorly of me."

"I don't know why. You're the only one who can even begin to understand what this is. But you have to know you're a hard man. That can't be a surprise to you."

"I was not always this way. I wish I could be a better support to you. But just rest tonight. Don't worry about the gate."

"Easy for you to say. You're not on probation. I made an oath to do better. Sure, *ha satan* instigated it, but it was true; I had been doing a poor job. I promised to do better, so help me. Now, so help me is coming."

"It will keep for one night."

"And what about tomorrow night will be better? I'll still be weak, on the verge of losing my child, and exhausted. Maybe I'll go to the gate but can't hold it. A stiff wind could blow me over right now. What kind of shape am I in to guard the gate?"

"Don't think ahead, just rest."

"You honestly think I can forget what happened here tonight? Just pack it away and march on? I try to be tough, but that's beyond me."

"You do a lot of talking for someone who is supposedly so exhausted."

Sheila opened her mouth, paused, then shut her mouth. She supposed he was right. She settled into bed and closed her eyes, wishing she could fly far away.

It happened on autopilot. Sheila had been coming near the gate in her dream state so regularly, she just found herself there at its edge again. The familiar sight made her sick. But she still felt it call to her. She might try to swear off of it, but it wouldn't quit her. How had her mother done it? The weight was so heavy.

She saw her grandfather's energy approach the gate.

"I knew you couldn't stay away, child."

"What are you doing here? This is not your dimension, and I have not let you pass." Sheila was perplexed to be talking to him here.

"I was a gatekeeper. I go where I will."

"Yes, but as you said, it's not without a cost. What is it costing you to be here right now? And for what, to catch me slipping up?"

"To stop you from going."

Sheila growled in exasperation. He was always pushing her to do better and be at the gate more often. What did it take to please him?

"I'm sorry you didn't have a chance to be taught by your mother and have a house full of children. You deserved that, but you got this instead. I'm here to give you a chance to have that child."

"What do you mean?"

"I will watch the gate until you are able."

Sheila's thoughts scrambled, and she struggled to set them right.

"So please, take my advice for once and get some rest. You need it."

"What are you talking about? This makes no sense. You're not of this dimension anymore, you *can't* guard it."

"And yet I will. I think I know a great deal more about this than you, so let me handle the matter."

"Handle the matter? Oh, that's all there is to it? I know you know tons more than me, but I still know some things. You're not supposed to be out of your dimension.

You belong in the heavenly realms, not here. And actually acting as gatekeeper? That is appointed to a person for a time. You don't just *decide* to do it. You've gone mad."

"I know I am a hard man, but this is how I show my love. Let me do what I have to do."

"No. This will cost you too much. This is out of the order of things. It will cause more chaos."

"You're right, a stiff wind could blow you over. Sleep, child."

Her grandfather's words filled Sheila's head. She felt herself irresistibly called to sleep, even as her mind was screaming no.

CHAPTER FORTY-THREE
HARSH LIGHT

Sheila woke up hard. She had a headache before she even opened her eyes. Her limbs were sore and tight. She was curled up in a ball and could not even imagine getting up.

Slowly, her tired mind put the pieces of last night together. She rocked herself as a small measure to soothe the hurt. It had all actually happened. For a few blissful hours of sleep, Sheila had forgotten about it.

Her eyes finally opened as she thought about the last part of her evening. Her grandfather loved her? He said he would watch the gate for her so that she could have this child. He had told her it was his act of love.

But it was too much. He was risking the placement of his soul for her. It didn't make any sense. Rather, it only made sense if he actually loved her—unconditionally. She had assumed he only cared about her in her capacity as the gatekeeper. He was relentlessly hard on her. Though their interactions were often those of a teacher trying to instruct a derelict, they had softened over the last several months. Sheila actually liked him, not a lot, but enough to make their relationship work.

She let out a long groan as she unfolded and stretched out her body. She felt as if she had watched the gate last night, though she knew she hadn't. Her grandfather had. What, was he trying to show her up? She tried to get herself to be mad at him, to distract herself from her feelings of worry, but she saw through her attempts and wound back at square one. She was worried about him.

When her mother had reached out to Sheila in this dimension, it had cost her passage to the ancestral plane. What would watching the gate cost her grandfather? Whatever the price, she would let him pay it. She had a chance to focus on her child now, not the gate. Besides, her grandfather was a wise man. She would not insult him by assuming he didn't know what he was getting into. She just had to let it be. Why invite trouble?

Sheila got to her feet and walked around her room, willing her body to feel better. She would have asked Naima for an energy treatment, but she was pretty sure Naima was mad with her and she was in no hurry to have that conversation. So, she spent some extra time working out cramps and knots until she felt more comfortable in her own body.

Looking around her room, it looked like Raines had not been back after their fight. Was he still in the house? She peeked out of her room as if she expected him to be just around the corner. After standing in the hallway for a while, Sheila finally got the nerve to open the door to her shrine room.

It looked no better in the harsh light of morning. An utterly destroyed ancestor shrine. The coffee pot was in pieces. There were splintered pieces of particle board sticking out every which way. It was a mess.

Sheila kicked a trash container toward the shrine, then sat down and started sifting through the debris. Raines had done a thorough job. Almost everything was broken. She put the pieces of the coffee pot in the trash bin. She took apart picture frames to get out the shattered glass and discarded of it. She put the white handkerchiefs that were soaked through with coffee to the side. She could wash those.

Finally, she had an overfilled trash bin and a pitifully small number of items she had salvaged. Her grandfather's coffee cup and saucer were broken and chipped, but a few of his cigars hadn't gotten wet. She didn't exactly have to start over, but this came close. It looked like the waist beads were intact, but the delicate lace that had draped the cupboard was torn and stained.

Sheila fanned her eyes rapidly. "Don't cry, don't cry,

don't cry!"

"Yeah, woman up and deal with it," came a voice from the doorway.

Sheila squeezed her eyes shut until she was sure they were free of tears. "Good morning." Sheila looked at Naima to see if she would have the look she had found on her face last night, the one spoiling for a fight.

"I would have done this for you, but some things you have to do yourself. I figured this was one of them."

Sheila nodded dully as she fingered one of the picture frames that had been on the shrine. She had thought she would feel better after she had cleared things away, but her feelings of despair seemed to have just further rooted in her. She couldn't figure out if she was mad at Raines or impressed with him. He had said there was nothing else to say, and then he had done something. He put his money where his mouth was, that's for sure.

"Do you know where my husband is?" Sheila saw Naima hesitate, which she thought was interesting.

"Yes," Naima said flatly.

"And where is that?" Sheila found she had to ask after Naima offered no further information.

"I don't think it's a good idea for you all to be in each other's company just yet."

"I didn't ask you that." Sheila was getting annoyed. Something seemed off to her. Naima was supposed to be yoked to Sheila. She should have been almost compelled to answer her truthfully. This resistance made no sense.

"Where is Raines?"

"In his studio."

"Why was that so hard?"

"Last night was more than enough violence for me."

"You think we are going to get violent?"

"I don't know what to think!" Naima broke out in a cold sweat. "I've never been around this level of discord in my life, and it's incredibly stressful." Naima's voice went higher and higher until she was just a squeak by the time she finished. "He broke stuff. And you just let him."

"I was at a loss. And he was determined. I don't know what to tell you. I suppose we were headed to last night from the very beginning. I must admit, though, I had assumed things would end with more of a whimper than with a bang."

"I feel unsafe, Sheila. What if he attacks me next because I've been healing you and enabling this behavior? Who knows what he could do?" Naima looked anxious and jumpy.

"Calm down, everybody's safe here. I know last night was scary, but it's over now."

"How is it over?"

"Because I don't have to go back to the gate until after I have my baby."

"What? How?"

"My grandfather is taking over the gatekeeping for a while."

Naima stayed silent.

"What?"

"That's not right."

"I'm trying to ignore that glaring fact, thank you."

"Messing around in other dimensions without permission is bad. He could lose his place on the ancestral plane. Why would he do that?"

"He said he was showing his love." Sheila massaged her temples. Her headache had returned. "And to be honest, I need a break. I need every bit of help I can get."

"Ok, then."

Naima's voice had the sound of being thoroughly unconvinced, but agreeing simply to move things along. Maybe Sheila was reading into things.

"I know he's paying a price for being there, for doing this. But I've paid too! I used to be more than just skin and bones, if you recall. I was perfectly healthy, yet here I am on bed rest. So I figure we've all paid for this.

"I just want to have this baby. I need to deliver this child healthy into the world. This is my only chance, and I'm gonna take it."

"So you admit that your plan to do both was never going to work?" Naima's voice had an edge in it.

"I really wanted it to work, but things have definitely taken a turn for the worse. I guess I was only fooling myself, huh? Was I really the only one that couldn't see it?"

Naima nodded her head.

"Well, all the more reason to appreciate my grandfather's gift. The odds were slim to none to start with. He is really rescuing me and my child."

There was a long pause. Sheila looked at Naima's unhappy expression.

"You're not going to let me enjoy this, are you?" Sheila threw up her hands in frustration. Finally, a way to give everyone what they want, but you're unhappy."

"You can't tell me you don't have concerns."

"I told you I was ignoring them. Naima, don't do this to me!"

"I'm sorry, I'm sorry. You're right. I'm on board."

"You're a horrible liar, but thank you for trying."

"I'm just going to shut up now." Naima mimed zipping her mouth shut.

"What am I supposed to do? He is *beyond* being a grown man. He has to know his own mind and be able to make his own choices. How can I look this gift horse in the mouth?"

Even Sheila realized people do crazy things in the name of love all the time. She just never thought her grandfather would be one of them. It seemed like this had become her problem.

But what was she supposed to do about it? Her grandfather knew far more about gatekeeping, perhaps more than Sheila ever would. And he was almost as stubborn as her. She couldn't just show up at the gate and sweetly ask him to stand down. Sheila didn't think she could handle another fight.

"If he's not watching the gate, that means I have to."

"Why can't you just let it slide for a few weeks? It's not like there's some alien invasion threatening to come through."

"I regret that I have to leave it a few days, much less a few weeks. Do you think Grandfather would be there if we could just let it slide? If he doesn't do it, I have to. Still feel like I have to do something about the situation?"

Sheila had worked herself into a state and had to spend a few moments breathing in and out to calm herself down.

"I need to get back in the bed. Can you order me another cabinet so I can start recreating my ancestor shrine? The least I can do is give him some support while he's doing this."

Sheila stood up clumsily, feeling lightheaded.

"It's been a full morning. I'm sensing I need more bed in my bed rest right now. But I heard everything you said, Nai. I'll figure something out."

With one hand on the wall for balance, Sheila made it back to her room and fell asleep almost as soon as she got into bed.

CHAPTER FORTY-FOUR
LOYALTY

Sheila was having a bad dream. In it, flames that were way too close for comfort surrounded her. She did not know where she was but she heard a voice crying out that sounded familiar. She just couldn't quite place it. It was one of those endless dreams where the scene just kept repeating, adding no clarity or additional information.

She felt too tired to control her dream. Instead, she forced herself to wake up, coming to with a start. Then she knew who the voice that had been crying out was.

"Grandfather? Are you there? Please talk to me."

She heard nothing in response, felt none of his energy in her presence. She never thought it would have happened, but she was worried about her grandfather. He was the toughest, most capable spirit she had ever encountered, after her mother ,of course. It was silly to think that he would need help. Yet the dream had seemed so real. She had heard his voice screaming.

Forcing herself to go slow, Sheila got out of the bed and went to her shrine room. She saw that Naima had cleared away the trash bin with the debris and placed a cabinet from the basement where her ancestral shrine had been. Sheila sat and set up her shrine, regretting the coffee stains that now marked her photos. There was no easy way to forget what had come before.

Finally, the shrine seemed a little bare, but it was serviceable. Sheila didn't have a cup for her grandfather or coffee to pour into it, and she had stopped using the cigars to call him when she had found out she was pregnant. But she had his photograph. Looking at it, she saw him smiling as he prepared to cut a cake. He looked a lot friendlier in the picture than he treated her in life.

Sheila cleared her mind, held the picture in her hands,

and focused. She let her mind stretch out in every direction. She had to find him, to know that he was alright.

She felt a tension brush up against her spirit and was put further out of joint.

"Grandfather, where are you?"

Sheila had never tried to find a spirit before. Occasionally she had surfed the astral plane, peeking in on boys she liked in her teenage years, but she wasn't well-versed in locating energy. She didn't have time to run a dragnet over all the dimensions and planes. She conjured the smell of coffee until it seemed to fill her. Letting that comforting scent pull her towards her grandfather, she smiled. Like attracts like, Sheila thought, though she couldn't remember where she had heard that.

It was hard for Sheila not to rush the process. She was impatient, and it felt like her search was moving at a snail's pace.

'Lord, show me the way,' she prayed. Sheila was delighted to see a pathway light up before her. The illumination was dull and rusty somehow. She followed the path and felt the air pressing in on her, as if there had been a significant drop in pressure. Her skin actually hurt. She stopped following the path as she tried to adjust to the change.

Finally, her system acclimated to the change, and she could move forward. She was only on the astral plane. She should be able to peek into other planes and dimensions but not enter them. She did not know why she was being so strongly affected. Yet again, she wished she had paid more attention to the things her mother had tried to teach her. The holes in her knowledge were so much more glaring now that she actually had to depend on correctly recalling and applying information.

Sheila refused to cry over missing her mom or from self-pity. She had work to do. She pressed forward in uncomfortable but bearable conditions in search of her grandfather.

The pull continued to draw her forward. She heard her grandfather's voice. That did not really help because, as always, his voice seemed to come from everywhere at once, but it let her know she was on the right track.

Grandfather groaned, and Sheila had difficulty staying focused. He sounded distressed, and it disarmed her. He was always in control and unbothered by anything but her. Was he hurt? What had happened? She cleared the rising questions and worries from her mind and held onto the smell of her grandfather's coffee. The pull continued to come.

Suddenly, Sheila reached the end of…well, the astral plane just seemed to stop, unceremoniously. She had never faced a barrier like this before. Yes, it was a barrier, not just an end. She could feel something on the other side. But was it keeping her out, or keeping something in?

Sheila resolved that if this was a barrier, she was just going to have to cross it. She had to follow the only key to her grandfather's whereabouts, wherever it led. She began to gather her energy. It wasn't enough, she knew that, but she had to try. Then Sheila had an idea. Bringing her focus to the interdimensional gate, Sheila pulled from the energy of the beings waiting there.

She hardly had the space to be pleased with herself as the energy overflowed. She pushed at the barrier and simply kept going, directing all the energy she had gathered into being relentless. Sheila sped forward at a disorienting speed.

She opened her eyes to…she opened her eyes. Looking at herself, Sheila saw that she had taken physical form. She pressed at her face as she realized her fingers didn't simply pass through her. Her form had actual matter to it. She had never heard of or experienced any experience like this before.

Sheila found herself in a darkness that was pierced by two torches. Beneath the torches were two large, fat human bodies with heads like pigs. They wore some kind of medieval-looking armor and held large axes. The axes formed an X across the entrance they guarded.

Those two…things were the only key to where she was. Slowly inching forward, Sheila cleared her throat.

"Where am I?"

They looked at her. She locked eyes with one whose eyes showed that he liked to make others hurt. They said nothing.

"Where am I?"

Sheila thought persistence couldn't hurt. She poured will and intention into her voice.

"Where am I?"

The two pig people flickered away. They had been projections. So had the torches. Sheila was standing in the blackest dark she had ever encountered.

"This is not the door for you, dear."

Sheila felt her lips tighten into a line.

"Hotep."

"I never thought I'd see you at my gates. Stay away."

"I'm in Hell?" Sheila had only just put two and two together.

"This is my domain, and I will not have you infecting this place with your spirit."

"Where is my grandfather?"

"With me, we have an arrangement. Bravo on penetrating my wall, by the way. I haven't seen that done in quite some time. Now you can go home."

"What arrangement?" Sheila was bewildered, not just because she seemed to be at the gates of Hell, but because none of this made any sense. Her grandfather would never have made a deal with *ha satan*.

"How you move him, Sheila. He would and *did* do anything for you."

Sheila's heart dropped into her stomach. "Go on." She could tell he was dying to share the story.

"You and your unborn baby mean the world to him,

but he would never be able to guard the gate. Being a gatekeeper is a role that you are blessed with, *for a time*. You can't just pick the mantle back up like a substitute teacher. He should have known better, but he didn't.

"I saw him at the gate struggling to survive. I found him, assaulted from every side and with no authority to even be standing there. They were going to consume him. But I swept in, picked him up, cleaned him up, made him like new again.

"And so he's mine now. I've agreed to lock down the gate until you have your baby. He has agreed to be my prisoner for six eras."

"Why do you even want him?"

"I want everybody!" The voice was suddenly amplified and rapacious. It shocked Sheila into remembering who she was dealing with, a spirit intent on proving God wrong about humanity.

"But you said you didn't want me here. Isn't it the same with him? You've got to be dying to get him out of here." Sheila felt like she was grasping at straws, but she had nothing else.

"Men like him are worth it."

"He doesn't belong here!" Sheila protested.

"He will. I intend to break him. The rigid ones snap like twigs. His fall from grace will fuel me for millennia. It will show that no one is beyond temptation."

"Can you and I come to some kind of arrangement?"

"No, we cannot, because you would lie. You're not nearly as principled as him. The agreement only means something if the person has honor."

"Let me see him."

"You don't just walk into Hell, and you don't go around ordering me what to do, I should add. You may not see him. He is lost to you, so I truly hoped you enjoyed him while you had him. I can't believe my luck. You are the best thing that's happened to me."

Sheila took the deep shame his words caused and the fear that it was true to produce desperate anger.

"We don't need your help guarding the gate. I can watch it just fine. I retract his agreement. Release him now!"

"Sheila, you know it doesn't work that way. Words were said. Now I really am going to have to ask you to go. You're dampening my dark. I mean for it to cut. Be gone!"

Before she could react, a force suddenly pushed her away, leaving her breathless. Sheila came back to her body with a start. She looked at her watch to see that only an hour had passed since she had gone in search of Grandfather. It had seemed like an endless night.

Everything looked just as it had when she had sat down, yet her world was upside down. Grandfather was in Hell because of her. It was almost too much to bear. How could she have let this happen? And there seemed to be no way to get *ha satan* to release him. She didn't know what to do.

Did she really have no options? Her mother had never taught her how to deal with *ha satan*, except to teach her to quickly agree with her accuser. But Sheila couldn't agree with this. She had to do something. Didn't she?

She couldn't just let her grandfather rot in Hell. Or was trying to save him like spitting on his sacrifice? He had arranged for the gate to be watched so that she could have this child. Would he rather be free from Hell, or have his wishes honored and the life of her child protected? She honestly didn't know.

Sheila felt paralyzed. Her grandfather had literally sold his soul to the devil, for however long six eras were, for her child. It weighed heavily on her. Could she live with this knowledge?

Sheila scooted over to the floor-to-ceiling shelves Raines had helped her set up when she moved Grandfather from her mother's shrine room to hers. She had combined a lot of their materials and needed more storage space. She pulled out a red case on the bottom shelf and opened it. It looked like it contained stacks and stacks of money.

They were Hell bank notes, the kind you found in Chinatown. You burned them to make sure your ancestors had enough money to be comfortable in the afterlife. It wasn't like ancestors had to pay for their groceries or anything, but it was a way to venerate them. Looking at the piles of money in front of her, she wondered if there was enough for what she had in mind.

Sheila dragged the case of money with her back to her ancestral shrine. She then went downstairs to her study and got the album with pictures of her biological father in it. She pulled one out, put the album away, and climbed the stairs. It was definitely harder going up than it had been coming down. She was tired already and felt the activities of the morning begin to weigh on her.

Back in her shrine room, she lay the picture of her father on the top of her ancestral shrine. Sitting down, she thought about what she wanted to do. There was a chance it would work. If not, her backup plan was always a possibility.

Sheila sat cross-legged with the case of Hell bank notes on her lap and cleared her mind. She traveled to the ancestral plane and then punched through the barrier at its edge. She stood impatiently with the two pig men, waiting for *ha satan* to appear. After a few moments, just as before, the two pig men disappeared. This time the torches stayed, at least. Hotep appeared in front of her.

"I have no desire for this to become a habit," he said.

Sheila produced a large, chest-high case and set it between them.

"How much to buy out his time with you?"

"Oh!" Hotep laughed. "No one has tried this in a long time. How quaint." He opened the chest and pulled out a fistful of hell bank notes. "I haven't seen these in a while. No one wants to use them for loved ones that are actually *in* Hell. Kind of missing the point, if you ask me. But seriously," Hotep said in a smooth, deep voice, "this doesn't begin to cover one era, let alone six. If he were no one, perhaps, but I'm in the middle of breaking an upright man. This is too dear to me. No. You may not buy him out of his agreement."

Well, it had been worth a shot. It was time for plan B.

"Am I right in thinking that my father is in your domain?"

"You father, the man whose absence taught you that you were never good enough."

Sheila's expression darkened. Her father meant nothing to her. Why was Hotep complicating the issue, she wondered?

"No. And I'm not here to be psychoanalyzed." Sheila took a deep breath and started over. "Is he here," she asked tersely.

"You know he is."

"I'd like to speak with him."

"Why now? You haven't spared a thought for him since you were a child."

"You don't get to know everything, *ha satan*."

"Hmm." Hotep stroked his beard thoughtfully. "I'll allow it." He grabbed the chest of notes and pulled it behind his back. "You could have gotten so much more," he chuckled. "But, per your request, you may speak with your father in private. It is agreed."

With that, Hotep and the hell bank notes disappeared. Sheila stood, bathed in the light of the two torches, waiting for something to happen. A short distance from her, a man appeared. He was tall and stocky, dressed in rags, and sat hunched over. This was actually happening. She took a breath and steeled herself. Sheila approached the man and lay a hand on his shoulder.

"Hi Father, do you know of a way to break me into Hell?"

I hope you enjoyed this book and I look forward to bringing you the rest of the series.

If you would like to keep up with my latest works, I invite you to visit my website at
www.ngozirobinson.com
where you can also sign up for my mailing list to get sneak peeks of current and future works and insight into my writing process.

Made in the USA
Columbia, SC
07 February 2025

52348192R00150